THE SCORPION'S STING

Concho Book Five

A.W. Hart

WOLFPACK
PUBLISHING
— EST 2013 —

WOLFPACK
PUBLISHING
— EST 2013 —

Text copyright © 2022 A.W. Hart
Special thanks to Charles Gramlich for his contribution to this novel.

Published by Wolfpack Publishing
5130 S. Fort Apache Road, 215-380
Las Vegas, NV 89148

Paperback IBSN 978-1-63977-506-4
eBook ISBN 978-1-63977-399-2
LCCN 2022931555

THE SCORPION'S STING

PART ONE
GHOST

CHAPTER 1

Sunday Morning. December. Concho Ten-Wolves climbed onto the sleek blue and silver Greyhound bus and walked all the way to the back before sinking gratefully into a seat. A week ago, he'd spent ten hours in his truck getting from Eagle Pass, Texas to New Orleans. With that same truck now a burned-out hulk, he would spend the next sixteen hours getting home by Greyhound. He brought along three freshly purchased books, which—besides his pistols, his Texas Ranger badge, his cell phone, and the clothes he wore—were about all he had to carry. Most of his gear had been in the truck when a rocket-propelled grenade fired by men who wanted to kill him blew it up.

It had been an eventful week.

Other than the several attempts on his life, he'd found the mother he'd thought dead for over twenty years. He'd also discovered a half-brother and half-sister. Very little of this was actually good news. His half-sister hadn't said a dozen words to him, for reasons unknown. His mother had been hit with a stroke two years before. She didn't even recognize him. Of course, she hadn't seen him since he was a year old. His younger half-brother and he had become friends. That *was* a good thing, though Bull Knife was remaining in the New Orleans area to be close to their mother. She did seem to recognize something about him.

All that had not been enough. Next came a text message from
Max Keller, his commander in Company D of the Texas Rangers
organization. It had permanently charred his memory:

> *This is to inform you that you've been suspended
> without pay from the Texas Rangers until a full inves-
> tigation is made of your actions in Louisiana. You may
> pick up documentation of your suspension at headquar-
> ters in Weslaco. – Keller.*

His actions in Louisiana?

Men had shot at him and missed. He'd shot back and hadn't.
He'd broken no laws, though he'd bent a few. And he'd been
cleared of any wrongdoing by the New Orleans Police Depart-
ment. Max Keller wasn't a fan of Concho Ten-Wolves, however.
This wasn't the first time Keller had tried to hang him out to dry.
It wouldn't likely be the last if Concho survived this time.

Keller really just wanted him to quit to avoid the potential media circus involved in firing a half black and half Kickapoo Ranger who some folks considered a hero after his role a few months
back in stopping a mall takeover by Neo-Nazis. Concho had no
intention of quitting. He'd fight the suspension. He thought he'd
win. Though, in the meantime, he needed to watch his spending,
which was why he'd bought a one-hundred-and-thirty-dollar bus
ticket rather than renting a car and paying for mileage and gas.

Half a dozen other passengers of various natures boarded the
Greyhound, and the bus pulled out of the station with a huff of
air brakes. Concho texted his girlfriend, Maria Morales, that he
was on the way home. He selected a book and started to read:
Murder in the Wind by John D. MacDonald. The story of a group
of diverse characters trapped in a house with a murderer during a
hurricane engrossed him.

He finished that book not long after they crossed into Texas and picked up his second novel, entitled *Bluebottle*. This was the fifth book in the Lew Griffin Mystery series by James Sallis, who'd once lived in New Orleans, where he'd just visited.

He was soon hooked anew and off and reading. Until the bus made a stop and trouble got on.

***

Concho glanced up automatically as the bus door opened. Without looking around, a teenaged girl in a gray hoodie came up the stairs and darted to an empty seat about mid-way back. A moment later, a second passenger climbed aboard. He started toward the back, then halted at the sight of Concho sitting there. A frown flitted across the man's face before smoothing away into blandness. He turned and sat in an empty seat a few rows up. The bus driver closed the door and pulled back onto the road.

A glance out the window showed Concho, the main street of a small Texas town rolling by in the late afternoon. He hadn't caught the place's name. It didn't matter. There'd be plenty more such towns before they reached Eagle Pass.

He tried to return to his book, but the weight of a gaze resting on him brought his head back up. The fellow who'd just boarded sat half turned in his seat, staring at him. A trick of the light made the man's eyes seem faintly luminous, with a blood-ruby tinge that summoned an image of the poised stings of scorpions.

Ten-Wolves wasn't wearing his badge or guns; he'd stuffed them into a carry-on backpack lying on the seat beside him. So, the new passenger's curiosity didn't have anything to do with the common curiosity people showed to armed lawmen in their midst. Something else lay behind it, something analytic. The man was calculating things, working them through in his head.

Concho didn't like it. He smiled into the man's analysis—offering the wide, toothy grin he reserved for people he wanted to put off their guard. The man smiled, too, but only to himself in amusement; he looked away toward the newly boarded teenaged girl who huddled across the aisle. His gaze lingered and lingered. Concho didn't like that either. He cleared his throat.

The odd passenger sighed at the sound but turned away from the girl and leaned his head back on his seat. He fell silent and very still. Concho frowned. The dynamic of the bus had changed. A few moments before, it had been peaceful. Now it resonated with chaos, though from the bored look of most other passengers, only the lawman and the girl could feel it.

He glanced out the window again. Afternoon shadows stretched long toward the coming night. The bus passed a field with cattle huddled at the far end. On the top strand of the barbed wire fence next to the road, a half dozen ink-feathered crows perched, watching the humans go by. Their beaks were open as if they were cawing. But eerily without sound.

CHAPTER 2

Concho had ridden a lot of long-distance buses in his life. They were a cheap way to travel. Only once before had he experienced anything approximating danger. It was right after deciding to leave the Army Rangers and return to Texas.

He'd spent six years in the military and served three tours of duty in Afghanistan. He'd been posted back to the states at Joint Base Lewis-McChord outside Tacoma, Washington, which was in the Puget Sound Region, a land of lakes and rivers and evergreen forests.

A Greyhound bus had been the least expensive way to get home. It had carried him from lush green Washington to brown and sere southern Texas, where he planned to work toward admission into the Texas Rangers. Seventy-two hours on the road for that trip. Four hundred bucks. On the way, he'd gotten into a fight.

He remembered—

The bus droned like a summer cicada as it carried him south. Then it stopped droning. It snorted once like a Clydesdale and quit. They were close to a small town called Lincoln. Every state seemed to have at least one. The bus driver managed to coax his mount past the city limits and off into the parking lot of a local

Walmart.

While the driver went to look for help, most of the dozen or so passengers got off to stretch their legs. One party ventured into the Walmart to shop. Concho and three others got back on the bus to wait.

As a newly minted civilian in jeans and a t-shirt rather than army fatigues, Concho felt displaced. For the first time in a long time, his minutes were not regulated for him. He fell back on one of the two things he'd learned best in the Army. Eat when you can eat; sleep when you can sleep. He reclined in his seat and let himself doze.

The whooping of beer and testosterone-fueled young men awakened him. Four locals, ranging in age from what looked like eighteen to twenty-four, forged onto the bus. They didn't see Concho lying back in his seat.

An older male passenger and a middle-aged woman sat near the front of the bus. They were first to be harassed. The man's hat was knocked off. The woman got a few leers and suggestive pelvic thrusts.

Concho sat up straight. The young men still didn't see him. They'd discovered an attractive young girl traveling alone. She was probably no more than sixteen, with dark Vietnamese hair. She wore a beautifully embroidered white tunic, split to the waist over red satin trousers—an outfit often called an Ao Dai. The men crowded around her, laughing. One plucked roughly at her silk sleeve. She flinched away.

"Gentlemen," Concho said softly as he rose to his feet.

He was six feet four and weighed two-hundred-and-fifty pounds. His shoulders were as broad as those of a Dallas Cowboy linebacker in full pads. Add his dark skin, shoulder-length hair, and the two-day growth of black beard just beginning to stubble his face, and you had a dictionary image of intimidation. At least for those smart enough to recognize it.

This group of young men didn't seem to include any smart ones. The two oldest, who looked to be only a couple of years *younger than Concho, had probably played high school football. They were big and broad, though already going a little to seed without their coach around to ride them. One had dark hair, the other blond.*

"Mind your business, Jig!" the dark-haired one said.

"Heck," Concho replied, still in a gentle tone. "I was going to give you fellows a chance to walk off the bus. Now it looks like you're gonna have to be carried."

The dark-haired one squared himself in the aisle and rolled his shoulders. "Guess we'll see, Boy!"

The blond-haired one pawed at the girl's tunic. She cried out as it tore. Concho stepped forward. The dark-haired man whipped a hunting knife out of a belt sheath and lunged toward him.

The ex-soldier caught the man's wrist as if the knife were moving in slow motion. He twisted the arm up, snapping it back hard against the edge of a bus seat. The man screeched as the elbow dislocated. The knife flew, clanking off the window and falling to the floor.

Concho whipped a kick from his right boot into the fellow's thigh; the man dropped to one knee. A slap to the head banged the fellow's skull off a seat. Concho shoved him aside and stepped past.

The blond-haired man froze in shock, then recovered enough to sling a fist as the ex-soldier walked into him. The punch slammed into Concho's open palm, and he closed his hand like a vice. Cartilage crunched; the man cried out.

"Get him!" the blond yelled at his two friends. He slung his other fist. It smacked into Concho's cheek, but with his body twisted by the grip on his other fist, there was little heat behind it. The ex-soldier shrugged it off, balled his own right fist, and hit the man about half as hard as he could right in the mouth.

Blood sprayed from smashed lips; blue eyes went wide. The man sagged and would have fallen if Concho hadn't picked him up and thrown him into the last two of his companions. They went down under their friend's weight, shouting in some combination of fear and outrage.

The big man stepped forward to stand over them as the two younger, and smaller bullies shoved desperately at the weight of their friend to get it off them. They managed and scrambled to their feet, darting back several steps from the stranger who'd just whipped their two bigger buddies in five seconds. Both had their fists up, but clearly, neither of them wanted to engage.

"Leave," Concho told them, still in the same gentle voice.

The two young men started backing away, nodding. In the next instant, they turned and fled. Ten-Wolves grasped the shirt collars of the two downed brawlers, dragged them both to shaky feet. He yanked them down the aisle as they stumbled and tried to regain their balance.

The bus door stood open. Concho hurled the men through it, one after the other, letting them thump down to the concrete of the parking lot like unloaded baggage. He stepped down after them.

The blond fellow lay on the concrete, moaning. The dark-haired man struggled to rise. One hand dangled below the dislocated elbow. His other was up palm open. He kept shaking his head. "No more! No more!"

"Either of you come back here, and I won't be so gentle next time," Concho said.

"OK, OK!" the dark-haired man practically shouted. He grabbed at his friend, half helping and half dragging as he got his buddy to his feet, and they wove away across the lot toward the store.

Concho stepped back on the bus. He smiled at his three fellow passengers, who watched him with big, rounded eyes. "Please resume your regularly scheduled relaxation," he joked.

The old man laughed. The middle-aged woman did not. "Good for you!" she snapped. "Those scum deserved every bit of beating you gave them."

"Just emptying the trash, Ma'am."

CHAPTER 3

Concho let the memories fade and came back to the pres-ent, to the Greyhound he rode now. The young woman who'd just boarded wasn't much different from the one he recalled from the other bus. If anything, she was even younger, though of European descent rather than Vietnamese.

After about ten minutes, she rose abruptly and stepped into the aisle, staying as far away from the man who watched her as she could as she came toward the back of the bus. Her head hung down, with her face hidden by long curly brown hair. She wore jeans with her hoodie; the clothes had seen better days and cleaner. She might have been as young as fourteen, too young to be traveling alone. She did not look at the Ranger as she entered the bathroom. His nose wrinkled. Not only were the girl's clothes dirty, but it must have been a few days since she'd bathed herself. Her body odor wasn't overwhelming but was definitely present.

Another ten minutes passed. Concho heard a few quick sobs through the wall and gritted his teeth. The girl finally emerged and walked back up the aisle. She didn't retake her original seat, though, but headed farther toward the front of the bus and slid into an unoccupied seat. She seemed to be reacting to the sense of being eyed by the man sitting across from her.

The new male passenger got up next. He stared after the girl for a moment, then turned and walked toward Concho. He stepped past and entered the bathroom. Water ran; a toilet flushed.

The man came out and paused to lean against the seat across the aisle, bracing himself easily against the highway sway of the bus. He was just over six feet and leanly muscled. Well dressed in new black slacks and a dark windbreaker over a collared gray nylon shirt.

It was starting to get dark in the bus as evening closed in, but the man's features were clear enough. They were even and handsome. His cheeks were cleanly shaven, his teeth straight and white. Only two observations suggested anything unusual about the man. For one, he had no scent. Neither sweat nor soap. For the other, even up close, the fellow's brown irises still had the blood-ruby tinge Concho had noted earlier. Again, the color made him think of arched scorpion stings.

"Kickapoo!" the man said, breaking the silence.

Concho would have arched an eyebrow if he could. He satisfied himself with "Observant."

The man's lips twisted into a smile, though not one to put anyone at ease. "And, given your undue interest in my every move," he added, "no doubt you're a lawman of some sort."

"Afraid we're not close enough buds for me to tell you."

The man nodded. He plucked a cell phone from the holster at his belt and patted it. "Guess I'll just have to do a little research on the world wide web. Can't be too many black Kickapoo lawmen in Texas. I bet I find out who you are pretty quickly."

"You'll let me know, I'm sure."

The man shrugged. "Maybe."

"If only I could identify you so easily," Concho said.

"Pity. But I doubt it."

"So why don't you tell me."

"No fun in that. Officer. Just call me… Mister Friendly." He grinned, touched his forehead with two fingers in a mock salute, and headed back up the aisle. He didn't return to his original seat either but slipped forward two rows to sit a few seats back from the young girl he'd been eyeing.

Concho's teeth ground together, but there wasn't much to do except keep an eye open for trouble. Mister Friendly leaned his head back on his seat and gave every appearance of relaxation. It was surely a lie.

The Ranger made a careful study of the other passengers on the bus. Various folks had come and gone across the day. Other than the lawman, the girl, and Mister Friendly, there were five remaining—a middle-aged white salesman with a suitcase of samples, a Hispanic laborer in jeans and a work shirt, a black man in overalls who appeared to be half drunk, a black woman in her sixties accompanying a girl of ten or so who was probably her granddaughter.

The woman and girl sat almost directly across from the teenager who Mister Friendly had been watching. The three men sat nearer the front of the bus. Concho flipped on his seat light and picked up his copy of *Bluebottle*. He tried to resume reading.

A sentence gave him pause: *Lives end, people die or walk away from you forever, lovers depart in moonlight with paper bags of belongings tucked beneath arms, children disappear.*

He glanced toward the teenaged girl, who fidgeted in her seat as if she still felt the eyes of Mister Friendly upon her.

"Children disappear," he murmured to himself. And then, "Not on my watch."

***

Half an hour later, Concho heard footsteps approaching and looked up from his book. The grandmother and granddaughter were headed his way, probably on their way to the bathroom. The woman was on the high side of sixty, with short, gray, curly hair. Her dress was old fashioned, in dark blue with a long skirt and high neck.

The girl looked younger than expected, probably no more than nine. She wore a short green and white dress with white leggings and white and black faux leather shoes. Her hair had been done up in cornrows. She paused as she saw the book in Concho's hands and her eyes took on a sparkle.

"Whatcha readin'?" she asked.

Concho showed her the plain blue-purple cover and smiled. "It's a mystery called *Bluebottle.*"

"*Bluebottle*! That's a funny title."

"It's a kind of fly," Concho explained. "It's part of a series, and all the books in the series have titles with insects in the name. Like *Moth* and *Black Hornet.*"

"Ahh," the girl said. "I'm reading a mystery series like that, too. It's all titled like the alphabet."

Confused, the Ranger glanced up at the grandmother.

"They're called A to Z Mysteries," the woman explained. "Like *April Fool's Fiasco* and *Colossal Fossil.*"

"Then she's absolutely right. It is like that."

"She really loves reading," the grandmother said.

"Good. Reading helps you in school. And just about everywhere else."

"I like school," the girl said. "My name is Toni, by the way." She held out her hand to shake, and Concho took it. His palm engulfed her tiny fist.

"Come on now, Toni," the grandmother said. "Let the man get back to his book."

"OK," Toni agreed. She smiled and gave Concho a wave as she enunciated with all seriousness. "I have to pee."

The lawman chuckled as the grandmother looked embarrassed.

***

Night encased the bus in a bubble of isolation. Concho dozed and dreamed. The bus was black inside, with no lights showing. A glow slipped in through the windows from a porcelain moon melted into the sky. The passengers all sat frozen in thin pools of pallid light—their faces blank, their mouths open to reveal rustling shadows gathered inside.

Only Mister Friendly remained unlit by any moon. He made an ebon silhouette in his seat, with his head bulking larger than it had any right to. His back remained turned, and a crunching noise came from him as if his jaws were cracking bones.

In the dream, Concho forced himself to his feet. His heart pounded. Blood rushed like a flood through his veins. He pushed himself down the bus's aisle. A sudden breeze buffeted his face. A flicking sound came, like a monstrous viper tongue testing the air.

Mister Friendly turned his head around, impossibly far. Curled horns adorned his skull. His ruby irises were elongated like those of a snake while his cheeks glittered with cornmeal-colored scales. Concho froze, mesmerized for a moment by the eyes. He recognized this being—Maneto, the horned serpent, an ancestral enemy of his people.

In the next instant, the engine song of the bus changed; the vehicle slowed. Concho snapped out of his dose and sat up straight. The dream evaporated, but his heart still pounded, and his mouth felt like the dry bed of a drought-stricken river.

The inside of the bus was softly lit, though, not turned to black. The passengers moved and breathed and began to stir as the driver swung the Greyhound off the freeway and took them down the exit ramp into the lot of a massive Texas truck stop. He pulled up in front of the diesel pumps alongside a couple of eighteen wheelers.

The Ranger made a visual check on Mister Friendly, but the man seemed sound asleep. No horns adorned his skull, and Concho shook his head as the images from his dream shredded away. It must have been his sense of the man's lethal nature that spurred his nightmare. His unconscious mind had turned the modern sociopath into an ancient devil from Kickapoo myth.

The final blow to his anxieties came as Concho recognized this truck stop. It was called The Lone Star. It sat just outside the edge of his normal patrol range around Eagle Pass. Elation swept him. He was less than sixty miles from home. It was going to feel good to sleep in his own bed again and see his own stuff. And to see Maria.

He took out his phone to check the time. 2:04 AM. But even in the middle of the night, the truck stop gleamed like a polished gem. The glass windows of the main store glittered with shiny merchandise; most of it was cheap but glitzy. Floodlights conquered shadows around the pumps while the yellow running lights on the many trucks looked like spider eyes outlining the broad faces of great beasts.

Concho rose and stretched. Other passengers did the same. Mister Friendly hadn't stirred. In contrast, the teenaged girl seemed animated as she bolted outside. Most of the rest of the passengers followed. Even if the air of the truck stop wasn't quite fresh, it was different from inside the bus. People needed the change and a bit of a walkabout after spending hours in a seat.

The lawman planned to join them, but his bladder urgently needed attention. He pushed his way into the bus's toilet. The light snapped on automatically. He handled his business, then splashed a little water on his face. A glance in the mirror showed a man who needed a shave and some solid sleep in a real bed.

His stomach growled, reminding him that he hadn't had a regular meal in almost a day and a half. There was beef jerky in his knapsack, but if they were here long enough, he figured to check the store and see what else could be found to eat. Even a microwavable hot dog would be worth a try.

Stepping out of the bathroom, he stretched again, listening to his joints and tendons popping and cracking. The air here *was* getting stale and a little too saturated with the odors of unbathed human bodies. He wanted something fresher, even if it contained the fragrances of various gasolines.

Reflexively, his gaze scanned the bus. He froze. He'd been in the bathroom less than five minutes, but Mister Friendly was no longer asleep. In fact, the man was nowhere to be seen at all. He had to be outside.

With the girl.

CHAPTER 4

Concho rushed down the aisle. The bus driver wasn't in
his seat; the doors stood open, and he leaped through onto the
concrete below. The brisk breeze of December slapped at him,
fluttering his long-sleeved blue shirt. It felt good after the stuffiness
inside. But he had no time to enjoy it.

No sign of Mister Friendly. He couldn't see *any* of the bus's
passengers, although the driver stood by the pumps wearing a
heavy coat as he filled the vehicle's dinosaur-sized fuel tank. Concho started walking rapidly toward the truck stop store, about seventy yards away.

Reaching the store, he entered and paced it lengthwise to in-
ventory the aisles and customers. Toni's grandmother stood in
front of a candy display filling a small hand basket with sweets.
Toni must be nearby. Two of the male passengers looked over a
display of collectible cups and keychains and various other items
proclaiming they were from "TEXAS!" But no Mister Friendly or
any teenaged girl.

Stepping back outside, Concho decided to circle the store. He
was halfway around when a commotion to his right brought him
to a stop. The lot was darker toward that edge, where big trucks sat
quietly while their owners slept. A shadowy figure darted between

two eighteen wheelers. Right behind it came a bigger shadow, one that shouted:

"Hey, stop! Thief! Thief!"

Concho sprinted toward the commotion. He found a husky-looking fellow bent down in a squat peering beneath a rig. In his right hand, the man held a "tire thumper," a short, sawed-off baseball bat many truckers used for checking low air pressure in their tires.

"What's going on?" the lawman demanded.

The man straightened, his face angry. He was thickly built, wearing jeans and a long-sleeved green and black flannel shirt. Several days' growth of beard made his cheeks look burned. His shoulders and arms bulged with muscle beneath his shirt.

"A damn chick stole from me," he said. "She ran off over here."

"I saw a shadow dart between these trucks," Concho replied. "But she could have gotten away by now."

The man smacked the thumper into his free palm. "Damn little thief!" he muttered.

Concho felt a sudden surety as to the identity of the "thief."

"This 'chick,'" he said. "How old was she? How was she dressed?"

The man stared; the tanned skin around his eyes tightened and wrinkled. "What business of yours? You her pimp?"

A fresh lightbulb powered on over Concho's head. "I'm a Texas Ranger. And it seems like you're telling me you tried to negotiate a deal with a hooker, and she cheated you. That about right?"

The man took an inadvertent step backward. He swallowed. "No hooker! That was just a joke. I was chatting up this girl. She got in the truck, but when I had my back turned, she grabbed my wallet and ran."

"Again, how old was she?"

The trucker's left eyelid jumped. Despite the chill, he wiped the back of his hand across a sweaty upper lip. "Eighteen. At least. Maybe older."

"Wearing a gray hoodie?"

"Maybe."

Concho spat on the ground. "That girl was fifteen at best. You could be in a lot of trouble."

"Hey, I'm the one been harmed here! She stole *my* wallet. And I never touched her."

"Seems like you got off lucky. Now get back to your truck. If I find her and find your wallet, I'll bring it to you."

The man started to bluster, thought better of it, and stomped away. Concho walked around the semi the man had been searching under. He kept his eyes and ears open but paid most attention to his nose. The girl had been a while without a bath. She smelled of old sweat and poor hygiene. He searched for that scent now.

From the direction of the bus came a long, agonized wail, followed by a shout that he recognized as coming from Toni's grandmother.

"Toni! Toni! Where are you? Toni!"

***

A bone-deep chill rippled up Concho's spine. In that in-stant, he suspected a trick. He gave up the search for the girl in the gray hoodie and raced toward the bus. The Greyhound driver and two other male passengers stood outside the bus trying to talk to the grandmother, who leaned over clutching her stomach as if in agony. The lawman sprinted up.

"I'm a Texas Ranger! What's going on?"

"Her granddaughter—" the bus driver started to say.

He was interrupted by the woman, who suddenly straightened and threw herself forward to clutch at Concho's chest. "Toni! Toni! She's gone. She disappeared. Somebody took her."

The woman's nails dug through his shirt. He caught her wrists, pulled her closer, and bent down to meet her gaze. "Tell me how! How?"

"I...she...she was tired. Sleeping. On the bus. I went into the store to get candy for her. She didn't want to wake up. She begged me to let her sleep. I covered her with my coat. I didn't think. I didn't know. I...I was only a few minutes. But when I came back, she was gone. Gone. Gone."

A quick blazing rage burned like a charcoal fire in Concho's ribcage. He *had* been tricked. He'd seen the grandmother's heavy coat on the bus; he hadn't realized Toni was supposed to be asleep beneath it. He'd imagined she was with her grandmother. But she was already gone.

Mister Friendly had never wanted the teenage girl. He'd wanted the younger child. Now he'd gotten her.

The Ranger slid his arm reflexively around the grandmother's shoulder as she began to sob against his shirt. He might have looked calm to the outside world, but his thoughts lunged against their reins. Yet, the three men standing in front of him looked to *him* for orders. They were the driver, the Hispanic laborer, who had his name—Armando—stitched in white across his shirt, and the white salesman who'd been riding the bus with him for hours. All looked scared and unsure.

"We checked the bathroom," the driver said. "She's not there."

Concho nodded. "She wouldn't be. It's Mister Friendly!"

"Who? What?" the driver asked.

"The last guy to get on. Black slacks. A gray nylon shirt. He's not here now. I think he's the one."

Everyone except the grandmother looked around suspiciously. She seemed hardly to have heard.

"Wow!" the driver said.

"We don't have much time," Concho said. He made eye contact with the driver. "Who was he? You've got a record of his ticket."

The driver's head bobbed vigorously. "Yes, yes, let me think. I..."

The lawman chafed but knew hurrying the man wouldn't help.

"I'll; I'll check my list," the driver said. He turned and rushed into the bus.

Concho spoke to the other two men. "You both saw the guy. Spread out. Look for him. Or anything suspicious. Call out if you see something. Hurry!"

He let go of the grandmother and pulled out his cell phone. Swiping his contacts, he found the one for Raul Molina. Raul was Concho's closest friend in the Texas Rangers. He worked as a radio dispatcher and would be off duty tonight. But, with Concho officially suspended, Raul was the only one likely to help him now. The call started to ring through. The bus driver came running back out of the bus.

"Roy Simms!" the man said. "With two 'ms.' That's his name. On his ticket."

Concho frowned. The name sounded familiar, but he couldn't quite place it. He held up a finger to the driver as Raul Molina answered his phone in a sleepy voice.

"Ten-Wolves! What in the world? You know what time it is?"

"I'm sorry, Raul. Listen! I didn't know who else to call. We need an amber alert. We've got a child abduction. It just happened. The Lone Star Truck Stop. You know it? A little over fifty miles north of Eagle Pass."

Molina was wide awake now. "I know it. I'll get the word out. What have you got?"

"A girl child. About nine or ten. African American. Cornrowed hair. Green and white dress. The man who took her was white. About thirty. Six one, maybe one seventy. Black pants, gray collared nylon shirt. A dark windbreaker. Dark brown hair. Brown eyes with a reddish tint. Going under the name Roy Simms. Two 'ms.' I know the name, though. From somewhere. It's probably an alias."

The sound of Raul furiously scribbling down information came through the phone.

"OK," the dispatcher said. "I'll call it in. Alert everyone."

"Thanks, man!"

"Call me later."

"Will do," Concho said. They hung up at the same instant.

"You think this guy is using a false name?" the bus driver asked the Ranger, who slipped his phone back in his pocket.

"Most likely. Look. Help our grandmother here." He patted the woman on the shoulder. "I've got to join the search."

The driver put his arm around the lady. Concho rushed past them into the bus, returning to his seat in the back. He yanked open his knapsack and took out his twin Colt Double Eagle.45s and buckled them on.

He also pinned on his badge, though he wasn't supposed to wear it, given his suspension. To hell with that now. To hell with Max Keller. If wearing the badge meant people would listen to him and move a little quicker, then so it had to be.

Returning outside, he surveyed the parking lot. Vehicles rolled in and out. Although he hadn't wanted to say it in front of the grandmother, it was quite possible Mister Friendly had kept a getaway car parked here and was already gone. He had to hope that wasn't true or that at least he could find a clue as to where the man might have taken Toni.

Despair tried to grab him as he wondered where in the wilderness of the Lone Star Truck Stop to start. He punched the emotion away. No time now for doubt. Toni's life was at stake.

CHAPTER 5

The passengers Concho had sent to search for Toni and Mister Friendly, or Roy Simms—or whatever his name was—were nowhere to be seen. They were probably checking the better-lighted sections of the truck stop. That left him the darkness.

He headed around to the back of the building. An iron fence formed a square directly around the store's rear entrance. The gate into it had been padlocked. Inside the fence could be seen a big generator, currently turned off, and a short metal staircase leading up to a small office. No glow showed through the office window. Everything here was shadowy, with only a few lights along the top of the building to provide illumination.

To Concho's right, the cement lot of the truck stop ended abruptly at a curb, with the gray silhouettes of mesquite and cactus and other scrubland bushes rising beyond. He smelled the dry, almost peppery scent that identified the plant life of this section of southern Texas. Small creatures rustled through the undergrowth.

To his left stood a cul-de-sac housing two large metal trash bins. A broken wooden pallet lay in front of them. Cardboard boxes of various sizes were piled to one side, including one large enough to hold a double-wide refrigerator. He stalked in that direction.

A noise brought him to a standstill. His heart sped. His hand dropped to the butt of one of his Colts as a stray cat broke from its hiding place and raced off into the field, dropping the half-chewed body of a mouse as it fled.

Feeling his heartbeat slowing again, he released the handle of the pistol. His head came up; nostrils flared wide. A stew of garbage smells filtered in, rotted vegetables, preserved half-eaten meats, gasoline, burnt cardboard, and plastic. He identified each one, isolated it, set it aside, then examined what lingered.

He remembered that Mister Friendly had no scent, but Toni's hair had smelled of some kind of gel. He didn't know what it was called, but it reminded him of beeswax. And, of course, the teen-age girl in the hoodie had exuded sweat. He hoped not to smell beeswax because it would mean, almost certainly, that Toni was already dead and discarded.

A scent did filter into his awareness, subtle but identifiable. He nodded his head, spoke loudly. "I know you're here. I don't know everything going on, but I'm not going to harm you. I'm a Texas Ranger. I can protect you."

Silence held for a dozen heartbeats. Then came a sudden sob. Ten-Wolves pulled out his cell phone, swiped a thumb across the flashlight app. A small circle of light appeared on the ground. He stepped toward the big refrigerator box and leaned down to shine the light inside. The girl in the gray hoodie huddled against the closed end of the box. Her face was dirty and tear stained.

"I won't hurt you," Concho repeated.

"He left me," the girl said. "Left me." Her voice took on a tinge, almost like jealousy. "And replaced me with *her*."

"You mean Mister Friendly left you?"

"That's not his name."

"Is it Roy Simms?"

"He uses that. Sometimes. But I call him Jericho. It's what he likes."

"Is he still here? At the truck stop?"

She shook her head, looked down as if ashamed. "I...saw him

drive off."

A tiny sliver of hope bloomed in Concho's mind if they could identify the automobile carrying Toni! "What kind of car was he in?" he asked.

The girl shrugged. "It was white."

The lawman's hopes shredded. He wanted to grab the girl, shake her until she gave him something of use. That approach wouldn't help. He strove to keep his voice calm as he asked,

"What's your name?"

The girl sniffed. "Mandy."

"How old are you, Mandy?"

A shrug.

"How old were you when…when Jericho took you?"

Again, she sniffed and shifted position, bringing her a little closer to him. "Ten," she said.

The muscles in Concho's jaws knotted. He forced them to soften. He couldn't give into his anger just yet.

"So it's been years," he said. "That you've been with him?"

"Yeah, I guess."

"Mandy. Listen. This is very important. I know he took you. I'm sure he hurt you. But now he's taken another little girl. Her name's Toni. You know that, don't you?"

"Yes."

"Were you supposed to provide a distraction?"

"Yeah. But I didn't really have to. Not so much."

"Right. You know, I don't want what happened to you to happen to Toni. I need your help to protect her."

"It's too late. Once he gets you, he keeps you." Her voice turned bitter. "Until he doesn't want to anymore."

Concho shook his head gently. "No, it's not too late yet. Not if we don't give up. You can be an important part of that."

"But I don't know anything."

"Maybe not, but will you answer some questions for me anyway?"

"I guess," Mandy said, in an even smaller voice than the one she'd been using up till now.

"It would be easier if you came out of the box."

Mandy nodded. She shifted to her hands and knees and crawled toward Concho. He offered his arm, and she grasped it. He stood, drawing her to her feet. She shivered in the cold, hugging herself. He drew her back a few steps against the wall where the breeze was partially blocked.

Concho swiped off his flashlight app and pocketed his cell. "You remember the town where you and Jericho got on? You recall the name?"

Mandy shook her head.

"Well, I can find out from the bus driver. Did Jericho leave a car there? At that town?"

"No. A man drove us. Dropped us off."

"Do you know this man's name?"

"Just Wilbur."

"Good. Very helpful. Was it a long drive to get there? Do you remember?"

Mandy gave a weak nod. "Very long. Hours."

"Great! That gives us a lot. And you're saying Jericho had a car here. And it was white. Was it a big car or a small one?"

"I don't know."

"Did it have four doors or just two?"

"Four. I…think."

"It would be really helpful if you could remember for sure."

"Maybe. I…."

"What?"

"I could probably recognize it if you showed me pictures."

"Good. That *will* be helpful." Concho smiled, making sure the girl could see it. "You're being very brave, Mandy. I just have a few more questions."

A rough voice shattered Concho's concentration. "There she is. The little thief!"

The lawman twisted around. The truck driver he'd confronted before—the one in the green and black flannel shirt who'd claimed Mandy stole his wallet—stood near the metal garbage bins. Two other burly drivers stood just behind him. All three carried wooden tire thumpers.

"The little bitch took my money," the leader of the three said. "And I'm gonna get it back, or I'll take it out of her hide!"

CHAPTER 6

At the trucker's harsh words, Mandy tried to bolt. Concho caught her arm, restrained her, pushed her behind him. "Stay there!" She cowered against the wall.

He looked back toward the three truckers. Moving a step toward them allowed the light from one of the roof floods to glint off his badge.

"Hey!" one of the men said, "you didn't tell us there'd be a cop."

The lead trucker, in his green and black flannel, smirked. "I doubt he's any lawman. I figure he's the chick's pimp. Probably got my five hundred bucks in his pocket right now."

"I don't know, Larry," the other trucker added.

Concho took another step toward the three. Eyes widened as they caught sight of the two pistols on his hips. The two men accompanying "Larry" took backward steps.

"I ain't confrontin' no Ranger," one of the two said.

Concho spoke softly. "You men go."

Larry's two companions slipped into drift mode and rushed away. Larry heard them moving and glanced around to find himself alone. He cursed. His hand hefted his shorn off bat, but then he shook his head. Lowering the club, he took a step away.

"Not you, Larry!" Concho snapped. "You stand right there. Mandy, did you take this man's wallet?"

"Ye...yes."

"Give it to me."

"I threw it away."

"Where?"

"Under that red truck by his."

Ten-Wolves glanced toward the girl and held out his hand. "Give me the money."

Mandy nodded. She stuck her fingers in the pocket of her jeans and pulled out a wad of greenbacks, which she passed over.

"It wasn't any five hundred dollars," she said.

Concho took the money, fanned it out to make a rough count. It looked like about three hundred in twenties, tens, and fives. He walked over to Larry, who straightened his shoulders and stood his ground, although he had to crane his neck to look up at the Ranger.

Concho tucked the folded greenbacks into the pocket of the man's flannel shirt. "Check under the red truck for your wallet," he said.

"Hey!" Larry said, pulling the money out of his pocket and swiping through it, "this ain't all of it. You pocket some for yourself?"

"I doubt it was more. But that's all you're getting anyway. Take it and leave. I don't want to see your face anymore."

"You ain't gonna get away with it!" Larry growled. "You'll be hearing from me."

"Later will be fine. Right now, I've got a missing child on my hands, and you're slowing the flow."

Larry jerked his chin toward Mandy. "That bitch ain't no child, and it don't look like she's missing."

Concho snapped a short jab into Larry's mouth. The man's eyes flew open in surprise as he took two steps backward and sat down hard on his ass. His tire thumper smacked the ground.

The lawman's teeth ground together as he snarled, "Not her. And that punch is for calling this young lady a foul name. Now get out of here unless you want more."

Larry winced as he pushed one hand against his bleeding lips. He forced himself to his feet, scooped up his thumper, and fled without another word.

Concho turned back to Mandy, whose face glowed white with surprise.

"All right," the Ranger said. "Where were we?"

Before either of them could say more, sirens began to blare through the distant night as the cavalry finally closed in on the Lone Star Truck Stop. Mandy's body shook violently at the sound. She tried again to bolt. Concho caught her with his arm, restrained her as gently as he could.

"It's OK," he said.

"They'll arrest me! Take me to jail!"

"No, Mandy! You're a victim. Not a villain. They'll only want to know the same thing I want to know. Anything to help us find Toni before Jericho hurts her."

"But I don't know anything," Mandy wailed.

"You probably do. You just don't know what's important. We'll get it straight." He reached out and enfolded her hand loosely in his. "Come on, let's go around front. I need to talk to the police when they arrive. You've got to keep being brave."

Mandy's hand was small inside Concho's. She twisted it around and grasped two of his fingers, squeezing hard.

"Don't leave me. Please!"

"I'll make sure you're safe before I do," he promised. "There are others coming who you can trust."

Mandy shook her head but allowed herself to be led toward the front of the truck stop.

As they walked, Concho asked another question. "Jericho told you to create a distraction. That why you stole the trucker's wallet?"

"I guess so. I didn't know what else to do. And I needed money."

"Did you know Jericho was going to leave you?"

Mandy shook her head. "He said...said if we got separated, I was to hide, and he'd come back for me. Or send Wilbur."

"Tell me about Wilbur."

Mandy gave a quick little shudder that told him some unpleasant things about Wilbur. "Dirty," she said. "He stinks. He never takes a bath or wears any deodorant. And he's mean. And fat. He likes to hurt. Jericho kinda kept him in line. Wilbur was scared of Jericho."

"How old is Wilbur?"

"Older than you. Or Jericho. I don't really know."

"Does he have gray hair?"

"Almost no hair. Just around the back and ears. He looks like a...a rotten cabbage."

The lawman nodded. "Thank you, Mandy."

They'd reached the front of the building now. Blue lights fractured the darkness, and rubber squealed as two police cars raced into the parking lot. Mandy's hand stiffened in Concho's grip, and he offered her a soft, "It's OK. They're our friends."

The lights in front of the truck stop glittered bright after the dimness of the building's rear. Concho blinked and raised his free hand high, waving it back and forth to catch the attention of the police.

Both cars swerved in his direction and screeched to a stop. State Troopers piled out of both vehicles, wearing their "Texas Tan" uniforms and tan cowboy hats. One was tall, one short. Their hands rested on the butts of handguns, but they didn't draw. Both men relaxed as they glimpsed Concho up close and saw his badge.

"We got a report of a missing child," the short one said. "Don't reckon this is her?" He jutted his chin toward Mandy.

"No," Concho answered. He explained quickly about Toni and the man he was now calling Jericho. Nodding toward Mandy, he added, "This young lady was his prisoner, too. She says he's already fled with Toni. He's driving a white car. Probably a four-door. One of you radio in an update. Then join me by that Greyhound bus." He pointed. "Toni's grandmother is there. We'll make it our base of operations for the moment."

The men nodded. The short one immediately slid back into his prowl car and grabbed the mic for his radio. Concho strode toward the bus, still holding Mandy's hand. He stuck his other hand in the air as a signal as more police vehicles, both state and local, began to pull into the truck stop. They saw his raised arm, turned in his direction. The lights and sirens made the girl flinch. Ten-Wolves squeezed her hand gently.

The driver of the Greyhound stood talking comfortingly to Toni's grandmother as the Ranger approached. The two passengers he'd sent to search the truck stop were also there, looking anguished. One was Armando. He didn't know the other's name.

The driver let go of the grandmother's shoulder and turned toward Concho.

"We've got another missing passenger!" he blurted.

CHAPTER 7

"What?" Concho demanded. "Who?"

"You must have seen him on the bus. Uhm…black guy. Thirty or so. Short hair and overalls. His name's Pete Cramer. According to the ticket. He was half drunk when he got on. Been sleeping most of the ride. He got off when we stopped here, but," he gestured toward Armando and the salesman, "none of us have seen him since, and he's not in the store or anywhere outside we can find."

Concho frowned. "I remember him. Haven't seen him either."

He considered the possibilities and could only come up with an unpleasant one. Maybe Cramer had been working with Jericho as some kind of backup. He could even have been the one who actually grabbed Toni.

Glancing at Mandy, he wondered if she had been holding out on him. "Cramer," he said to her, his voice rougher than he wanted it to be. "Was he working with Jericho?"

The girl looked scared. "I don't…believe so."

Concho didn't think she was lying, but he had more questions. "What about when you saw Jericho leave? Was there another adult in the car with him?"

"I didn't…I didn't…see one." Her voice rose in pitch. "I don't know!"

Concho fought a little bit of calm back into his voice to keep from frightening Mandy further. "It's OK. OK. I don't suppose you saw Toni either?"

Again, Mandy used her small voice, the voice of a child. "No," she whispered. "But..."

"But what?"

Mandy looked down. "She would have been...in the trunk."

"Is that where you were put when he kidnapped you?"

Her voice grew even smaller. "Yes."

The lawman slid his right arm around the girl and gave her a squeeze. "Thank you, Mandy. I'm sorry we have to ask you these things."

"I...I understand."

Concho let go of Mandy and stood looking at the people around him, policemen and civilians. They all looked sick to heart or boiling angry, or both.

"I could be wrong," he said. "But my bet is Pete Cramer was working with Jericho. Probably had his own car. And it might be the one Toni is in. Jericho seems smart enough to cover himself that way."

"Means we have zilch as far as a lead goes," one of the gathered police officers said. She was a local cop rather than state. Looked to be in her late thirties. Her badge identified her as a deputy of Kinney County, Texas—this county—which lay directly north of Maverick County, where Eagle Pass was located. The name tag over her right shirt pocket read Wiebke.

Concho didn't want to reply because he'd seen Toni's grand-mother step closer to hear what they were saying. He didn't want to add to her pain. But she'd already heard the deputy. She vented a wail; her legs gave out. Concho leaped forward and caught her before she could hit the ground. He picked her up; her head lolled back. She'd passed out.

"Is there an ambulance coming?" Concho demanded from the

crowd of officers.

"On the way," Wiebke answered. "Here, put her in my car."

Concho followed the policewoman. She opened the back door of her unit, and he lay Toni's grandmother across the seat. As he straightened, he glimpsed Mandy inching away from the other people by the bus. He called her name. She startled, then came toward him with a guilty look on her face.

"Mandy," he said. "I've got a very important job for you. I know I can trust you."

"What?"

"Can you watch over this lady?" He pointed toward the unconscious woman in the police car. "If she wakes up or cries out, let someone know right away."

Mandy chewed at her lower lip but bobbed her head in agreement.

"I also have another couple of questions for you," Ten-Wolves continued. "What kind of house did Jericho have when you were with him?"

"What do you mean? It was just a house."

"I mean, was it near other houses? In a town? Or out in the country?"

"The country," Mandy blurted. "Pretty far out. Nobody else around. They had a pond. It was scary."

"Why?"

The girl shrugged.

"It sounds like you remember the place pretty well. You think you could describe it for someone who might try to draw it?"

"You mean, what it looks like?"

"Yeah. How big it was. Whether they had a barn, a windmill. The pond you mentioned. Any other buildings around."

"I guess I could."

Concho glanced at Deputy Wiebke. "Can you get a sketch artist out here? I can describe Jericho for them. Pete Cramer a little. Though I never got a good look at his face. Mandy will be able to help with the house, Jericho, and a man named Wilbur, who also seems to be Jericho's accomplice."

"Wiebke nodded. "Will do."

"If we get a description of the house, we should get some helicopters in the air to search for it. I bet it's within a hundred miles. Probably less."

"Why do you say that?" Wiebke asked.

"One reason is just a feeling. I think Jericho wanted this kidnapping to end close enough to home to get there fast. Either to hide out or to try and throw any police off the trail."

"But you have another reason?"

Concho nodded. "I realized something about what the man said to me. He knew I was Kickapoo and a lawman. He acted like it was just a guess, but I'm pretty sure now it wasn't. He knew *exactly* who I was. Which probably means he's watched the local news over the last few months."

"Makes sense. You've been on it enough. I'll send for the sketch artist."

Fresh sirens shrieked along the main highway. Red lights mixed with blue. An ambulance coming. Concho stepped closer to Mandy to help keep her calm. She was the key to it all right now, to whatever chance they had left of finding a little girl named Toni alive and unharmed.

***

As was usually the case when Jericho was in action, the crimson thoughts slipped into the background of his mind. Killing those who deserved it would come later, and he'd welcome it. But now he needed to focus, to keep his thoughts on the now.

A glance into his rearview mirror showed no car lights behind him. He hadn't expected any. After leaving the Lone Star Truck Stop, he'd taken only surface streets, which soon led to local roads where few traveled, particularly at this very early hour of the morning. The "taking" had worked just as he'd planned it.

Only one thing had surprised him. Concho Ten-Wolves. He'd recognized the half-black, half-Kickapoo Texas Ranger the moment he'd seen him sitting on the bus. The man's face had been pasted all over the local news in the last few months, from his bloody shootout with Neo-Nazis in the Eagle Pass Mall to breaking up an all-female gang of bank robbers. The man was famous hereabouts or near to it.

Fate was fickle, it seemed. It was surely no coincidence that Ten-Wolves had chosen to ride the same bus Jericho had picked for his work. But, if so, the Ranger had appeared unaware of the significance. It was clear the man sensed the power inside Jericho, but also clear he had no clue as to the nature of that power.

And so, a challenge! Fate had thrown a gauntlet down in front of Jericho, a steel glove with the name Ten-Wolves etched across it. And with his imagination spurred, he'd left Mandy behind to be found by the Ranger. He had no clear idea where that might lead, but the possibilities intrigued.

Jericho grinned into his mirror while shadows bled from the corners of his mouth.

CHAPTER 8

7:07 AM. Monday. Concho stepped out of the Lone Star Truck Stop holding his third cup of coffee in the last two hours. He didn't really like coffee, but after a night with almost no sleep, he needed it.

He sipped, made a face at the bitterness even though he'd laced in enough sugar to choke a buffalo. The Greyhound bus sat almost alone now, in a parking space near the highway. The ambulance and most of the police cars were gone. Only the local officer's vehicle remained, Deputy Wiebke, who'd given her first name as "Perse." Concho guessed it was short for Persephone. It made him wonder what kind of folks named their child after the Queen of the Underworld and the wife of Hades.

The ambulance had taken Toni's grandmother to the hospital. The police cars had gone off to look for any sign of the man or men who'd taken Toni. The child's last name was Everett, he'd discovered. The Greyhound was also reloading its few remaining passengers. The police had finished fingerprinting the inside, at least the seats occupied by Simms/Jericho and Pete Cramer, and had finally released the commercial vehicle to continue its journey. Concho's paid-for seat would remain empty.

Switching his cup to his left hand, Ten-Wolves pulled out his phone. Maria would be awake now, getting ready to go to work.

He needed to tell her he couldn't get home quite as soon as he'd planned. He hoped she'd take it well. The phone rang twice before Maria answered.

"Lover!" she purred.

Her voice sent shivers traveling the length of his body.

"Hello, baby," he replied. "How's your mom?"

Maria's mom, Rosa, had gotten sick while he was in New Orleans and had been hospitalized with a breathing issue the doctors hadn't been able to identify. At least that had been the case the last time he'd talked to Maria.

"She's a lot better. We brought her home yesterday. The doctors are just calling it pneumonia. They've got her on oxygen, but she was up and moving around a lot last night, so I think she's turned the corner."

"Good to hear."

"So, are you home? Can you come by my office this morning? I've got a meeting at 10:00. Should last about an hour. Otherwise, I'll be…available." She chuckled as she breathed heavily into the phone.

Concho sighed. "I…I'm sorry, baby, but I'm not quite home yet."

Maria's voice sharpened. "What? Why?"

"A little girl. Nine years old. She was kidnapped off the bus I was riding. I've got to help find her. Before the kidnapper hurts her."

"Oh my God!" Maria said, gasping. "I'm sorry. Do you know who took her?"

"I think so, and I'm the one who can best identify him. I've got to see it through. I don't know how long it'll take."

"Of course," Maria said. "Of course. I understand."

"Thanks. I really want to see you. I'm only about fifty miles away, and it's agony not being able to cross that last distance."

"I understand," Maria repeated. "You've got to do what you have to. What's her name? The girl?"

"Toni Everett. She's a reader. We talked about books on the bus. She was with her grandmother."

"You talk about books with everyone," Maria said fondly.

"Not so much with you," Concho teased.

Maria snickered. "Yes, I well know the kinds of things *we* talk about." Then she huffed a hard breath. "You got a name on the scumbag who took the girl?"

"Roy Simms. With two 'ms.' Though he also goes by Jericho apparently."

"*Simms!*" Maria exclaimed. "Roy Simms? You sure?"

Concho frowned. "Yeah. Why? You know the name? I thought I recognized something about it but can't remember."

"I know it. And you should, too. I told you about Roy Simms. From my college days at Texas A&M."

A very different kind of shiver coursed the lawman's body now as he recalled a story Maria had told him. Roy Simms had managed the meat locker for a while at Texas A&M's animal industries building. One day in 1959, he'd accidentally cut himself with a knife. Cut an artery, actually. That hadn't quite been the end of his tale, though.

"Roy Simms is a ghost!" Maria said.

***

Roy Simms, aka Jericho, pulled down the long dirt road leading to the farmhouse he'd occupied for the last five years. It was dangerous returning here now, especially if his enemies had caught Mandy and questioned her. He'd expected them to do so when he left her behind. No doubt she'd reveal this place. And once revealed, it wouldn't take long for the police to locate it physically. Perhaps they already had. They could be waiting for him.

The thought made him chuckle. What was any game without risk? After pulling up in front of the house and putting the car into park, he leaned over and opened the glove box inside nestled a beautiful snake of a pistol, a Manuhrin MR73 Sport .38/.357 with a 5.25-inch barrel. It had been produced by Beretta in coal black with a gold hammer and trigger. He pulled it out and held it down by his right side while exiting the vehicle.

No one responded to his arrival. He glanced around. The house and barn were silent. The breeze stroked him pleasantly. It was a nice day for December. Of course, he didn't much mind cold.

Stepping up on the porch, he unlocked the door and pushed inside. Immediately, he relaxed. The place was empty. Almost. The presence in the house was the same one he always felt. If anyone else had visited, he would have known.

He walked down the hallway and turned into the dining room, ignoring the five naked mannequins sitting in a family group around the scarred oak table. The big kitchen lay through another doorway beyond. A clock ticked; the refrigerator hummed. He opened the fridge and took out a can of Dr. Pepper, wishing it was the old Dublin cane sugar variety. Unfortunately, those were no longer made.

Sliding up a window to let fresh air into the place, he stared out while sipping his soda. The black dog stood near the barn, watching him. Shadow smoke rose from its back. He toasted it with Dr. Pepper, and it turned its head toward a wood pile that had once been a small shed, long since collapsed on itself.

Jericho followed the dog's gaze, glimpsed movement near the pile. A wild rat nibbled at something on the ground. The brownish rodent was nearly as big as a cat. On impulse, he lifted his pistol in one smooth movement and fired through the window screen. The rat leaped into the air with a high-pitched squeal, crashed back to earth, and lay still after a few twitches.

Jericho closed the window, dropped his empty can into the trash and washed his hands, then went upstairs to pack. He was leaving this place. He'd already found a new one. The black dog would follow. He'd call Pete Cramer, who'd bring Toni. A little business would be conducted, and after that, they'd be a normal family. For a while.

***

Concho had spent most of the early morning hanging with Mandy, trying to keep her calm and cooperative as the police sketch artist arrived and questioned her about Jericho's appearance and about the house where she'd spent time with him. The artist had gotten good information. The drawings of the farmhouse and of Jericho had already been reproduced and emailed to every law officer in a ten-county area.

Now, Mandy was talking to a social worker who'd been dispatched by state social services. Her name was Beth Pennebaker. Her office was apparently in Eagle Pass, though Concho had never met her. She seemed a good choice, likable on first meeting. But Mandy still wanted him nearby and kept glancing in his direction, though her glances had been getting less frequent as Pennebaker worked with her.

A white Dodge Durango came tooling down the off ramp from the highway and pulled into the Lone Star Truck Stop. It braked to a halt next to Deputy Wiebke's prowl car. Concho recognized it and blinked in surprise.

Special Agent Della Rice climbed out of the driver's side of the SUV. She wore black pants and a black shirt with a blue windbreaker over it, reading FBI in white. A Glock.40 hung at her right hip.

Della Rice stood six feet tall. Lean, dark skinned, and dark haired. Her mother had named her after Della Reese, the actor, and singer. Or so it was said. Concho had a history with Rice, much of it unpleasant. Rice had investigated him on suspicion of using his position to help smuggle drugs from Mexico through the Kickapoo reservation into the United States. She'd based her suspicions on a series of anonymous tips called into her agency, as well as on some circumstantial evidence she'd given more weight to than it deserved.

To her credit, she'd finally admitted she was wrong after Concho had a shoot-out with the crooked cop who'd been providing those tips. Turned out the cop was in league with the Aryan Brotherhood, who still held a grudge against Ten-Wolves for his role in crushing their plans to take over the Eagle Pass Mall some months back.

Concho hadn't completely forgiven Rice yet for how easily she'd swallowed the faked stories about him. But, he liked some things about her and had developed respect for her commitment to the law. Plus, as she'd told him the last time they'd seen each other, they still had to work together as professionals.

Rice strode up to Concho and shook his hand as a second FBI agent climbed out of the passenger side of the Durango. Concho had met this one only briefly. Special Agent Binh Bui was of Vietnamese descent. He wore dress slacks and a white shirt with a dark blue tie. His weapon of choice was a Sig Sauer P365 9-millimeter.

A final agent slid out of the SUV's back seat. He looked to be in his late twenties, strongly built with crewcut brown hair and a slightly ruddy, open face. He carried a Glock as well. Rice introduced him as "Special Agent Will Bolin."

The two men shook hands, then Bolin stepped back and crossed his arms in front of himself as his non-stop, serious gaze began to scan every inch of the parking lot.

"Where, pray tell, are Duke and Voight?" Concho asked, mentioning the two agents who'd worked with Rice during her investigation of him. They hadn't taken to the Kickapoo lawman very much, and the feeling had been mutual.

"Sent them back to the main office," Rice said. "They didn't seem particularly suited for the work down here."

"Oh, too bad. I really liked those guys."

Rice snorted. She knew exactly how Concho felt about Duke and Voight.

"Now," Rice said. "What's this about you being suspended from the Texas Rangers?"

"News travels fast."

"Gossip certainly does." She gestured toward the two Colt semi-automatics on Concho's hips. "I guess you know you're not supposed to be carrying those under the circumstances."

The lawman shrugged. He'd actually taken his badge off again and put it in the pocket of his jeans, but he'd continued wearing the pistols. "You here to arrest me for going armed?"

Rice flashed a smile, which softened her stern face considerably. "Nope. Here to offer you an excuse for carrying them. A temporary consulting job with the FBI. If you want it? Unless you've got better things to do."

Concho frowned. "What kind of consulting job?"

"On a certain case involving a kidnapped nine-year-old girl," Rice said.

"I thought drug abatement was more your thing."

"Not since we heard about a missing child. You in?"

"I'm in," Concho said.

CHAPTER 9

Concho glanced away from Della Rice as he heard Man-dy's voice rising. She was talking to the social worker but kept looking in his direction with anxiety on her face.

"Excuse me a minute," the lawman said. He hurried over to Mandy, who grabbed for his hand. He let her squeeze it.

"What's up?" he asked, keeping his voice upbeat.

"She says I have to go with her," Mandy blurted, pointing at Beth Pennebaker.

Pennebaker's short red hair was mussed as if she hadn't had a chance to comb it this morning, but her voice remained mild as she said, "I told her I could help find her parents, but we'd need to go to my office in Eagle Pass."

Concho squatted to bring his face closer to Mandy's. "You want to see your parents, don't you?"

It took a few seconds for Mandy to respond. "I guess. But I'm scared!"

"Of what?"

"He— Jericho took me from my yard. My parents couldn't do anything. I don't think they even knew."

"And you're afraid he'll come take you again?"

"He will. Or someone will. He has all kinds of friends. Everywhere! I want to stay with you."

Concho rested a big hand on Mandy's thin shoulder. "I understand. We can make sure you have a police officer with you. But right now, Jericho is on the run. He's got to worry about himself and not focus on you. And if you go with Ms. Pennebaker, he won't know where to look for you anyway."

"Until I go home."

"We can arrange for both you and your parents to have police officers around 24/7. Jericho won't get to you again."

"Why can't you come with me?" she pleaded.

"I wish I could, but I have to try and find Toni. Now that we have the great information you gave us, we need to move fast."

Mandy's voice turned sullen. "Why is she more important than me?"

"She's not *more* important. But she's in greater danger than you are at the moment. You understand, don't you?"

Mandy sighed. Her head hung down as she scuffed her worn tennis shoes on the concrete. "I guess."

Concho glanced up at Pennebaker. "Can you get a police officer to help you take Mandy to your office? Preferably someone who's good with young folks?"

Beth nodded. "I can." She smiled. "My husband is a police officer. And we have two girls just a little older than you, Mandy. I'll call him right away."

"Does that sound alright, Mandy?" Concho asked.

Mandy's eyes darted back and forth like minnows racing for shallow water to avoid a predator. "I guess," she said again.

Concho smiled, though he worried about Mandy's fear. It seemed excessive, but who knew what years of being held by a kidnapper could do to a child's mind. Beth Pennebaker pulled her cell phone out of her purse and swiped a number. She moved away as a man's voice answered on the other end.

Concho rubbed his thumb over Mandy's thin shoulder blade as he met her gaze. "I'm really impressed by your bravery. Not many fourteen-year-olds are this tough."

"I still wish you were coming with me."

"Tell you what. When Ms. Pennebaker comes back, I'll give her my cell phone number so you can call me anytime you need me. I promise I'll answer unless we're actually about to rescue Toni. And if I *don't* answer right away, I'll call you back the second I can."

"OK."

"And as soon as we get Toni, I'll come see you. But I can tell from talking to her that Ms. Pennebaker is a good person. You can trust her. And her police officer husband."

"OK. If you say so."

Concho patted her shoulder again and rose to his feet, his legs rejoicing at the change in position.

"There's one other thing I guess I could tell you," Mandy said.

"What's that?"

"Something I didn't think about until now. Or include for the drawing guy. But it might help."

"Go on."

"The burned church."

Concho frowned. "What burned church?"

"I just remembered. Right near the road that turns into the farm, there's a church. Or there was. It burned a while back. But parts of it are still standing. It's got a stone cross in front. It's broken. One of the arms fell down, so it looks wrong."

The lawman liked the feeling of hope springing up inside him but didn't completely trust it. "That's really helpful. And it's right next to the road where you turn to Jericho's farm?"

Mandy's lips flipped up and down in a quick and tentative smile. "Yeah. I just remembered because I was thinking about what Jericho said when we left. For the bus, you know."

"What did he say?"

"He pulled over there. Pointed it out to me. He said...'that shows the fo...folly of faith.' You can't believe in anything but me."

Concho's anger at the man named Jericho burned like a barbecue inside his chest. "You know that's not true, don't you?"

"I do now. I believe in you."

The Ranger wasn't sure whether to be pleased or terrified at Mandy's words. But he dared not let her down.

***

Beth Pennebaker finished the call to her husband and came back to Mandy. Concho exchanged phone numbers with her, then walked quickly toward Perse Wiebke, motioning for Della Rice and her fellow FBI agents to join them. Wiebke was talking into the mic of her radio but signed off when she saw the other law officers coming.

"How can I help you?" she asked.

"I hope you can. Is there a burned-out church anywhere nearby you know of? It would still be partially standing. With a stone cross in front that has one arm broken off."

Wiebke gave a small gasp. "There is about forty miles from here. It was called *The Old Rugged Cross* church. Why?"

Mandy just told me about it. It's right near the road that turns onto the farm where she was held by Jericho."

Wiebke bobbed her head furiously, her eyes alight. "I can show you. Follow me!"

She spun and piled into her car, grabbing for the keys in the ignition. Concho glanced at Della Rice with triumph.

The FBI agent nodded. "Let's go!" She leaped for her Dodge Durango.

"No lights or sirens when we get close," Concho shouted to Wiebke before rushing toward the SUV as well. He waved to Mandy and Beth Pennebaker before scrambling into the passenger side of the FBI vehicle. Agents Bui and Bolin were already buckling themselves in the back seat.

Wiebke pulled out, lights and sirens blazing. Della Rice wheeled the SUV out behind the deputy as they began a desperate but hopeful race against the threats of time and terror.

CHAPTER 10

Jericho hauled two small suitcases out to his car, but not to the white 2016 Ford Fusion he'd driven here in. That was strictly a discardable. Meant for temporary use and to serve as a distraction. His real car sat hidden in the barn, a 2018 Mazda Miata MX-5 convertible. Also white.

After sticking the cases in the trunk of the Miata, Jericho went back upstairs in the farmhouse and took a last hot shower, dried himself, then dressed in clean khakis and a white polo shirt. He threw a linen jacket on over that.

He studied himself in the mirror in his bedroom. The jacket was cut a little big and successfully hid the shoulder holster slung under his right arm. The Manuhrin Sport revolver went into this and made only the smallest of bulges. He smiled at his reflection. He looked like a young, wealthy heir to some robber baron's old oil empire, which wasn't far from the truth.

Glancing around, he saw little else to remember from this place. Other than the clothes, his laptop, and a few special items he'd already packed away, everything else was expendable. Some things he *wanted* to leave behind. Others he simply didn't care about, such as the art on the walls, which were only reproductions of original work and not worth hauling along.

Straightening his collar, he took a deep breath. He was ready to leave forever. Just one more thing to do, one order to give. He spoke to the presence in the house. His voice echoed.

"Enemies will be along soon. Stop them. The way I taught you. But one thing. Among them will be a very large black man with hair to his shoulders. Do nothing to him. He's my kill. In time."

The presence did not speak. But it never did. Not anymore.

***

Winter sun glittered off the windshield of the Dodge Durango as the FBI vehicle followed Perse Wiebke's police cruiser down one of Texas's many straight highways at a high rate of speed. They'd had to take back roads to get here, and it had cost them time. Now they made it up.

They'd also radioed for chopper support, but nothing was close. For now, they were on their own. Concho's phone rang. He recognized the caller; he'd exchanged cell numbers with Wiebke earlier.

"Yes?" he answered, swiping on his speaker so everyone in the Dodge could hear.

"We're about twenty minutes out," Wiebke said. "I'm shutting down my lights and sirens. You'll see the burned church on the right; there's a dirt road off to the left that must be the way to the farm. I'll take it as fast as I can, but it's likely to be rough."

"Gotcha. We're right behind you."

Wiebke swiped off. Her siren went quiet, her blue lights dark. Concho heard a lot of movement in the back seat of the Durango and turned to see Bui and Bolin pulling on their bullet-proof vests. Bolin also had a scoped hunting rifle leaning against the seat next to him, barrel down—a bolt-action Savage model 111 in .30-06, painted in camouflage colors.

Bui handed a vest to Concho but said, "For the boss. I'm afraid we don't have one for you. I should have thought of it."

"No problem," Ten-Wolves replied. He plucked at the pocket

of his blue shirt. "This is a tactical garment."

Della Rice glanced over, amused. "So, it repels bullets? That what you're saying?"

"Right," Concho said. Then he frowned. "Or is this the magnetic one? I can never remember."

Bolin laughed. Bui only blinked.

Rice shook her head. "Anyone ever tell you you're crazy, Ten-Wolves?" she asked.

"Just you. I'm pretty sure."

"I was right."

"Hmm," Concho said. And, "Why are you doing this?"

"Doing what?" Rice asked.

"Helping me stay involved with this investigation even though I'm officially suspended from the Rangers?"

"Just using resources effectively."

"Raul Molina called you, didn't he?"

Rice glanced over, then back at the road. "Yeah. He contacted every law enforcement agency around. He mentioned you were involved. And a nine-year-old was missing. Whether you believe it or not, I know you well enough to know what that kind of thing means to you."

"Thanks!"

"Besides," Rice added. "I've met your boss. Max Keller."

"Nuff said," Concho replied.

***

Jericho opened his front door and stepped onto the porch. He paused, then sighed as he realized one *more* thing he would have to do. He walked back inside and over to the basement door. Pulling it back, he flipped on the light switch. The single bare bulb was old and starting to brown, but at least it created a dim and dreary glow to push back the piled-up shadows below.

He started down the steps into a pool of hollow voices whose words his ears could not quite make out. It did not matter. Those voices were the past and need not be paid any attention.

A long pinewood table and a single folding wooden chair were the only furniture in the room, but a fireplace stood cold and empty against one wall. He reached to the underside of the fireplace mantel. His fingers searched for certain grooves and found them. He slid a short square of wood backward and felt into the hole behind it. The warmth of soft leather caressed his fingertips.

He grasped a small sack and drew it out. Fawn colored, with a rawhide tie of yellow, it fit comfortably in his palm. Its contents rattled as they settled against each other as if it were full of marbles.

He'd thought he could leave certain things behind as he transitioned into a new life. But the ache in his chest told him he wasn't ready yet to abandon all his recent past. He tucked the bag into the inside pocket of his jacket before returning to the stairs.

Halfway up, a sound cut into his awareness. This was no voice he could ignore but the howl of the black dog. It came from the speaker of his personal phone. He didn't need to see the accompanying message to know what it signaled. It galvanized him into action.

***

Concho saw a blackened spire of brick and wood rising ahead on his right, and his adrenal gland clicked into high gear. His body tingled. Every sense grew heightened. Vision sharpened to absolute clarity. He felt the weight of his shirt on his skin and the heavy bulk of the pistols on his hips. His nostrils flared, taking in the soapy clean scent of the agents in the car with him, mixed with the first beads of sweat as their own fight or flight instincts began to pump.

A narrow dirt road split off the highway just past the burned church, crossing a cattle grate and then surging up a hill. Deputy Wiebke's police car took the off road at speed, kicking up dust.

Della Rice followed. They hit the cattle grate with a teeth-rattling thud, then bounced on the rough road beyond. Inevitably, they slowed, but Rice handled the SUV like a pro as she wrestled it along in the wake of Wiebke. They were headed up a rise, which peaked and dipped half a mile ahead. He couldn't see the house, which must sit in the dip. He hoped it wasn't far. The tension of impending action was nearly unbearable.

His left hand slid to the seat belt button, preparing to release it as soon as they were in sight of the house. His right fist curled around the butt of a Colt.

***

At the signal of the howling dog, Jericho launched him-self up the stairs from the basement, raced through the house and out. The door to the barn already stood open, with his Miata parked just inside. He ran for it.

A glance at the dirt road leading from the highway to the house revealed a double glint of jagged light coming fast in a wave of dust. Maybe two miles away. Concho Ten-Wolves was surely inside that light.

Piling into the Miata, he gunned the engine. One more thought curled his lips. He grabbed a book from his glove box, tore out a page, and tossed it into the dirt of the barn. Something for the Ranger. To tantalize him, to taunt him. Then he sent the Miata hurtling into the open, turning away from the road and pushing the quick little car around the backside of the house.

Dirt spun up from under his wheels. A thought came with great clarity. *For dust you are, and to dust, you will return!*

CHAPTER 11

Still following Deputy Wiebke's racing police car, Concho and the FBI agents in the Durango crossed a low, mesquite-laden ridge and saw a two-story farmhouse below them standing next to a faded gray barn. A white car sat parked about thirty yards from the front door of the house. A four-door Ford Fusion.

Concho released his seat belt and drew a pistol. Wiebke slid her vehicle to a stop to the left side of the Fusion. Della Rice drew up on the right side. Doors on both law vehicles slammed open. Men and women leaped out and ducked into the cover of those doors.

For the moment, the day lay silent. Dust hung in the air, barely stirred by a small breeze. Despite it being mid-December, the day felt hot to Concho, no doubt due to the rush of blood and adrenaline through his system.

"Deputy!" Della Rice shouted to Wiebke. "I want you to take one of my agents. Drive around the back of the house to make sure no one runs. OK?"

"Will do," Wiebke replied. She slid back into the driver's seat of her car, keeping her head low. Leaning across, she pushed open the other door.

"Bui!" Rice called. "You're with Wiebke."

"Yes, Sir," Bui called back.

The dark-haired agent circled around the Durango and the Fusion, then rushed up the side of the police car toward the "shotgun" seat. Just as he reached the door, Wiebke twisted on her ignition, and the quiet of the day shattered as a barrage of bullets suddenly slammed into the cruiser's passenger side, shrieking into metal and sending safety glass spraying.

Wiebke cried out. Bui grunted. Concho rose from his crouch and double actioned his Colt, emptying a clip into a window on the farmhouse's second floor, where the first shots had come from. A shadow at the window ducked back as panes of glass in the window splintered apart.

"Bui!" Rice shouted. "You OK? Wiebke?"

"Bui's hit! He's down!" Wiebke shouted, her voice pitched high but not in panic mode.

"I'll get him," Agent Bolin yelled. He ducked around Jericho's Ford and started at a crouch up the side of Wiebke's car.

To keep the shooter back, Concho drew his left-hand Colt and emptied it at the same window as before, deliberately aiming high. Rice fired too. Bolin reached Bui, who was on the ground but trying to get up. Bolin pulled the wounded agent into a fireman's carry and rushed him around to the back of the Durango.

"Bolin!" Rice shouted. "How is he?"

"I'm OK!" Bui replied himself, though shock roughened his voice.

"He will be," Bolin said. "His vest stopped a few. He's shot in the arm. With some glass cuts."

As Concho slapped fresh magazines up the wells of his Colts, Wiebke bailed out of her vehicle and duck walking to the back of the cruiser. Specks of blood spattered her brown uniform top, but it looked like most or all of it came from Bui.

"Cover me," Concho said to Rice. "I'm going for the back. But shoot high. Toni might be in there somewhere."

"Wait!" Rice snapped.

"Can't!" Concho replied.

He lifted his guns, fired at the top of the window, where the shooter had yet to reappear. Rice snarled but opened fire, too. The Ranger launched himself into a sprint. He was fast for his size and faster now with the thought of being shot at to spur him. His long strides ate the ground. No bullets sang his way, and in a moment, he'd reached the corner of the house.

Scarcely slowing, he circled the building, ducking beneath any windows. They'd only seen one shooter so far, but there could be more inside. A burst of renewed firing came from the second floor of the house. It sounded like the same gun, an AR-15 probably, though with the shots coming from a different place this time. It wasn't clear what that meant, except at least one shooter was still active.

Was it Jericho? He hoped so, though something about the indiscriminate spraying of bullets made him think it wasn't. Jericho seemed more organized, more controlled. This was likely an ally. Didn't mean Jericho couldn't still be inside, though, hanging back.

The Ranger reached the rear of the house. A set of three concrete steps led up to a screen door and a small back porch. He darted up them and crouched. The screen wasn't locked; he stepped inside. The porch was floored in concrete, and six steps took him across it to a wooden door leading into the house proper.

Pushing up from his crouch, he glanced through the square window of the door. A spotless kitchen revealed itself. No one was in sight. Concho twisted the knob, eased the door open, and slipped inside.

The kitchen was more modern than expected, with a big block table in the center over which hung copper and iron skillets and various cooking and serving ware. The refrigerator and stove were of stainless steel, the floor, and counters of natural wood. The microwave had enough buttons on it for the cockpit of a fighter jet and looked like it could reheat an army's worth of food.

One window stood open near the refrigerator, and a cool breeze stirred the lace curtains framing it. The curtains evoked an earlier age and didn't fit the rest of the décor. Through the window, he could just glimpse the corner of the barn. A bullet hole marred the screen.

Everything here smelled of soap and disinfectant, which made Concho wonder about how dirty Mandy and her clothes had been. Why would Jericho keep his house so clean but let the girl he'd kidnapped be so slovenly? Unless it had been part of the trick? *An act?* He'd think about it later.

Two doors led out of the kitchen. The one he could see clearly connected to a hallway. He chose that one, moving silently with a pistol in his right hand. He came to a bathroom on the left and a utility room on the right. Both were clear.

Another door looked like it led to a cellar. He ignored it for now. Just beyond stood a living room, which looked more like a Hollywood set piece for a 1950s sitcom than a living space.

Next up on the right came the dining room. It was shadowy, with a set of heavy blue curtains drawn shut. Concho peeked through the doorway. Five figures sat at a long oaken table. The Ranger's finger tightened on the trigger of his Colt, but he held fire as he recognized what he was seeing. Mannequins, not people. They were of various sizes, naked and bald, gleaming white against the dimness of the room. Their heads were all turned in his direction; their motionless hands rested on the table.

Against the wall to his right rose the steps leading to the second floor. Another burst of AR-15 fire came from up those stairs, followed by the answering bellow of Will Bolin's hunting rifle. A high-pitched cry vented from above. It didn't sound human at all but like the shriek of a wounded elk.

Bolin shouted from outside. "I hit him! Don't know how bad."

Concho started up the stairs, crouched over, walking lightly, fist tight around the butt of his Colt. He heard panting. Whoever was up there might have been hit, but they were still alive.

He went to his belly as he reached the top of the stairs and peeked around the newel post. In front of him was a single open room with virtually no furniture. A man sat on the floor, leaning back against the wall near a bullet-ridden window. He wore tattered shorts and no shirt; blood stained him from chest to waist, and fresh crimson bubbled from a bullet wound in his chest below his left shoulder.

A closer look revealed the man was no man at all but a boy, maybe sixteen or seventeen. Small for his age, with long tangled blond hair. Slat thin with ribs showing. An AR-15 lay across his lap, and he clutched for it as Concho's head appeared at the top of the stairs. Then he thrust the weapon away to clatter on the floor.

The lawman turned to scan the rest of the upstairs. There were two other rooms, both with their doors open. And no other sounds but the harsh, nasal breathing of the dying boy. The Ranger rose to his feet. He ignored the wounded shooter as he padded over to check out the other rooms to make sure he wasn't going to be ambushed from one of them. Both appeared empty of danger.

Turning back toward the youth, Concho yelled out through the shattered window to his colleagues: "Shooter is down. Call an ambulance. I didn't see anyone else in the house, but there's a cellar. Someone will need to check it."

"All right!" Della Rice yelled back. "We're coming in."

Concho stepped over to the boy, whose hazel eyes followed his every move. He squatted down. The wound still pumped blood, but it was slowing. The youth's skin was gray, already taking on the color of the dead. Concho had seen plenty of fatal wounds in the Army. This was one. And not a thing to do to stop the end from coming.

"Jericho!" Concho said.

The boy's eyes flared; he recognized the name, meaning he was another victim of the man.

"Who are you?" the Ranger asked, at least wanting to know what to call the youth. Someone should remember him.

The lad tried to talk. His purplish lips worked back and forth against each other, but nothing came out but gibberish. Concho saw why. He saw what had been done to the boy. His lips had been sewn shut, so he couldn't speak.

After a moment, the youth stopped trying, and his suffering ended.

CHAPTER 12

Deputy Wiebke winced when she saw the dead boy. Della Rice frowned.

"Damn!" Will Bolin said. "Didn't know he was just a kid."

"No way you could," Concho replied.

"And he was shooting at us," Agent Rice added.

Bolin nodded at the comments but still looked sick.

"The ambulance is on the way," Rice said. "Not that it matters to this one."

"How about Agent Bui?" Concho asked.

"He'll be OK," Rice answered. "One serious wound. But not life threatening. Some superficial cuts in addition."

"You find anything in the basement?"

"Maybe," Rice said. "There's a table down there with some ugly stains. Could be blood or…other fluids. The forensics people will need to take a look."

"What's up with those dummies at the living room table?" Wiebke asked.

Rice answered she'd once mentioned having had behavioral science training at Quantico. "Hard to tell, but maybe some surrogate for a family he never had, or never felt like he had. Could explain why he kidnaps kids, too."

Concho thought it might be more complicated. "Five manne-

quins," he said. "Two adult sized. The others smaller. One of the
adults must represent Jericho. Then we have, in descending size,
this kid," he pointed at the dead youth, "Mandy from the truck
stop, and Toni. The littlest."

"Makes sense," Rice said. "But what about the second adult?
Pete Cramer?"

"Maybe. Or the 'Wilbur' Mandy mentioned. Anyway, we know
Jericho was here. So he switched cars, and we have no idea what
he might be driving now. Where's our helicopter support?"

"En route."

"All right. I'm going to check the barn. That's likely where Jericho parked any getaway car."

Rice nodded. "I'm gonna have another look around the house.
See if anything else jumps out at me. Not literally, I hope. Wiebke!
Would you wait outside for the ambulance and any cops that show
up?"

"Yes," Wiebke answered. She glanced once more at the dead
boy before turning away. "A shame," she said.

Concho couldn't think of anything else to add.

                              ***

By the time he'd driven a dozen miles down the road
away from the farm, Jericho began to relax. He'd beaten Ten-
Wolves again—proof the Ranger's magic was no match for his
own. A final confrontation between them had already been fated.
But from now until then, the lawman would only fall farther and
farther behind.

Jericho turned on his radio and pushed in the waiting CD. *Re-
quiem* began to play, the last work of Wolfgang Amadeus Mozart,
incomplete at the time of his death and yet still a masterpiece.

Jericho hoped to finish his own masterwork *before* he died.

                              ***

Ten-Wolves stepped into the barn. A single-story affair,
probably used as a garage rather than to house animals or feed. The

only scents were of dust and gasoline. He saw where car tires had spun in the dirt as if someone had pulled out quickly. The tread of the tires was visible in places, and it wasn't from the Ford Fusion parked outside. As he'd figured, Jericho had kept a second vehicle, which was now missing.

Squatting near the tracks, the Ranger studied them and took a few pictures with his phone. The tracks were typical, with no distinguishing features he could find. No way of telling what kind of vehicle these tires were on.

He let out a quick, angry breath, then stood and let his gaze slowly roam the entire building. A scrap of paper caught his eyes. He moved over to it. It was partially folded, and he spread it open with the barrel of his Colt to avoid marring any fingerprints left on it.

It was the dedication and copyright page of a book. *This is dedicated to my young readers. You are my inspiration! – R.R.* Further down came mention of "Random House" and "A to Z Mysteries."

His fist clenched on the butt of the pistol. He holstered it and stood, shaking his head. According to Toni's grandmother, the girl was reading a series of books called A to Z Mysteries. This had to be a page from one of those books. And it hadn't landed here accidentally. Jericho must have left it to be found. He didn't know why, though it seemed likely to be some kind of taunt.

He also didn't know whether the page meant that Jericho actually had Toni with him or if it were just her books. He began searching the hard ground of the barn for any human prints. Scuff marks were plentiful, but only in spots did he see the imprint of a heel or the toes of a shoe. All were larger than Toni's feet, probably about a size nine. Of course, Jericho could have been carrying Toni if he'd had her here.

Stepping outside the barn again, the Ranger glanced around. It was nearing noon, with the sky a wintery blue despite the mild temperatures. Down the hill, from him, a good hundred yards stood a long, muddy pond. A large log lay half buried in muck on one bank. No doubt, this was the pond Mandy had mentioned as being "scary." It didn't look scary, though it had a thick chick-en-wire fence around it—possibly to keep anyone from venturing too close and falling in.

He turned back toward the house, and for just an instant, the hair stood up at the nape of his neck. He heard the hint of a low growl. He smelled ashes. Spinning around, he saw only a breeze playing with dust near the corner of the barn. The scent was gone as well.

Nothing had been there, he realized. His mind had created the phenomenon. But it probably had a reason for doing so. He just wished it would let him know what the reason was.

***

"There's a back exit out of here," Will Bolin told Concho as the two men stood next to their SUV. "I saw tracks cutting through the grass out behind the house and followed them. They lead to a shallow creek you can ford. Just beyond is a gate onto the main road. It was open, so I figure that's how Jericho escaped. He surely had it mapped out ahead of time."

"Most likely. We're dealing with a planner. Gonna make it harder to catch him."

"We'll get him. I want his hide nailed to the barn door for what he did to those kids. To Mandy. And…that boy upstairs."

"The boy tells me we're looking at something more complex than we'd first thought."

Bolin frowned. "How so? He's a serial sex offender. He needs to be off my planet."

"A sex offender?" Concho replied. "Almost certainly. But that's not the only reason he's taking these kids. And keeping them. It may help us catch him if we figure out why."

"You and Rice figure it out. Just give me ten minutes alone with him once we get hold of him."

Concho nodded grimly. "Sure. But the line starts behind me."

CHAPTER 13

Della Rice came out of the farmhouse on the phone with her agency. She finished her call as she approached Concho and Will Bolin.

"We're going to set up a temporary field command post here," she told them. "The house has WIFI, and we need to complete our sweep of the place for evidence. Help is on the way."

"Gotcha," Bolin said. He popped the rear hatch of the Durango and started pulling out bags. He handed a laptop carrying case to Concho, who took it with one hand while covering a huge yawn with his other. Rice noticed.

"You sleep at all last night?" she asked.

"Dozed a little."

"Look," the special agent said, "why don't you grab an hour or two in the house. It's going to take a while for our help to get here and even longer before we can start gathering intel and planning our next step. You'll be worth more to us after you're rested a bit."

Concho nodded. The woman was right. He'd had times, both in the Army and as a law officer, when no sleep was possible because of impending danger. And it cost you in concentration and creative thinking. Going without sleep when you had a chance to get some wasn't toughness; it was stupidity. It didn't serve oneself or others. And he'd need all his faculties on high alert when they got within striking distance of Jericho again.

"All right," he said. "I'll try for a couple of hours. But someone needs to get in touch with whatever officers are watching over Mandy. See if they can get her to describe Jericho's other car. Whatever he had in the barn here."

"I'll take care of it," Rice said.

"OK, wake me if we get any breaks."

"Of course," Rice said.

Taking another bag of supplies from Bolin, Concho carried them and the laptop into the house and placed them on the table in the dining room. Starting up the stairs, he made a quick phone call to Beth Pennebaker to check on Mandy.

Mandy was asleep. Concho felt grateful. Her parents, Lewis and Linda Callimore, were on the way and tremendously excited to see their daughter again. He told Pennebaker to give them his cell phone number and get theirs for him. She agreed.

Carrying his phone, Concho turned to the right at the top of the stairs and went into one of the rooms he'd looked in on earlier. A queen-sized bed sat against one wall, just beside a wide window hung with more lace curtains. It was made up with sheets, a blanket, and a quilt on top, with no sign it had ever been slept in. The only other item of note in the room was a broken grandfather clock against the wall farthest from the bed.

He put his phone down on the bedside table and took off his boots and guns. Leaving the rest of his clothes on, he lay down on his back on top of the covers, placing his gun belt and guns beside him. In three minutes, he was out, and the sounds of vehicles arriving and people coming in and out of the house did not disturb him. He'd slept in war zones before. This was nothing.

Forty-five minutes into sleep, though, something happened that did disturb him. Once more, he began to dream.

***

Jericho pulled up to the isolated cabin he'd rented two weeks before and frowned. There were no lights inside and no sign of occupancy. There should have been. Pete Cramer should have already been here with Toni.

Climbing out of his Miata, Jericho walked over to the stand-alone garage. It was locked, but he had the key. Opening it revealed…nothing. No car or any sign one had been here. A mewl of anger spilled from his lips.

He pulled his own car into the garage, took out his suitcases, and headed for the cabin. That, too, was locked, and once he got inside showed no evidence of having been visited at all since the last time he'd been here. Putting his cases on the floor, he pulled out his cell phone and keyed in a number. The phone rang and rang before going to voice mail.

"You know who this is, Cramer? Where are you? I need to hear from you now."

He hung up, feeling as if he were about to explode. Only gradually did a glacial calm flow over him. He'd chosen Cramer for two reasons. First, he needed to replace Wilbur, the man who'd worked with him for years but was becoming increasingly recalcitrant. Cramer seemed a possible alternative.

Second, Cramer's dark skin might come in handy in extracting the girl, Toni. And it had. But now, Cramer had proven himself unreliable, too. Despite being given every bit of information, he could need as a ferryman.

There should have been no problems. Jericho doubted there *were* problems. This had to be Cramer's choice, which meant Jericho had been betrayed. Such could not be allowed to stand.

An idea occurred. *Two birds with one stone*, he muttered to himself. He turned on his laptop and called up a certain program he'd installed for just such a possibility.

***

Concho found himself standing beneath a ghostly moon riding high in a pale morning sky. He stood at the back of the barn on Jericho's farm, looking down toward the fenced-off pond. A trail of wildflowers bloomed between where he stood and the pond, though they were curiously colorless as if faded by the odd light. There was no sound, no scent. He couldn't feel a breeze or any sensation in the air of heat or chill.

As he looked up, the face in the moon began to alter until it no longer looked human but like the muzzled face of a beast, a bear perhaps, or a feral hound. The black blot of the mouth began to spread as if opening. Inky splotches of darkness spilled forth, then broke into a flock of hundreds of crows. These swept down toward him, silent though their mouths were open.

The Ranger felt a threat in those diving shapes; he grabbed for a pistol at his hip and found it gone. Found both guns gone. He lifted his hands, palms out in a warding gesture. The crows broke to either side of his upheld arms, circled in a whirl of forms and shadows.

A dozen feet in front of him, the two flying columns of crows dove straight into the earth and disappeared. It didn't mean he was safe. His breath came fast, his heart pounded. Where the crows had melted into the ground, a bubble of blackness began to grow. It took on shape, stretched out limbs, grew fur.

A black dog manifested. The fur horripilated along its back, and the tips of it smoked with the remnants of fire. Its face was flattened, its muzzle short, its ears cropped and standing up like those of a pit bull.

The dog stared with eyes like empty holes in which maroon dots floated. It growled, the first sound the Ranger had heard in this dream. Strangely, the growl quietened his fear. It made him angry instead, and he growled back.

The hound snorted and shook its head. It turned and stalked stiff-legged to the edge of the pond, walking straight through the fence as if it didn't exist. The hound stepped into the water and sank down. As it sank, it dissolved as if made of clotted ink.

Black streamers spread, turned the water obsidian. And yet, Ten-Wolves could see through the darkness to the bottom of the pool. A face floated there, wavering. Its eyes snapped open, as silver and reflecting as mirrors.

Concho startled awake and sat up just as Della Rice stepped through the door of the bedroom. "What's up?" he asked as he swiveled onto the side of the bed and began to pull on his boots.

"Thought you might want to know; the coroner is about ready to leave. I asked him to wait a minute to see if you needed to speak to him about anything."

The Ranger stood and slung his gun belt around his waist. "I do. Unfortunately."

"You OK?" Rice asked. "What's wrong?"

Concho took a couple of deep breaths. "I'm OK, but I just had a very bad dream."

Rice frowned. "About this case?"

"Connected. You know of the 'Black Dog?'"

"I've heard people refer to depression as a black dog."

Concho shook his head. "Depression has been described that way, but the black dog I'm talking about comes primarily from British folklore. It's a hellhound. Associated with the devil and usually signifying death. Some Indian legends mention the black dog, too. I've known about it since I was little."

"Didn't know that. But what does it have to do with this case and the coroner?"

The lawman wiped his mouth with one hand and sighed. "We need to drag the pond out back of the barn. I don't think it's empty."

CHAPTER 14

Brackettville, Texas. The county seat for Kinney County, population about sixteen hundred. If it weren't for the modern cars, traveling through sections of Brackettville would make you think you'd slipped through a time warp into the early 1900s. Big, yellow stone buildings. Mexican style arches and roofs. Boots and cowboy hats. Dusty roads.

Jericho had been here often. In fact, he'd taken his name from a movie filmed at Alamo Village, just outside Brackettville. Alamo Village had been the first film location built in Texas, back in the late 1950s for the movie, *The Alamo*. Directed by and starring John Wayne.

Jericho had never cared much for John Wayne, although his father had loved "The Duke." Not that anything about his father mattered anymore. Putting past thoughts out of his head, he turned down a dirt side road, pulled off at a small park, and got out. It was late afternoon. A chill tingled in the air, and he pulled his jacket tighter around himself.

Down a slight hill from where he'd parked ran a stream spanned by a narrow walking bridge. Jericho crossed the bridge and headed up a dirt trail beyond into the woods. Fifteen minutes of travel brought him close to the edge of the trees. He paused and crouched, then inched forward to see into the field beyond.

A metal pole fence separated the woods from the field. About fifty yards farther in stood an isolated farmhouse. Pulling a compact pair of bird watchers' binoculars from his jacket pocket, he studied the back of the house.

The yard area was separated from the rest of the field by a fence of yellow pine boards. There were two sheds, one for the water well and another for maintenance tools. A dozen people milled about, most of them men but with a woman or two in the mix. All of them looked middle-aged and well-to-do. All had drinks and seemed to be waiting for the smoking grill to render up meat.

Jericho couldn't see Pete Cramer among the group but figured he was in the house. He had to be close. Before he'd let Cramer put Toni in his trunk, Jericho had secretly installed a GPS on the man's car. The car was here, meaning Toni was here. Probably in the basement. He hoped to have a chance to get her back, though that seemed unlikely. But he certainly intended to see that Pete Cramer and his cronies could never interfere with his plans again.

Besides, he'd been intending to deal with this group for a long time. All it would take now would be a phone call. But not quite yet. Jericho settled himself against a tree and waited for evening.

***

Concho opened the gate leading through the fence to the farm pond. Della Rice, Will Bolin, and the Kinney County coroner followed him. The pond was big, almost an acre. The smell of muck permeated the air. The banks were muddy, though there were no signs that cattle or any other animals had been coming here to drink. Nor could they have gotten through the fence anyway. Runoff from the banks had turned the water into a stew of silt-heavy brown liquid that seemed to be equal parts water and earth.

The coroner's name was Frank Port. He stopped at the edge of the water to study the pool. "So you think this Jericho may have dumped bodies in here?" the man asked.

"I'm very much afraid so," Concho replied.

Port shook his head. Della Rice stepped up beside him.

"An ugly job," she said. "We'll have to get the water drained. Dredge the mud."

Port nodded. He didn't seem enthused. He pulled a phone out of his pocket and turned away to make a call. Della Rice continued to stand by the pond, her hands on her hips as she surveyed the water.

Concho glanced around the banks. A frown creased his face. When he'd looked out here earlier, there'd been a big log lying on the opposite bank of the pond. It was gone now.

"Look out!" Concho shouted as he leaped toward Agent Rice.

The woman turned her head. An expression of surprise was still forming on her features when the water boiled at her feet. A broad, scaly head exploded from the pool just as Concho reached Rice. He hooked her across the belly with his left arm and flung her backward as if firing her from a slingshot.

The big alligator's jaws snapped shut where Della's legs had been an instant earlier. Now, Concho was in its sights. It twisted its upper body toward him; the jaws sprung wide. Muddy water poured between its savage teeth.

The Ranger smashed his size twelve boot into the side of the monster's head, then leaped backward. The gator hissed; its short legs churned as it lunged after Concho. He backpedaled as if his feet had sprouted wings.

Gunshots slammed into the muck around the alligator's head. A bullet slashed across its skull between the eyes, leaving a gouge of pinkish-red behind but not penetrating through the thick bone.

Concho had one of his Colts out now but held his fire. The gator's forward charge had stopped as it was struck. It shook its head, flipped its heavy body completely around, and dove back into the pond, disappearing beneath the brown water in a roil as a couple of last shots dimpled the pond's surface.

"My God!" Frank Port exclaimed his face bone white.

Concho took a few deep breaths and holstered his pistol. He glanced over at Della Rice. She was almost gray with shock; her eyes looked like saucers in her face. Will Bolin stood beside her, the barrel of his Glock still smoking.

"Hit it, but the lead practically bounced off!" he said, his voice higher pitched than normal.

"You got its attention," Concho replied. "I'm grateful."

"How big you think it was?" Bolin asked.

Concho grinned. It was only a little forced. "You want to call him back out and hold him while I measure?"

Bolin shook his head and holstered his pistol.

"You saved my life," Rice said. "How did you know…it was there?"

"Earlier, I saw a big log lying on the bank," Concho answered. "I didn't realize at first, but the log was gone when we came down here. Should have recognized what it was sooner. You don't usually expect gators in a Texas farm pond, but it's been known to happen. I don't think this one got in here by accident, though."

Rice took a deep breath with a hint of shudder in it. "I'm just glad you realized when you did. I don't like the thought of being eaten. You figure Jericho put it there?"

"Likely."

"This is gonna make my job harder," Frank Port complained. "Not that it wasn't already with the weird crap we saw inside the house."

"If you need someone to commiserate with," Concho said, "give Earl Blake a call at the coroner's office in Eagle Pass. He's had some experience with weird cases."

Port looked up. "*Your* cases, I'm guessing?"

Concho just smiled.

***

As Concho and the others headed back for Jericho's farm-house, a second FBI SUV arrived carrying four fresh operatives. That made seven, with Concho adding an eighth to the mix. Agent Bui had been taken to the hospital. One bullet had passed through the muscle of his left arm, and he'd need surgery to repair it. His other wounds weren't overly serious, mainly fragments of safety glass embedded in his face and upper body that would have to be removed. But he was out of commission for the moment.

Two more local county officers had joined the group as well, with Deputy Perse Wiebke making three. They had the manpower now to run Jericho to earth. But they didn't have any idea where to start. Even getting a description of Jericho's second car had proven impossible. Mandy only knew about a sports car kept in the barn. She couldn't give any reasonable description of it, except that it was white.

Concho chafed at the delay and the cold trail. It was growing late, with evening shadows starting to fill in low spots in the landscape. His concern didn't stop him from helping himself to some of the KFC fried chicken, biscuits, and French fries the FBI reinforcements had brought along. He was so hungry the scent alone made him salivate.

He was on his second drumstick when his phone rang. He pulled the cell out of his pocket and frowned. He didn't recognize the number but never felt free to ignore a call coming through. Civilians might get away with responding only to numbers they recognized, but a law officer could never be sure it wasn't someone who needed his help.

He swiped to answer, and everything changed.

CHAPTER 15

"Ten-Wolves," Jericho said rather jovially over the phone. "I trust you weren't injured by the greeting I left behind at the farm?"

Concho was less surprised by the call than he might have imagined under the circumstances. Somewhere inside, he must have been expecting it. And he couldn't afford to blow this opportunity.

"Which greeting you talking about? The boy with the gun? Or the gator in the pond?"

Jericho hmmed, then chuckled. "I completely forgot about the gator. I trust you still have all your limbs?"

"And soon a new pair of alligator boots," the Ranger replied.

Again, Jericho chuckled. "You're welcome."

"Your other little greeting is dead!" Concho added in measured tones. "But I don't imagine you care."

Silence. Then, "You'd be wrong. Of course, I care. The boy was, to turn a phrase, like a son to me. I'd hoped he would be taken alive."

"He opened fire on police officers. The fire was returned. We had no idea he was a kid until I found him bleeding out."

Rice and Bolin had stopped eating. They stared at Concho, recognizing by his words and tone of voice that something important was happening. He lifted a finger to let them know he needed time.

Jericho winced audibly. "That is too bad. But in any grand game, certain moves are fated, and the results are...necessary. If not always to our personal liking."

"And did you like or dislike the part where you sewed the boy's lips shut?"

"Part of his maturation. I would think you might understand. Do not the Kickapoo go through certain...rituals as they reach for adulthood?"

"By choice."

Jericho snorted dismissively. "I know you must be smarter than that. If one's upbringing limits one's choices to a bare few, do you truly *have* a choice? I gave the boy as much choice as you probably had."

"And what about Toni? Why don't you give her the choice of staying with you or going home to her grandmother?"

"Eventually, I *will* give her that choice. But right now, it's beside the point. I don't have Toni. Which is one reason I'm on the phone with you."

"Pete Cramer has her."

"Cramer has her. Yes. I badly misjudged him, I admit. Although...he's already delivered her to a group I don't like. She won't last long with them. And that was not what I wanted." Jericho's voice turned savage for an instant. "I'm sure Cramer was well paid for his act of betrayal."

"Couldn't control your own ally, eh?"

Now came an overly dramatic sigh. "Good help and all that. But, if you want Cramer and his new buddies, I can tell you how to get them."

"And Toni?"

"Afraid not. I should have her back by the time you get here. But, you know, there's always a chance something goes wrong. The great hero might save the day and the girl after all."

"Where do I go?"

"Brackettville. You know it?"

"No."

"You can find it on a map. Just outside the town, there's a ranch called Stone Creek. Cramer is there. Along with some other unpleasant people. You should be aware, many of them will be armed. In addition to their predilections, most are quite anti-government and anti-law enforcement in stance."

"You seem to know a lot about them."

"We've brushed shoulders."

"I'm on my way," Concho said.

"Counting on it," Jericho replied. "I'll be in touch."

The call cut off.

Wasting no precious time, Concho explained quickly to his companions what was happening. In minutes, two local police cars and two SUVs loaded with FBI agents and selected others were en route to Brackettville, Texas. A confrontation was coming, and the chances it would end peacefully had to be zero.

Or less.

***

Apparently, Deputy Perse Wiebke's family had come from Brackettville. She knew the town. She knew Stone Creek Ranch. She briefed everyone over speaker phones while they drove.

"It was a working ranch until the 1980s," Wiebke told them. "Then a fellow named Eli Sands bought it. A Texas oil man. With all that implies. You still hear gossip about the parties Sands and his wife threw. After Sands died, his wife sold the place to a group of investors called the Stone Creek Consortium, who use it mainly to host their own parties for prominent and wealthy people who want privacy for…whatever it is they do there."

"Is the wife still alive?" Concho asked.

"Died a few years after her husband."

"Any idea who is on the Stone Creek Consortium board?"

"No idea," Wiebke said, "but I imagine the FBI could find out."

"I'll look into it," Rice said.

"From my conversation on the phone with Jericho," Concho said, "it sounds as if child abduction and worse is scheduled entertainment at Stone Creek."

The Ranger's words brought all discussion to a temporary halt. Then Della Rice added, "We better be ready. Deputy Wiebke, stop us somewhere outside Brackettville so we can make final adjustments to our strategy."

"Will do," Wiebke said.

Concho swiped off his phone and glanced at Rice. Her face was grim as she kept her hands tight on the wheel of the SUV. Ten-Wolves fell off into his own thoughts. He'd seen far too many children afraid, hurt, dead. He'd never grown numb to it. Each new case was like a thorn under his eyelids.

It was horrible enough when it happened in battle zones when children were the collateral damage to the war games of the adults around them. But when people deliberately targeted children.... When people *chose* to hurt them.... It was almost more than he could bear, and he had to fight hard to maintain enough calm to do the job that needed to be done.

Concho fought for that calm now as the small convoy of law enforcement officers pulled into an abandoned quick stop a few miles outside Brackettville to finalize their plans. They'd called for backup, and it was on the way, but for Toni's sake, they decided not to wait for the help. From what Jericho had said, the people who had Toni now were extremely dangerous, with every intention of hurting the girl.

Concho and Will Bolin joined Wiebke in her prowl car while the rest of the agents and local officers filled the two SUVs. They were headed off to kick in the ranch's front door while Ten-Wolves and his two companions took a back way. They'd coordinate actions by radio and cell phone.

The direct approach to the Stone Creek house was along a well-maintained gravel road, which ended in a circular driveway for parking. However, there was a less visible way in, as well—a hiking trail running about a mile through the woods up to the ranch's long backyard.

When the FBI reinforcements arrived at Jericho's farmhouse, they'd been carrying a bullet-proof vest for Concho—in extra-large. He was slipping into it when Wiebke pulled off the main road through Brackettville and down into a small roadside park.

The three law officers stepped out of the vehicle, and everyone followed Wiebke as she crossed a walking bridge over Stone Creek and led the way into the trees along a pathway that seemed little better than an animal trail. They moved at a jog and quickly reached a barbed wire fence, which separated the woods from a field beyond.

The local water table must have been pretty close to the surface here because the field grew thick with prairie grass in all shades of green and brown. It would have made great fodder for cattle if there'd been any. The target ranch house stood about fifty yards across the field, with very little in the way of cover other than the tall grass.

It was 5:34 in the evening, with night descending quickly. Lights already burned in the house and on the back porch where four men stood talking while they smoked cigars and drank beer. Two were white, one black. Possibly Pete Cramer, though it was hard to tell at this distance. The other looked Asian. All appeared relaxed, and no one noticed the watchers in the woods.

Concho studied the layout they'd have to negotiate. A low picket fence separated the ranch house yard from the field. Inside the fence were two sheds, one of concrete blocks that had to be the well house, and the other of wood and tin and much bigger—probably a tool shed.

He also looked for any sign of Jericho. Saw none. Had the man really been here? Had he recovered Toni from Pete Cramer, as he'd claimed he would? There'd been debate among the law officers as to whether Jericho was telling them the truth or merely playing them for fools.

Ten-Wolves had to admit this might be a wild goose chase or even a trap. But, on the other hand, it was the only lead they had.

And any chance to save Toni was worth taking. Besides, there'd been something in Jericho's voice and demeanor on the phone. The man would happily lie to him, try to trick him, but he didn't think he'd done so now. It was a strong feeling, and one soon to be verified as yeah or nay.

The men on the porch all turned their heads toward the house at the same moment, as if someone had called them from inside. Cigars were dropped and ground out underfoot. One man opened the back door and held it for his companions as all four entered the house. Ten-Wolves took it as a signal.

"All right," he told his colleagues. "I'm going in. Once I reach the tool shed, I'll signal you. You call Agent Rice and tell her to move in from the front. Then give me backup. I'll bet when the sirens and lights hit; there'll be a few of these folks hoofing it out the back door."

"Gotcha," Bolin said. "I'll cover you." He hefted his .30-06 hunting rifle. It had an ATN night-vision scope for shooting in the dark.

"You want my shotgun?" Wiebke offered.

Concho shook his head. "It'll only get in the way of my crawl."

Before Wiebke could respond, the big Ranger went down on his belly in the tall grass and began to squirm rapidly toward the back of the ranch house. Bolin was in a squat, aiming through his scope to provide cover. Wiebke lay the shotgun down on the ground and drew her service pistol. It would be hard to hit anything at this distance with a pistol, but it would be better than the shotgun at fifty yards.

When Wiebke looked back toward Concho, she could see no sign of him other than an occasional sway of grass or bushes. She wondered how such a big man could move so silently and stay so hidden.

"One dangerous fellow," she whispered to herself.

CHAPTER 16

Ten-Wolves reached the tool shed and rose into a crouch.
The stench of cigars lingered in the air. So did the scent of charred meat from the barbecue grill. Lifting his fist, he waved it back and forth to signal Deputy Wiebke and Agent Bolin to call Della Rice and give her the word to go. His heart began to speed up. Adrenaline dried his mouth. No matter how many times he prepared for a fight, his body made itself ready.

He slipped around the side of the shed, working forward to get a better view of the ranch house's back exit. The porch was screened in, giving him a good view of the actual wooden back door to the house, which was closed. Light and music filtered through.

Beneath the porch, at ground level, he could see several rectangular windows marking the basement. The windows were frosted; you couldn't see through them. However, one of the windows toward the back of the house stood open slightly. A faint glow came from behind it. He wanted a look, but there was no cover at all between here and there.

He passed a side door leading into the shed. It invited him to explore in hopes of finding a better view and better cover. He drew it back with the faintest of creaks and slipped inside. The whole front of the shed was open, letting in enough ambient light to reveal the shadows of a mower and a four-wheeler. Tools hung on the walls. The floor was of wooden planks, thick with dust.

He ducked behind the heavy-duty riding mower and drew his Colts. From here, he had a clear sight on the house and at least some protection from any gunfire from that location. A nearly ideal spot for what might be coming.

Adding to the scent of cigars and barbecue from outside, his nose now detected motor oil, gasoline, and grease. And something else. He frowned and lifted his head to sniff the air.

Beeswax!

On the bus, Toni's hair had smelled of whatever gel her grandmother had used on her. It had reminded him of beeswax. Concho twisted around suddenly to study the interior of the shed. He could see nothing out of place. But the smell… It was strong, recent.

"Toni!" Concho whispered. "Are you here? I'm Concho Ten-Wolves. We met on the bus. We talked about books. You remember? I'm a Texas Ranger. I'm here to help you."

He thought he wasn't going to get an answer. Maybe Cramer or some of the others had brought Toni out here for an unknown purpose and then taken her back inside. Or maybe the smell came from something else entirely—some cleaning product.

Then a small, quiet voice said, "You're a Ranger?"

Concho's chest fluttered with joy and relief and with questions. It *was* Toni's voice. But how had she gotten here?

"Yes," he said.

"I remember your book on insects. Or named after an insect."

"After a fly. A Bluebottle."

"I remember."

Concho followed the sound of Toni's voice. A large wooden work table stood against the back wall. The little girl's voice was coming from underneath it, from behind some boxes.

"How did you get out here?" the Ranger asked.

"I scaped," Toni answered. "I was in the basement, and I climbed out a window. But I didn't know where to go. I don't really like the woods."

"They didn't have you tied up?"

"They did, but when they tied me, I made myself big. And when they left me alone later, I made myself small again, and the ropes slipped off my hands. I had to work on the ones on my legs a while. They were tight."

"I understand," Concho said.

He was remembering the horse he'd learned to ride on. A pinto named Abooksigun, which had belonged to his grandfather. The horse's name meant wildcat, which was appropriate. Anytime you tried to ride him, it was like climbing aboard for the first time.

Another thing Abooksigun was known for was sucking in air and holding it when you put on the saddle cinch. As soon as you climbed aboard, he'd let out the breath, and the cinch would come loose. When the horse shifted positions, the saddle would slide right down one side, dumping the rider on the ground where Abooksigun would promptly try to step on him. It had happened to Concho a couple of times before he learned to wait the pinto out and let the horse release the air before tightening the cinch.

When the people inside Stone Creek Ranch had tied up Toni, she must have kept her hands and wrists as wide apart as possible, so when they left her alone, she'd have a little slack in the ropes to work with. She'd then used the slack to work the ropes off her hands. Pretty smart for a nine-year-old. Or any year old, for that matter.

"You did good," Concho said. He was squatting near the table now and moved one of the boxes to the side to look underneath. Toni was virtually invisible in the corner beneath the table. He smiled at her. She smiled back with a quick gleam of teeth.

"You've done perfectly so far," Concho continued. "But in a few minutes, there's likely to be some loud noise and possibly some shooting. I'd like to get you out of here, but there's no time. Can you stay hidden just where you are until either I or another police officer comes for you?"

"Of course," she said. "I'm nine years old."

"You are. And a very brave and resourceful nine-year-old. Did you see any other children inside?"

"Too many," Toni replied, suddenly sounding much older than nine.

Concho suppressed the angry hiss trying to escape his lips. Holstering his pistols, he quickly stripped off his bullet-proof vest. He leaned into Toni's cubbyhole and draped the vest over her. It was large enough to nearly swallow her.

"This is important, Toni," Concho said. "You stay behind this vest. Keep it wrapped around you and keep your head and arms and legs inside. Can you do that?"

"All right," the girl said.

"Good. I'll—"

The wail of sirens interrupted him. The FBI had arrived.

"Stay put!" Ten-Wolves said to Toni. He pushed the box back to cover the gap under the table and turned toward the house, drawing both his .45s and preparing for a war he hoped wouldn't come.

CHAPTER 17

Night now. Only the last glow of the sun lingering. From his position behind the mower in the shed, Concho heard a sudden thunder of running feet in the ranch house as blue lights strobed and sirens wailed from the front of the building. An amplified voice ordered:

"This is the FBI! Everyone in the house! Exit through the front door with your hands up and empty!"

The house's back door swung wide. Feet pounded on the planks of the porch, and the screen door nearly tore off its hinges as two men and a woman burst through. An outside light still burned, showing Concho everything he needed to see. The woman dragged a small child behind her by the arm.

Ten-Wolves rose from his crouch. "Freeze!" he shouted. "Texas Rangers!"

The woman screamed. She let go the child and threw herself to the ground, covering her head with her hands. The man on her left spun back toward the house. Concho let him go because the man on the right had a shotgun and brought the big-bore weapon swinging up to fire.

Concho shot him in the chest. Twice. The man grunted; the shotgun dropped with a thunk to the ground; the woman screamed again at the gunfire; the child, a little boy of eight or so, stood bewildered.

If not for the child, Concho would have held his position. But the boy needed help. He reached the child in a few steps. The wounded man lay shuddering on the ground, striving for breath and unable to find it. The woman kept screaming.

Considering the circumstances, he felt no pity for her. He pressed the barrel of the Colt against the side of the woman's head. "Shut up!"

She shut up.

Concho holstered his pistols. Dragging out his handcuffs, he twisted the woman's right arm behind her and cuffed her right wrist to her left ankle, leaving her prone on the ground. He scooped up the little boy and spun back toward the shed.

At that instant, gunfire exploded from within the house. Galvanized, Concho almost did a broad jump into the shed. Even as he reached the mower and tucked the boy behind it, he realized the shooting was all from the front of the house. And now the FBI agents began shooting back. He recognized the crack and whine of their standard-issue Glocks.

The boy, a skinny towhead, seemed in shock. He kept licking his lips as he tried to talk but couldn't get a word out. Just as the lawman was about to try talking to him, he heard movement at the side of the shed and turned swiftly.

Perse Wiebke whispered loudly. "Ten-Wolves. It's me. I'm here."

"Good," Concho replied. He watched the young officer slip in the side door of the shed, moving in a crouch with her pistol drawn. She squatted beside him, her eyes on the child.

"Bolin?" Concho asked.

"Still covering us from the woods."

"Gotcha. Listen, I found Toni. She got away herself. She's safe in this shed. Relatively safe." He pointed toward the little girl's hiding place. "And this," he indicated the boy, "well, I don't know his name. But I need you to watch over him and Toni and cover my backside. You up to it?"

"Where are you going?"

"In the house."

"Doesn't seem like a good idea!"

"Maybe not, but from the sound of it, there's a lot of guns in there, all firing at our friends out front. They need help."

Wiebke nodded. "I'll cover."

"Thanks," Concho said.

He reached out, patted the little boy on the shoulder, then rose without another thought and took off in a run for the ranch's back door. As he raced past the dead man in the yard, he leaned down and scooped up the dropped shotgun.

The screen door on the porch hung off of one hinge. He stepped around it and moved to the side against the back wall of the house. Gunfire still exploded from inside but had died back slightly as both sides sought openings and targets. The firing clustered near the front of the house, but the back had surely not been left unwatched.

Beneath the porch light, Concho took a moment to examine his confiscated shotgun. A Remington 1100, 12-gauge with a high-gloss walnut stock. A hunting weapon rather than an offensive one. But it would do. This one was loaded; shells glinted in the magazine. But how many? Such weapons typically held four, though if the choke had been removed, it would hold up to eight. He flipped off the safety.

The wooden back door opened outward and was slightly ajar. Concho used the barrel of the shotgun to push it further open. It creaked; a gasp came from inside as someone drew a quick, panting breath. That someone likely had a gun.

Other kids were in the house. He didn't dare fire the shotgun through the door without knowing what was there. But it would be risky finding out. He inched toward the door, swiftly glanced around it, and then jumped back even faster.

A man cried out from inside and started shooting at where Ten-Wolves' head had been. It wasn't there anymore, but the Ranger's eyes had registered enough. A hallway, with doors opening to left and right. A heavy sideboard table—with a mirror above and thick, square legs below—had been wedged across the hallway as a barricade. Through the gap beneath it, he'd seen a set of shoes. Adult size. Only one pair.

The man behind the sideboard stopped firing. A mumbled curse was followed by the sound of a clip falling on the floor. While the gunman was reloading, Concho stepped into the open frame of the doorway and opened fire with the 12-gauge directly into the sideboard.

The roar of the Remington filled the hallway. The shotgun was a semi-automatic. It fired every time you pulled the trigger, and the lawman kept pulling. Waves of lead pellets, barely spreading at this distance, slammed into the piece of furniture. Splinters flew. The mirror shattered like a scream.

And then a real scream came from behind it as pellets from the third and fourth shot of the 12-gauge sleeted through the shattered table and ripped into the man hiding behind it.

The fourth shot emptied the Remington. The trigger clicked; Concho hurled the gun down the hall, blue smoke trailing from its barrel. He drew both his Colts. The man behind the sideboard leaped to his feet, still screaming. Blood spattered his face and white shirt. He still had a gun in hand, and Concho shot him at ten-yard range, putting one .45 slug through the top of his head, taking off a large piece of skull and scalp.

Concho spun to his right. Through the doorway there, he could see kitchen cabinets. He dove through the door, twisting to his right side with his guns leveled. He slid on the linoleum floor.

A woman stood in the kitchen behind a big oak worktable. She was older, at least in her sixties, with one long gray braid half pulled over a shoulder. Her left hand gripped the chin of a young Asian girl of eleven or twelve. Her right hand held a butcher knife to the child's throat.

"Drop your guns, cop!" the woman screamed. "Drop your guns, or I cut this little bitch from ear to ear!"

CHAPTER 18

"Don't!" Concho said to the woman with the knife to the child's throat.

He rose slowly to his feet, his gaze darting everywhere, taking in any other dangers. A smashing sound rolled in from the front of the house, no doubt the FBI kicking in the door. Gunshots boomed in a flurry.

"It's over," Concho continued. "We've got cops everywhere. Don't add murder to your other crimes!"

"Screw you! You drop your guns, and I'm going out the back."

"There are more cops there. One with a hunting rifle. You step out with a weapon, and he'll take the top of your head off. Drop your knife. Let the girl go. Don't make us kill you. Please!"

The woman's eyes were pale gray and glittered. She looked crazed, perhaps drugged. "I'm the one that kills," she said in a suddenly solemn and prophetic voice.

She twisted the knife in her hands, bringing it into a stabbing position. Concho was too far away to reach her. He fired once before she could put the knife into the child. The slug punched right between her eyes, spraying a gruesome serum of blood and brains and skull against the flowered wallpaper behind her.

Her eyes blinked, rolled up. She took a step back. Her hand

spasmed on the knife, and it dropped to clatter on the floor, but as she fell, her other hand tightened across the little girl's face and pulled her down on top of her. Now the girl began to scream.

Concho holstered his left-hand Colt as he leaped toward the child. The still dying woman was on her back, the girl on top of her. A liver-spotted hand kept scrabbling at the girl's face like a pale, bloated spider.

The Ranger's nostrils were filled with the stench of gunpowder and blood and with some kind of lavender scent the older woman wore. The combination was horrid, but not so horrid as the woman's fingers scritching, scritching at the child's face. Ten-Wolves grabbed the dying fingers, pried them away. He scooped the girl up in his left arm. She still screamed, the sound like a buzz saw in the small room.

A figure filled the doorway behind where the woman had been standing with the child. A man. Balding in the front. Pony-tailed in the back. He had a rifle, a lever-action .30-30. He started to lift it as he glimpsed the tableau in front of him. Concho shot him twice in the chest at point-blank range. He folded like a suit of empty clothes.

The sound of gunfire from the front of the house died away. Della Rice's stern voice could be heard ordering, "Get on the floor! Face down!"

Still carrying the girl, who'd exchanged screaming for whimpering, Concho stepped past the two corpses on the floor and glanced into the next room. A man wearing an FBI windbreaker stepped into the room from the other end at the same moment.

Concho pointed his gun to the sky and yelled out, "Texas Ranger!"

The agent had obviously been briefed. He motioned the Ranger forward. "We've got them, I think," he said. "Half a dozen kids, too; I see you've got another one."

"Yeah, and there are a couple more in the tool shed out back. With a local Deputy named Wiebke. Several bodies, as well."

The agent nodded. "We'll get there."

Still holding the girl, Concho stepped past the agent into the next room. This was the living room, a long wide space half filled with people. Della Rice stood with legs braced in the center of the room. She wore body armor over her black shirt and held her Glock.40 in firing position.

Three other FBI agents stood scattered around her, and more than half a dozen men and women of the house lay flat on their bellies with their hands behind their backs while agents cuffed them. Several appeared to be wounded and moaned in pain or fear.

Against the far wall sat four children, ranging in ages from eight to thirteen, white, black, Hispanic. Their clothes were a mismatch of items too big or small. None of them appeared to be shot, but all had the thousand-yard stare Concho had seen in exhausted and war-shocked villagers in Afghanistan.

The Ranger looked down at the prisoners who'd been keeping these children here, doing things to them to create that stare. They were as physically diverse as the kids themselves, but in another way, they were all alike. For a moment, it almost seemed he could see inside these people, see the maggot-twisted thoughts squirming through their brains.

A white-hot rage exploded inside Concho—an incandescent flame that threatened to consume every ounce of restraint he had. His muscles contracted against their bones. He shook, the gun in his hand shook. He wanted to scream, to kill....

"Mister, you're squeezing me."

The voice cut through Concho's awareness, splashing a tsunami of cold water onto his thoughts. The little girl in his arms was looking at him, seeing him. She'd spoken because his arm had tightened too much around her. He instantly relaxed his grip.

"I'm sorry, honey." He lowered her slowly to the floor. She started walking on her own toward the other four children. She had on white tennis shoes, scuffed and with splotches of blood from the dead woman in the other room.

Concho bit at his lip, trying to calm down. He turned to Della Rice, who was staring at him.

"Thought you were about to go nuclear," she said.

"Almost," he agreed. "There's an upstairs. And a basement."

"I'll take the basement," Rice said.

"The upstairs for me then," Ten-Wolves replied.

"Horn," you're with me," Rice said, gesturing to one of the FBI agents. Causey, you go with Ten-Wolves. Everyone else keep an eye on the children and our prisoners."

Causey was a young blonde woman. Her service issue Glock hung in a holster at her belt; in her arms, she carried a tactical shotgun with a pistol grip. Looked like a Benelli M series. Concho gestured for her to follow him. They started up the stairs, which rose against the wall to the right side of the living room.

Concho drew his second Colt. Pete Cramer had not been among the prisoners captured below. Nor had the Ranger seen him elsewhere in the house. He hoped the man was upstairs; He wanted a chance at the son of a bitch who'd supplied a group of violent pedophiles with a potential nine-year-old victim.

CHAPTER 19

Ten-Wolves and FBI Agent Causey reached the top of the stairs. There'd been enough creaks and cracks on the steps on the way up to warn anyone who might be waiting for them. But the landing stood empty. Two hallways led off from the landing, one long, one short. Both were carpeted, with closed doors along them.

Concho pointed down the short hallway, which had two doors on the left-hand side, with a railing and open air on the right. He gave Causey the nod. She returned it, moved in that direction.

The Ranger stepped into the long hallway, which had two rooms on each side. He was reaching to open the first door on the right when he heard a noise at the end of the hall, from behind the last door on the left. It sounded like someone wrenching at a stubborn window.

Leaving any closed doors behind him could be dangerous, but someone was trying to escape from the last room. And they could have a child with them. Concho rushed forward, his feet silent on the carpet. The door to the last room was pushed to but not closed. A light burned through the crack. Concho kicked it open with his left boot and leveled both his Colts into the room beyond.

A standard-issue bedroom greeted his gaze. A double bed against the wall, a chest of drawers, a lamp table, one window.

At the window stood Pete Cramer, bent over as he yanked at the wooden frame, trying to raise it.

The glass slid up a few inches and screeched to a stop as Cramer heard someone enter the room behind him. He turned quickly, his right hand dipping for the butt of a big, nickel-plated revolver stuck through his belt. Concho triggered his left-hand Colt and put a slug into the wall just over Cramer's head. The man froze.

"Dump the pistol," the lawman snarled. "Left hand. Two fingers. Throw it on the bed."

Cramer looked as if he were considering taking his chances on a draw but then shrugged and did as he was told. Using the thumb and forefinger of his left hand, he pulled the weapon out and tossed it onto the bed.

"Guess you got me, Cop."

A voice called from the hallway. "Ten-Wolves!" Concho recognized Agent Causey.

"It's all right," he called back. "I've got Cramer. But I didn't have a chance to check the other closed doors."

"I'll get them," Causey replied.

Concho focused on Cramer again. "Where's Jericho?"

Cramer offered a small smile and another shrug. "In case you didn't hear it, Jericho and I had a bit of a falling out."

"Because you brought Toni here instead of taking her to him." Concho forced himself to take a deep, slow breath. "Brought her here to *sell!* To *these* people!"

"Business," Cramer said.

Concho held the barrel of his left-hand Colt vertically up in front of his lips in a shushing motion. "You don't justify. You answer questions. You had some place you were supposed to meet Jericho before you changed your mind. Where?"

"Why? He won't be there anymore. He may be freaking weird, but he's not stupid."

"Tell me anyway. Who knows what clues might have been left behind?"

A crafty look suddenly masked Cramer's face. "Maybe so," he said. "Maybe we could work out a deal?"

Concho's right-hand Colt was pointed directly at Cramer's face. He let the barrel drop a little and cocked the hammer, though it wasn't necessary. The metallic click certainly provided an accompanying backbeat for the savage words he uttered:

"You ever mention the word 'deal' around me again, and I'll shoot you in the crotch and watch you bleed out. I don't deal with sociopaths who traffic in children. You tell me where you were supposed to meet Jericho, or I'll pistol-whip it out of you with a happy little smile on my face."

Any cunning look on Cramer's face fled to be replaced by shock as he realized how close the Ranger was to carrying out his threat. He lifted his hands, put them both out in front of him with palms flat as if trying to calm the law officer.

"OK, OK! I'll tell you."

***

Jericho had climbed a tree. He sat like a perched raven against the upper trunk of a large oak as he waited for the gunfire from the ranch to die down. It was full dark now, but there were enough lights on around the house to see what he needed to see. The bird-watching binoculars he carried helped.

One last shot sounded from inside the house. Then silence. A few moments passed, and more lights came on around the ranch. Officers wearing jackets bearing the letters FBI came out the back door to examine the scene. It would appear Cramer and his buddies had fought the law, and the law had won.

Jericho hoped Cramer was dead and that Concho Ten-Wolves had killed him. It would be appropriate. The Texas Ranger came off as something of an avenging angel after all, albeit a rather large and darkly hued angel. Even if Cramer was alive, he'd been told nothing to hurt Jericho.

About thirty yards from Jericho's tree, the FBI agent named

Will Bolin rose to his feet from where'd he'd been covering the back of the ranch. He stretched, slung his hunting rifle over his shoulder, and started walking toward his colleagues. Jericho could have killed Bolin at any time but doing so would only throw suspicion in a direction he did not want it to go.

Jericho put the binoculars back to his eyes as a very large dark-skinned man stepped out of the house now. He smiled at the sight of Ten-Wolves. He smiled even more, when a tiny little black girl came running out of the tool shed and threw herself onto the Ranger.

Toni!

Concho scooped the girl up and seemed to be laughing, though the sound didn't carry this far. Despite what Jericho had told the Texas Ranger on the phone, he'd never expected to be able to get Toni away from Stone Creek Ranch and back into his possession. He'd merely wanted to spur the lawman to greater efforts. It had worked.

But an actual chance had come. He'd seen one of the basement windows open and the tiny little girl climb out and dart across the yard to the wooden tool shed. Somehow she remained unseen, though several men had stood talking on the porch less than thirty yards away. But people do not see what they do not expect to see.

Toni, it seemed, was quite the resourceful child. Jericho believed he could have retaken her then. It would have been tight, but he'd come through more difficult "eyes of the needle" before. But something much better had occurred to him, something so sublime it had to be fated.

From a source no one would suspect, Jericho had learned much about the lawman's recent days. He was on the outs with his boss in the Texas Rangers. He'd been suspended. The hero Ranger had been *suspended!*

But what if the *former* hero became a hero again? What if he led a daring raid and rescued a child kidnapped by evil people? Destroying a ring of pedophiles and human traffickers, would that not cure all Ten-Wolves' ills?

Jericho pocketed his binoculars and pulled a burner phone from his jacket. He punched in a number memorized courtesy of a colleague. He expected to have to leave a message. Who answered their phone these days unless you knew the caller? But a voice did answer, a man who sounded just like who he was supposed to be, a commanding officer in the Texas Rangers.

"What is it?" Max Keller snapped roughly into the phone.

"Commander Keller," Jericho whispered. "I was afraid I'd have to leave a message for you. Thanks for answering."

"Who is this?"

"Not important. What is important is some information I can give you."

"If this is a spam call—" Keller threatened.

"Information about Concho Ten-Wolves," Jericho interrupted.

Silence. Then, "Go on."

"I understand you've suspended the good Ten-Wolves. Very foolish. You're going to want to reinstate him immediately."

"I don't answer to you," Keller snapped. "Did Ten-Wolves put you up to this? I still want to know who you are."

Jericho ignored the last comment. "I'm staring at the man right now, but he has no idea I'm here or that I'm speaking to you. I'm sure he'd disapprove of both. But as to who you answer to. You answer to your bosses, and *they* answer to the public. The public is going to be furious with you once they find out what happened tonight?"

"What are you squawking about?"

"Concho Ten-Wolves, along with a few colleagues in the FBI, just took down a pedophile ring and rescued half a dozen children, including a very charismatic and photogenic little girl named Toni. I'm sure her clear affection and appreciation for the Ranger will play well on the news. It won't reflect well on you."

"This is bull!" Keller fired angrily into the phone.

Jericho ignored the anger. "You've suspended a hero!" he continued. "People will not forgive you. Your days in law enforcement are numbered. But you might have a chance to salvage a little something if you act quickly."

"I'll not be threatened!" Keller shouted.

Jericho chuckled. "Good night."

He hung up and tucked the phone back in his pocket. He'd discard it as soon as he got away from the ranch. Soon, Ten-Wolves would be on top of the world again. From hero to goat to king dragon in a few short days. Then would be the time to bring him into the fold. Or tear him down and take everything of his before killing him. And to wrap himself in all the resulting glory.

Sliding down from his tree, Jericho melted back into the woods. The black dog followed; it snuffled among the dead leaves. The dog wasn't the only specter wandering here. A dozen shades paced him, shrieking in their silent voices. He walked among them. Unafraid. Just one more ghost among the ghosts.

PART TWO
HERO

CHAPTER 20

Concho brought Toni to see her grandmother in the hospital. They talked to a doctor first, who said the woman would be OK. Her collapse had been triggered by mental exhaustion. As soon as the Ranger walked into the woman's room with Toni in his arms, she began a remarkable recovery.

The reunion between the two was joyous, a reason to smile. Concho's own exhaustion faded for the moment. Good work had been done tonight by many people. He was glad to have done his part.

Plenty of Toni's family members were at the hospital. The girl would be well taken care of. As Concho finally escaped the hugs from Toni and the pervasive "Thank you, thank you, thank you's" from the grandmother and other relatives, he made his way downstairs to the hospital's main waiting area.

Della Rice and Will Bolin were visiting Binh Bui, who was in the same hospital. But Perse Wiebke sat in one of the waiting area's worn chairs. She'd insisted on tagging along, and he was grateful when she handed him a brown paper bag with the gold McDonald's M all over the side of it.

"Thought you might be hungry," she said, grinning. "And there's drinks." She pointed to a nearby table where a cardboard tray of fast food sodas stood. "Hope Coke is OK."

"You're a Godsend," Concho replied, pulling open the bag and grabbing a handful of still hot fries. He stuffed these into his mouth.

"You get you something?" he muttered around the mouthful of crispy, delicious potato.

"Ate it on the way over. Was pretty hungry myself."

Concho nodded, ate more fries, unboxed one of the two Quarter-pounders she'd brought him, and bit off half with one chomp.

"Didn't know how you liked yours, so I just let 'em put everything on them," Wiebke said.

"Mhmm," Concho replied.

The nearby elevator dinged, and Rice and Bolin came out. They were smiling as they walked over to their fellow law officers. Wiebke handed them each a McDonald's sack of their own.

"Bui OK?" Concho asked before stuffing the rest of his first quarter-pounder into his mouth.

"Good as can be expected," Rice replied as she glanced into her own bag and delicately pulled out a couple of long fries. "The arm wound might be an issue down the line. The doc's not sure if he was able to repair all the damage or not."

"Hope so," Concho said. "He seems like a good officer." He picked up one of the tall sodas Wiebke had brought, ignored the straw, pulled off the lid, and drained about half the drink in one gulp.

"He is," Rice replied. "Been my right-hand man."

"So, what's next?" Wiebke asked.

Rice answered. "Now," she gestured around at their four-person crew, "we all go home. Let the next shift take over with grilling the perps and seeing that the other children are identified and either returned to their parents or placed appropriately."

Concho had started on his second quarter-pounder but was taking smaller bites. "With Jericho still out there," he said, "we have to make sure Toni has protection. I don't see him as the type to give up."

"I've given a full report to my Sheriff," Wiebke said. "He's sending over a couple of officers to relieve me in watching the girl. Should be here shortly. I get the feeling you're right about Jericho. He's not the kind to give up. But he's not stupid either. I doubt he'll go after the girl again with so much attention focused on her."

Concho nodded. "What about the state police?"

"They're informed," Wiebke said. "I imagine they've got a heavy presence all around here."

Concho finished his second burger and the last few of his fries. He tossed his garbage in a nearby can. As he turned back to the group, Della Rice took a step away from him and put her hands protectively over her own bag of goodies.

"Yes," she said forcefully, "I *am* going to eat all of mine."

Bolin laughed around a mouthful of hamburger. Wiebke grinned. Concho tried to arch an eyebrow and couldn't manage it—as usual. "I'm wounded to the quick at your distrust of my motives," he said.

"Uh-huh, right," Rice said. Then she smiled. "You can have some of my fries if you want."

"Appreciate it," Concho said. He yawned. "But what I need now is to get some shut-eye." He sniffed himself and added. "And maybe a shower."

"How are you getting home?" Della Rice asked.

"Hmm. Good question."

"We're headed that way in a few minutes," Rice said. "You're welcome to ride along."

"I'd appreciate it."

Rice and Bolin tossed their trash and picked up their drinks to take along. Wiebke rose from her chair and shook hands all around.

"Let me reimburse you for the food," Rice offered.

Wiebke waved her off. "Charged it to the department. No problem. I just appreciate being able to ride along with you guys today."

"We were lucky to have you," Concho said.

Wiebke's green eyes met his. "I learned a lot. Sure hope you'll all keep me in the loop on this Jericho thing. After what I saw today, I'd like to be in on the kill." She grinned. "So to speak."

"Will do," Rice said. "Will do."

***

Concho let Will Bolin take the front passenger seat and climbed in the back of Della Rice's SUV. They were soon on the road to Eagle Pass. The time on the vehicle's clock read 10:57 PM. Much had happened in a short while.

They hadn't been able to get to the cabin Pete Cramer had described the place where he was supposed to bring Toni to Jericho. Too much had to be done at Stone Creek Ranch. Rice had sent another team to the cabin, and though they were still checking the place out, Jericho was nowhere to be found. That was to be expected.

Concho glanced at the time again. 10:58. Maria Morales was probably still awake. He tugged his cell phone out of his jeans. His charge was down to twelve percent. Still plenty. "Gotta make a call," he told the others.

Bolin turned around in his seat and grinned. "You better. I already called my wife and told her how much of a hero I was. That'll keep her waiting up for me."

Della Rice snorted but said nothing. Concho merely grinned back and punched up the number he wanted. The phone began to ring.

"Baby?" Maria's voice answered. She sounded anxious.

"Yes, Maria. And I'm fine."

A flood of relief rang through Maria's next words. "Thank God. I was having a bad feeling about things. Did everything go OK? What about the little girl?"

"We got her. She's safe. And so are several other children."

"Wonderful. What about the bad guy?"

"We arrested some bad ones but not the one who started it all. But he's on the run, and eventually, we'll get him."

"I'm glad."

"I didn't wake you, did I?"

"Just how old do you think I am?" Maria asked, chuckling. "I don't usually go to bed before midnight."

"Really?" Concho said. "I've seen you get in bed a little earlier."

"Mmmm," Maria purred. "Maybe. If the company is right, but not to sleep."

The lawman felt his face flush with heat. From the front seat, Della Rice made a gagging noise. Concho blushed even more.

"Are you coming home now?" Maria asked.

"On my way. Catching a ride with some FBI jokers. Should be about an hour. Maybe I can see you in the morning?"

"I'll meet you at your trailer."

"Don't you have to work tomorrow?"

"I think they can handle a day without me. Besides, I *am* the boss. And what good is that if you can't abuse the position a little?"

"I'd love to see you."

"You will," Maria said. "All of me." She hung up.

"Ooh la la," Bolin said.

Rice pretended to gag again.

Maria's voice did carry. The agents must have heard both sides of the conversation. Concho just grinned and leaned back in his seat.

CHAPTER 21

It was right at midnight when Della Rice turned her SUV
onto the Kickapoo reservation outside Eagle Pass. Prior to 1984,
the Texas Kickapoo had lived like squatters beneath the International
Bridge connecting the US and Mexico. In 1983, the tribe
was officially recognized by the United States government as the
"Kickapoo Traditional Tribe of Texas" and thus became eligible
to own land. They chose some one hundred and twenty acres just
south of the town of Eagle Pass, which was where the reservation
was located today.

Even after finding land for their new home, money had remained
short for the tribe for a long time. Most tribal members
lived in poverty, in cinder-block houses, trailers, or even in traditional
Kickapoo homes called wickiups. Then, in 1996, a casino
and hotel called the "Lucky Eagle" opened. It was one of the first
casinos in Texas and still one of only four.

The casino paid every tribal member a monthly dividend, significantly
raising the standard of living for many. New buildings
and houses had gone up on the reservation, many of brick. Most
people drove better automobiles and had more of both the necessities
and luxuries of modern America.

Unfortunately, no gambling enterprise comes without attendant problems. Concho had something of a love/hate relationship with the casino. He appreciated the financial help it gave the tribe but resented the drugs and crime that too often came along with the money.

As Rice drove her SUV through a quiet Kickapoo Village, the glittering lights of the casino/hotel showed off to the right. It didn't really matter what Concho thought of the place. It was here, and he'd learned to play the world's cards the way they were dealt. He'd live with it.

Rice turned onto a well-maintained dirt road leading out of the main Kickapoo settlement and cruised along it. Concho's trailer lay out this way, and she'd been to it several times. It was about a fifteen-minute journey.

The Ranger looked out the window, watching the nearly full moon rain silver onto the mesquite trees and dryland scrub to either side of the road. After a couple of weeks away, he felt a surge of homecoming pleasure in his belly. He belonged here, a part of the land just as the land was part of him.

They turned off into his long driveway, which was much rougher than the main road, and traveled about half a mile into the heart of the Rez before Concho saw the lights of his trailer shining up ahead. He smiled. Maria was here before him. It would be so good to see her.

The Kickapoo lawman's trailer was a large double-wide, with three bedrooms, one full and one-half-bath, a living room, and a den. His last trailer had been burned down in a case of arson. Before that, he'd grown up on this same plot of land with his grandmother in a much smaller trailer.

Rice pulled her big Dodge Durango up beside Maria's tiny little 2017 Ford Focus. Concho slid out on the driver's side, carrying the backpack he'd boarded a Greyhound bus with two days earlier. About the only thing in it now were the books he'd bought to read on the bus. One of those remained unfinished.

The Ranger took a deep breath. The scents of mesquite and

juniper made a heady and familiar perfume for the night. He nodded to the two agents in the vehicle. "Thanks for the lift."

"Don't do anything I wouldn't do," Rice replied.

"I've got no idea what that might mean," Concho said. "But I'll give it some consideration."

Both agents chuckled. Rice slipped the SUV into reverse, backed up, and turned around. Concho started for the front door of his trailer. It opened. Maria stood framed there. She was, as some say, "sky-clad." Others just describe it as a "birthday suit."

***

The first bout of lovemaking was short and intense. The second lasted only a little longer. After the second time, Concho lay back on his massive king-sized bed, panting for breath, sweat beaded across his face and chest.

Maria panted beside him; one sculpted leg draped across his waist. Her long dark hair hung damp and wavy over her shoulders, half covering her right breast. Concho turned with a groan toward her and brushed the hair away, then kissed the taut nipple. She groaned herself and gently pushed his face away.

"Mercy," she said.

The lawman lay back with a chuckle. "I don't even know the term."

Maria rose onto her right elbow and stared at him. She ran the fingers of her left hand through the curly hair on his chest and suddenly plucked one out.

"Ouch!" Concho said, wincing. "Why did you do that?"

Maria pinched another chest hair between her forefinger and thumb but only gave it a light tug. "Sure you don't know what 'mercy' means?"

"Mercy."

She laughed and lay back down with her head pillowed on his broad shoulder. She sniffed and made a face, though she didn't switch positions. "You need a shower," she said.

"Told you that when I came in the door."

"I don't think my ears were hearing too well right then," she said. "All the blood must have been rushing elsewhere."

Concho twisted a little bit toward her. His right hand cupped the back of her head as he slid his shoulder from beneath her cheek and lay her down on the pillow. He brushed his lips lightly across hers, then turned and slipped out of bed.

"I'll be back in a few minutes."

"Don't tarry," she replied.

"Baby, if time-efficient bathing was an Olympic sport, I guarantee I'd bring home the gold tonight."

Maria smiled and whipped the sheet off herself for an instant to flash him before covering back up just as quickly. He groaned and went to take a shower.

***

By habit, Concho awoke at 6:00 AM. Normally, he'd get up, get dressed and fix himself some breakfast before starting his day as a Texas Ranger. Not today. He was suspended, even though he'd gone ahead and recorded a report on the Jericho affair last night and sent it to Ranger headquarters anyway.

He rolled onto his left side. Maria was asleep, facing away from him, with only the tip of one shoulder and the top of her black-haired head showing from beneath the sheet. She snored in gentle little peeps that sounded like a newly hatched chicken.

He smiled, recalling the long, slow intimacy they'd shared after he came back to bed from his shower. Sighing pleasurably, he closed his eyes again. To heck with it, he wasn't getting up. That thought quickly led back to sleep.

The next time he awoke, it was 8:14 AM, according to the clock on his side table. Maria was no longer in bed; he heard her moving around in the kitchen and smelled bacon frying. Sliding from under the sheet, he slipped on a pair of loose boxers and a white t-shirt, then padded into the other room.

Maria bustled around the stove, wearing the black satin robe she'd left here for such mornings. She'd pulled her mass of midnight hair back and tied it loosely. The thick ponytail hung down between her shoulders in a tangled mess. Concho didn't care. She was beautiful enough to flutter his heart.

Ten-Wolves could move silently but didn't want to startle his lover. He cleared his throat to warn her; she turned and smiled brilliantly at him. The robe was only loosely belted at her waist, and very attractive shapes moved beneath the satin. He bit his lip, greeted her with a peck on the forehead.

She was having none of that and pulled him into a stormy kiss on the mouth before finally letting him go. They were each breathing a little roughly when the kiss was done. Maria turned back to the stove where bacon sizzled in an iron skillet.

"I had to dump your milk," she said. "What little you had left was sour. Your three eggs didn't look too good either, so I tossed 'em. However," she smiled at him again, "your bacon was fine, and I'm fixing most of it now. Along with," she gestured toward the stove and opened it slightly before closing it again.

"Biscuits," Concho said, catching the scent. "I'm certainly glad my bacon and biscuits met your approval."

Maria picked up a home-fired clay cup from the counter that Concho had bought for her from one of the local Kickapoo sculptors. She sipped at the liquid inside. The Ranger smelled the bitter black brew and made a face, but Maria did not go without her morning cup of java. It was the main reason he'd bought a coffeepot.

Over the rim of her cup, Maria's electric eyes met Concho's gaze. He held out for just a moment, then took the cup from her gently and set it aside. Sliding both of his big hands around the back of her head, he threaded his fingers through her hair and drew her up on her tiptoes for another kiss, a long and lingering sharing.

Maria finally broke the kiss. She panted slightly, and her pupils were dilated. "Let's eat first," she said. "There'll be plenty of time for more later. I'm going to be with you all day."

"I know," Concho replied. "I couldn't let you go now anyway. I always have to finish any investigation I start."

Maria used a pair of tongs to flip the bacon. "Oh, am I an investigation to you now?"

He grinned. "You're what we in the law biz call a 'hot case' file."

Maria laughed and gave him a once over. "And you'll be more like a crime scene when I'm finished with you."

Before Concho had a chance to reply, his cell phone rang back in the bedroom. It startled him for a second. He squeezed Maria's shoulder and trotted toward the ringing. Plucking the phone up from his bedside table, he glanced at the caller ID and was startled anew. A look of distaste crossed his face. He swiped the phone to receive.

"Hello," he said.

CHAPTER 22

"Ten-Wolves," **Max Keller said into the phone. "Glad I** caught you."

"Major," Concho said.

An awkward pause followed. Then, Keller added, "I just got off the line with Special Agent Della Rice of the FBI."

"I know her, Sir."

"Yes, well…she indicated to me that you assisted her and her group yesterday evening in arresting a group of human traffickers and freeing half a dozen children from their clutches."

"A ring of pedophiles, Sir. And there were eight children. And I was invited by Agent Rice, so I did not violate my suspension."

"Uhm…yes. Well…about that suspension. I also spoke yesterday to an NOPD homicide detective named Solly Burstein. I believe he was the man you worked with primarily in New Orleans?"

"Yes, Sir."

"He also assured me your actions in that city were all above board."

Concho's teeth ground together. Keller had received the same word officially from the New Orleans Police Department several days ago. It hadn't stopped him from signing the suspension statement originally. But Ten-Wolves wasn't going to remind the man of that right now. He said nothing, and another pause filled the air.

Keller cleared his throat. "At any rate, I've decided to cancel the suspension. In fact, I'm going to clear it completely, so no record of it remains on your service sheet."

Will surprises never cease? Concho thought. But what he said was, "I appreciate it, Sir."

"Good. Then we're pretty much done here. Take the rest of today off. I'll expect you back on duty tomorrow."

"Yes, Sir."

"Oh, and I understand the primary suspect in the kidnapping that started this ball rolling has not yet been apprehended?"

"No, Sir."

"Has the FBI given any indication they'd like you to keep working on the case?"

"They have."

"Well, good. You're free to do so. Just keep me closely informed. This could be an excellent opportunity for the Rangers. Taking down human traffickers is an important service. I don't imagine there's been any mention of a trial yet for the ones you caught?"

"No. I'm sure I'll be called to testify. But some of the perps were wealthy. They'll have good lawyers, and it'll be a while before anything happens."

"I'll expect you to represent us well. Let me know, too, if there's going to be any press conference."

A lightbulb went off inside Concho's head.

"I'll do my best," is all he said into the phone before swiping off.

***

As Max Keller laid his phone down on his work desk, he reran the conversation with Concho Ten-Wolves through his mind. He matched it with the one he'd had the night before with a mysterious caller who'd suggested he reinstate the Kickapoo officer.

Ten-Wolves had played it perfectly, giving away nothing of whoever he was working with behind the scenes. But Max had a sixth sense about such things. The black Indian was up to something. No doubt, something that skirted the rules of the Texas Rangers organization. And that meant Max would have a chance to catch him at it and finally pluck a thorn from his side.

"Give them enough rope to hang themselves," he muttered before turning to the pile of papers on his desk.

***

Maria had breakfast on the table when Concho returned to the kitchen. She'd poured him a glass of orange juice, piled his plate with bacon, and even buttered a biscuit for him. He immediately buttered two more.

"Everything OK?" she asked as Concho folded two strips of bacon between the golden halves of a biscuit and took a big bite. He held up one finger for time, then chewed and swallowed before answering.

"That was my boss. Max Keller. He has officially expunged my suspension?"

Maria arched an eyebrow. "Sounds like good news. But...."

"But it's not like him. Seems he wants me to keep working with the FBI. I believe he figures it could be good publicity for the Texas Rangers. Or else he's giving me enough rope to hang myself. And if something good *does* come out of it, he'll be able to grab some of the credit."

"Asshole!"

"Nail head, meet hammer. I've heard rumors he plans to run for political office. This would seem to corroborate that idea."

"I don't like that man," Maria said. "I wish someone would get rid of him."

Concho just ate more biscuits and bacon.

***

Completing errands was the plan of the day for Concho. And avoiding phone calls from the press, who'd already learned of last evening's human trafficking raid and were looking for interviews.

Unless it was clearly the number of a local news outlet, he answered most calls. Someone desperate might need his help. But upon hearing the requests and learning it was a news source, he quickly gave them his well-practiced two-sentence response and hung up.

"Thank you, but I was just doing my job. I don't need recognition for that."

Since Concho had no vehicle, Maria drove him to his first errand, which was to rectify his biggest problem. They stopped at the local Ford dealership, and the lawman bought a gently used 2018 F-150, in white with an extended cab. It had less than 20,000 miles on it.

He hadn't gotten the insurance money for his previous F-150 yet but took three thousand out of a meager savings for the down payment. When the insurance money came in, he'd put it down too, although he was still going to have a monthly note. At least he wasn't still suspended without pay.

While Maria left for the store to pick him up some groceries, Concho drove his new truck around to *Camino del mal*," a small bar in Eagle Pass catering mainly to Hispanics. The owner, Piero Almanza, was an old friend from Army Ranger days.

Piero also dealt in weapons, mostly of the legal variety. After drinking a Dos Equis with Piero and swapping a few tall tales, Concho left the bar with a Remington semi-automatic .30-06 hunting rifle, ammunition for it and for his Colt .45s, a Kevlar vest big enough to comfortably fit even his shoulders and chest, and a pair of military-issue night-vision goggles. These, he stored in the extended cab section of the F-150.

Feeling about half whole after replacing the weapons and some of the tools he'd lost when his old F-150 was blown up, he headed back for the reservation and stopped off at John Gray-Dove's automotive shop. John was another friend, and in addition to his garage, he kept a woodworking shop for building furniture.

Concho borrowed the shop on occasion to make arrows for his bow. Now, he needed to remake the bow itself since it, too, had been in his destroyed truck. He didn't have time to work on the weapon immediately but picked up various wooden staves and loaded them into his truck along with a few tools so he could start the process at home. He also picked up a small metal tin containing red ochre, which made excellent warpaint.

Despite the chill in the December air, Concho headed for home with the windows down in his truck. He liked the feel of the fresh wind. His phone rang, the caller ID indicating it as Della Rice.

"Hey," he said into the phone. "Thanks for putting in a good word with me to Max Keller. He's decided to reinstate me."

"Good!" Rice said. "Surprising, but good."

"I'm pretty sure he's hoping for some publicity from it all."

"Ahh, makes more sense."

"So, what's up? Why'd you call?"

"The crew that investigated Jericho's cabin found something I wanted to mention to you."

"Oh?"

"A handwritten note. Addressed to you.'"

"I see."

"I wrote it down. It read: 'Ten-Wolves. You won. Congratulations.' It was signed, 'Jericho.'"

"That it?"

"Mostly. It was on the kitchen table, sticking out of the top of a children's book."

"A to Z Mysteries."

"What?"

"It's a mystery series for kids. Toni was reading one on the bus. Jericho may have sent Toni with Cramer, but *he* had her books. Or one at least. Anything else notable?"

"Not that they said."

"I need to see the place."

"Gotcha. I can swing by and pick you up in about an hour. That OK?"

"Can you make it two hours?"

"Miss Morales still visiting?"

"Indeed."

"All right. Two hours." She signed off.

Concho frowned to himself. He spoke out loud to the truck. "So, what now? What kind of game is Jericho playing? Whatever it is, I don't like it!"

CHAPTER 23

Maria was waiting for him at his trailer when Concho arrived. She'd already put up the groceries and had steaks ready to grill. She offered him a kiss and a glass of cold chocolate milk as he came in the door.

"You're spoiling me," he told her.

"I'm glad to have you home. I missed you while you were in New Orleans."

"I missed you too."

"Just don't get used to the spoiling!"

He grinned. "Too late. I've already adjusted."

She slapped him on the arm, then went to start the steaks. They had time to eat *and* make love before Della Rice arrived to pick him up.

***

Della Rice turned up a paved driveway through wintery brown fields thick with mesquite and thorn trees. About a hundred yards in, the road curved sharply around a thick grove of mesquite, and they saw Jericho's "cabin" just ahead. It was a small house, white with blue trim. Recently painted. A separate garage in the same colors stood to the left.

Rice pulled her Durango up next to another police vehicle already on the scene. A state trooper climbed out to greet them with a wave. He wore a heavy coat. Rice and Concho got out. Rice shivered and pulled her windbreaker tighter about her shoulders. The news had indicated a cold front coming, and they must have driven through it on the way here. The temps had dropped into the forties, with a wind. Concho zipped up his own light jacket.

After handshakes and introductions, the state trooper—named Dan Holtzen—peeled back the police tape blocking the cabin's front door and unlocked it. He followed the others inside. A bedroom stood to the left of the door, a combination den and living room to the right.

"The kitchen is where the note was found?" Concho asked.

Holtzen offered a 'thumbs up.' "This way," he said, taking the lead down the hall and turning to the right into a small but well set up kitchen.

"Right there," Holtzen said, pointing to a small, round dining room table sitting almost in the center of the room.

"And it was tucked into a book?"

"Yes. There were two books. Kid's books. The note was in the top one. I took some pictures." He pulled out his phone and opened his gallery app. He swiped through a couple of images and handed the phone over.

Concho saw two books stacked on the same table. The title on the top read: *A to Z Mysteries. Colossal Fossil.* A drawing of a dinosaur skeleton filled most of the cover, with the name of the author, Rob Roy, at the bottom. About an inch of notebook paper stuck out of the book.

"You can see the top of the note," Holtzen said. "Swipe left, and you'll see some more pics."

Concho did as suggested. The next one showed the note itself. Handwritten in blue ink, in a nice script. Agent Rice had quoted it to him correctly. A congratulations from Jericho.

A third picture showed the cover of the second book, another *A to Z Mystery. Operation Orca.* The next picture was apparently

of Holtzen's wife and baby girl. Concho handed the phone back
to the trooper.

"Nothing else around of interest?" he asked.

Holtzen shook his head.

"And the house was rented to Roy Simms?"

"Yep. The owner's a retired oil exec. Described this Jericho to
a T. Said the guy was clean cut, friendly, and seemed like a perfect
renter."

"Hiding in plain sight," Concho said.

"Yep," the trooper said again.

"Everything's been fingerprinted?"

"It has."

Concho looked around the kitchen. He opened the refrigerator
door. The electricity had been turned on in the house. The fridge
hummed. An untouched gallon of milk sat on the bottom shelf,
along with some cans of Dr. Pepper. He saw an unopened package
of turkey lunch meat. Rectangles of margarine and some condi-
ments rested in the door shelves, along with a dozen eggs—all of
them there.

The freezer had pork chops, steaks, and several packages of
chicken. The pantry contained cans of chili, beans, corn, and
soup, along with a box of rice, several cereals, and various packs
of mac 'n' cheese.

"He was planning on being here a while," Concho said. "And
the food selections certainly suggest with a child."

"The question now is, where did he go?" Della Rice asked.

"Yeah. Maybe you have a look around in here. I'm going to
check out back."

"All right."

Concho stepped out of the kitchen into a combination laundry
and mud room. He opened the back door and pushed through the
screen to stand on top of a set of concrete steps. A fenced-in yard
greeted his gaze. It was small but pleasant enough.

The fence was of wood, some six feet high. A gate opening
to the outside caught Concho's interest. An open lock dangled

from it. He removed it and stepped through into a field of tall brown grass full of scattered scrub. No other houses were visible anywhere around, although off to the north, a thin trail of white smoke rose from someone's chimney.

To his left was a pile of debris, leftover from the construction of the cabin, it looked like. As the Ranger moved in that direction, something stopped him—a covered-over well. Thick planks had been nailed to a wooden frame blocking the opening of the well. They wouldn't be hard to remove.

Concho studied the structure, seeing no recent sign of it having been tampered with. He could smell nothing but a faint odor of dampness coming up out of the well. There were no sounds from within.

"Hasn't had a chance to use it yet," Ten-Wolves muttered to himself.

He closed his eyes for a moment, listened with more than his ears. And now he did hear a faint sound, a tinny, echoing howl that seemed to come from the bones of the earth. It was only his imagination but was not without meaning.

"The black dog," Concho murmured. "And hungry."

The screen door slammed on the house behind him, and he stepped back through the gate into the yard. Della Rice stood there, clearly looking for him.

"You find something?" Concho asked.

Rice shook her head. "No, but I got a call. From the house where we first tracked Jericho."

"The pond!"

"Yes. They've started dredging it. They've already found three bodies. At least they believe it's three. Some were only parts. There's a reason that gator was so big."

Concho winced but added, "And?"

Rice knew what he was asking. "All adults so far. No children."

Concho shook his head in confusion. "I need to talk to Mandy again. We're missing something. Something big."

CHAPTER 24

Uvalde, Texas, was the county seat of Uvalde County, which lay north and east of Concho's own Maverick County. The town had a population of about fifteen thousand. Mandy's parents, Lewis and Linda Callimore, lived in a duplex up on a small rise near the outskirts of the town.

On Wednesday morning, the day after the first bodies were found in Jericho's farm pond—the parts of two more had been discovered since —Ten-Wolves drove up to visit the Callimore family. He'd called ahead, and they were waiting for him. Della Rice had been unable to accompany him, but Beth Pennebaker was visiting as well.

Lewis and Linda were young professionals, but both had taken off a few days to help reacclimate their daughter to home. Both were polite if a bit standoffish. Both seemed a little awkward around their daughter, who'd been missing for over three years and who they'd given up for dead. They were awkward around Concho, too, who made a large reminder of what had happened to their Mandy.

Both parents were willing to leave the room while he talked to Mandy. In fact, they seemed eager to be gone. Beth Pennebaker asked to stay, and the Ranger did not object. The Callimores had probably requested her presence.

Mandy sat on the couch while Concho perched rather awkwardly on a too-small dining room chair pulled into the front room for that purpose. The room smelled of candles recently burned, of cinnamon and orange and lemon. A Christmas tree in one corner showed signs of some haste in having been put up.

Mandy looked a lot different today. Her face had been scrubbed clean, and her curly brown hair trimmed and tamed, apparently with a strawberry scented shampoo. She wore a long cotton dress rather than jeans and a hoodie. She'd given Concho a hug when he came in, to the apparent consternation of her father, but now sat primly on the couch without really looking at him.

"So, how are you, Mandy?" Concho asked.

She didn't look up. "I'm good."

"I wanted to come by and check on you. Like I promised."

"I'm glad you did." She glanced at him. "How are *you*?"

"I'm doing all right." He smiled. "I finally got something to eat and got some sleep."

Mandy sighed. "They're treating me well here," she said, which seemed a rather odd thing to say. But, she'd been through enough trauma to discombobulate anyone.

"Glad to hear it. I also had a few more questions to ask. I hope that's OK."

Mandy's eyes were hollow, with dark circles beneath. She clearly wasn't sleeping well herself.

"I told you everything I know," she said. "And the other police too."

"Yes. You were very helpful—"

"And you got the girl back," Mandy blurted. "Didn't you? That...Toni?"

"Yes, we did. Thanks in large part to you. But...Jericho is still out there. And if he took you and Toni, he's likely to try the same thing with other young ladies. I really don't want that to happen."

Mandy nodded; her gaze dropped again.

"You told me you didn't know Pete Cramer was working with Jericho. But did you ever hear his name mentioned?"

Mandy shook her head. "No," she said in the small voice Concho had heard her use before. He winced inwardly at hearing that voice come back but felt he needed to push on. Too many things, in this case, didn't add up, and, right now, Mandy was their only first-hand source of information.

"That's OK," Concho said. "I wanted to ask another question. When we—me and the other FBI agents—got to the house. The one past the burned church. There was a young man there. You know who I'm talking about?"

A hint of animation sparkled in Mandy's eyes as she met the Ranger's gaze and flashed him a quick smile.

"Jeff!" she said. "Is he OK?"

Concho shook his head. "I'm afraid not, Mandy. He shot at us. We didn't know who it was. We weren't expecting him. We thought it might be Jericho. We shot back. One of the agents hit him. He didn't make it."

Mandy's small voice returned. "Oh."

"He was a friend of yours?"

Mandy nodded slowly.

"Why didn't you tell us about Jeff?" Concho asked, trying to avoid sounding judgmental.

Mandy shrugged. "We were told *never* to talk to anyone about the family."

"The family?"

"Me and Jeff. And Jericho.'"

"Speaking of families, we haven't been able to identify Jeff's. Did you know his last name?"

Mandy shook her head. She'd clasped her hands in her lap and twisted her fingers back and forth.

Concho glanced over at Pennebaker, who sat on the couch a few feet removed from Mandy. The social worker offered him a noncommittal smile, indicating that she wasn't sure how to proceed either.

"Jeff was older than you," Concho said. "Was he there when Jericho first took you?"

"Yeah. For a couple of years, I guess."

"Did he ever tell you anything about himself? Where he was from or anything?"

"We never talked about before."

"Before Jericho?"

"Yes."

"When we went into the house, I saw five mannequins sitting around the dining room table. Can you tell me what they were all about?"

Mandy chewed at her lower lip. "The perfect family," she finally said.

"Perfect?"

"They never fought. Or argued. Or hurt each other."

"Two of them looked like adults," Concho said. "And the other three were children. That right?"

Mandy nodded.

"The tallest of the children was probably Jeff, I'm guessing."

"Yes. And I was the middle one."

"What about the youngest?"

"Supposed to be Toni." She shrugged. "Or whoever."

"And the adults? Was one Jericho?"

"Of course."

"And the other?"

Mandy shrugged, and she wouldn't look at him. "I guess... guess it was Wilbur."

"You sure."

Again the shrug. "Yeah, it was Wilbur."

For the first time, Concho was sure Mandy was lying to him. But he still had one more question, the most important one of all. And he didn't want to confront the girl about a lie first and have her clam up.

"I see," he said. "I just want to ask you one more thing, Mandy. It may be the hardest for you to answer. And I understand if you don't want to answer. But it is something we need to know."

"OK," she said in her small voice.

Concho took a deep breath. He glanced at Beth Pennebaker, then back to Mandy. "Did Jericho ever...touch you? In ways, he shouldn't have?"

"You mean sex?"

Concho's heart lurched. Beth Pennebaker flinched. It seemed neither of them wanted to hear Mandy's answer. But they needed to.

"Yes," the Ranger said.

And Mandy did answer. Not in her small voice but in a strong one. "No!" she said. "Never. Wilbur tried...one time. But Jericho caught him and punished him. He said we were family, and family didn't do that kind of thing."

Pennebaker looked confused. It clearly wasn't the answer she'd been expecting. But Concho had begun to realize this case was much more convoluted than it appeared at first. And he believed Mandy now.

"How did Jericho punish Wilbur?" he asked.

"Beat him with a stick."

"Is that how he punished the rest of you? Jeff? And you?"

"Only if we did something bad. But never like he punished Wilbur. I remember him staying in bed for a couple of days after. Cause he was all...hurt inside."

"When we found Jeff," Concho continued. "His...his lips were sewn shut. Was that another punishment from Jericho?"

"Partly. For using a bad word."

"What else?"

"A lesson," Mandy said. She swallowed.

"What kind of lesson."

Mandy met his gaze again. "That silence is the greatest gift the world can give."

CHAPTER 25

After a few minutes of more casual conversation, Concho
gave Mandy a hug, shook hands with the parents, then headed out.
He was on the sidewalk, striding toward his new truck at the curb
when the door to the Callimore house opened behind him. He
turned to see Beth Pennebaker step out.

"Officer," she called.

He waited for Pennebaker to catch up. It was still cold today.
She wore a stylish brown leather jacket over a long black silk skirt
and a sweater with horizontal stripes of red and yellow. Her short
red hair was cut in a "pageboy," with short bangs over the eyes
and slightly longer sides. Although Concho tended to feel that
long hair better complimented most women's faces, the shortcut
worked for Beth with her small, narrow features.

"Yes Ma'am?" Ten-Wolves asked.

"Maybe I could speak to you a moment?"

"Sure."

Pennebaker took a quick breath. She looked toward the house
and back. She crossed her arms over her chest, hugging herself
against the chill. "Do you...believe Mandy when she says she
wasn't sexually abused by this Jericho?"

Concho considered, then gave a brief nod. "I guess I do."

Beth puffed a longer breath between her lips as she digested his words.

"Don't get me wrong," Concho continued. "What Jericho did to Mandy and the boy, Jeff, was abuse. I just hope Mandy can recover. But I don't think it was overtly sexual in nature."

"She wouldn't talk to me about it," Pennebaker said. "I'd assumed it was sexual. Until today. You seem to have gotten more out of her in ten minutes than I've gotten in two days."

"Outside of Jericho's 'family,' I was the first person she'd interacted with in a long time. And there was a lot of intensity in that encounter. Jericho had just driven off. A trucker was harassing her. She was terrified, and then I came along. Those kinds of experiences form a bond."

"One going both ways," Pennebaker said.

"It does. I very much hope she'll be OK. Doesn't mean she won't lie to me, though. She lied to me about at least one thing."

"What she said about those mannequins?" Pennebaker asked.

"Yeah." He quickly explained the setup of the mannequins they'd found in Jericho's house, then continued with his point. "Mandy said the second adult mannequin represented the man named Wilbur, who we know is an ally of Jericho. But," he shook his head back and forth, "I don't think so. I think it's someone we haven't seen yet. Which feels very dangerous to me."

"This whole mannequin thing. I…I've never encountered anything like it."

"I once saw a bunch of dummies and dolls shot up with high-powered ammo. But this is very different. I don't understand it either, but it means something to Jericho, and I have a feeling we need to know what."

"So what is this Jericho? I mean, if he's not a standard issue sexual predator?"

"He's a serial killer. And a serial kidnapper. But the kidnapping is different than the killing. He's trying to…achieve something."

"Do you think he might be a paranoid schizophrenic?"

"I think that label is too convenient. He's disturbed, I'd agree."

"In most cases like this, there's a terrible childhood at the heart of it."

"I suspect it's true here, too, though the exact nature of that childhood eludes me."

Pennebaker sighed. "Thanks for talking with me, Officer Ten-Wolves. I think Mandy is going to need a lot of help, and I hope I can depend on you for support."

"You can. And I hope you'll let me know anything she says relevant to this case as far as confidentiality will allow, of course. Jericho is not going to stop killing or kidnapping. We need to stop him!"

Pennebaker smiled. "Of course."

She shook the Ranger's hand and turned back toward the house. Concho climbed into his truck and headed home for the Rez, his mind churning with thoughts leading nowhere.

***

Concho was on Highway 277 headed toward Eagle Pass when his cell phone rang. He glanced at the caller ID: Persephone Wiebke. Traffic was light; he swiped to answer the call.

"Yes, Deputy?"

"Ranger Ten-Wolves," Wiebke said. "Maybe we know each other well enough now for you to call me Perse."

"Sure. Perse. And you call me Concho."

"Will do. I was calling to update you on the scene over at Jericho's farm. The pond."

"Right. I appreciate it. Whatta you got."

"It's not pretty."

"I don't imagine so. But I was in Afghanistan."

"Yes," Wiebke said. "I know. But did you see a lot of bodies that had been…chewed on?"

"Not a lot," the lawman admitted.

"Anyway, the coroner insists things are still preliminary, but he has pieces of what he says are six bodies. All adults. Likely between the ages of twenty-five and sixty. Two men, four women. None of them have been identified yet, and some probably won't be because of the state of decay."

"Hmmm. What about fingerprints inside the house?"

"Plenty of them. We've matched prints with the girl and the boy Jericho was holding prisoner. But the ones believed to be from Jericho himself haven't been matched to anything. He seems to have kept his nose pretty clean. At least as far as the law knows."

"We'll just have to spread our net wider and keep hoping for a hit."

"Of course. However, I'm not feeling very confident about catching him that way. He's too smooth."

"Unfortunately."

Wiebke sighed, then added, "I don't know much about serial killers, by the way. Is that what we're calling Jericho now?"

"That's what *I'm* calling him."

"Isn't it unusual to have a mix of genders? I mean, for serial killers. I thought they usually had a kind of…target group for victims."

"Usually. But a lot of things are *unusual* about this case."

"You're telling me. Any idea why there's both men and women?"

"Don't know. Only Jericho is going to be able to answer that question."

Wiebke chuckled. "I doubt he's going to volunteer a treatise on the subject."

"I think it's possible he will. If I ask."

A pause hung on the line. "You're confusing me. *Ask?*"

"He's already called me once. I have a feeling he'll call again."

"You think he's that stupid? He seems fairly bright to me."

"Not stupid at all. But…for lack of a better term, he and I made some kind of connection. At least in his mind. We were together on the bus. He chose to speak to me, to…challenge me.

It meant something to him. He's the kind of guy who makes connections. Maybe spurious. But they mean something to him."

"Are you saying he's superstitious?"

"Not quite. Or maybe it is in a manner of speaking. You ever have one of those moments when everything is right? The sky, the land, the people? The world? You just know something significant is happening or is about to happen. There's no logic to it. You just *feel* it."

"Yeah, I've had that. But the feeling doesn't last long. Because it's not real, it's only some random moment when the combination of chemicals in our brains is just so. Like a bubble. Here for an instant and then gone."

"You may believe that. Sometimes I believe it. But I don't think Jericho believes it. He's the kind to endow everyone and everything with meaning. For him, even a random encounter is drenched with significance. I have a good friend who is much the same. However, he's not a killer. It's clear from my phone conversation with Jericho that he's endowed our meeting on the bus with meaning. I don't know what, but he's not going to just let go of that connection."

"Interesting. Weird but interesting. Maybe we should make a side bet as to whether he calls you again."

"I'd win," Concho said.

Again, there came a pause and then a "I believe you."

"Did the coroner learn anything else from the bodies?"

"Hey, turnabout is fair play. You have anything for me from the other end of the investigation."

"Not much. I did just get through talking with Mandy."

"The girl Jericho had before taking Toni?"

"Yeah. She said the boy whose mouth was sewn shut was named Jeff. She liked him. She also said Jericho did not sexually assault her."

"I was wondering," Wiebke said. "I mean, him taking Toni suggested a sexual predator. But something about the boy... Jeff, you said? That…changed my thinking."

"Yeah. It muddied the waters. And the bodies in the pond muddy it further."

"Anything else from Mandy?"

"She lied to me about the mannequins."

"Oh? How so?"

"Five mannequins. Mandy told me they represented Jeff, her, Toni, Jericho, and Wilbur.".

"You don't believe it?"

"I don't believe the 'Wilbur.'"

"Then who? Pete Cramer?"

"No. Not him either. Someone we haven't seen. Someone, we better keep an eye out for."

"That's…scary."

"Yes. But now, what else did the coroner say about the bodies?"

"He took your advice by the way and contacted Earl Blake, the coroner out of Eagle Pass. They both agreed they couldn't find any sign of bullet wounds. Though plenty of rips and tears. They believe the men were likely killed with a blade of some kind."

"And the women were strangled?" Concho said.

"That's their guess. Probably at least. How did you know?"

"For a serial killer, the killing is intensely personal. They like to be close, to get their hands dirty, so to speak."

"Pretty awful."

"Killing is an awful business."

"I….guess so. I've…never killed anyone."

"Be glad you haven't."

"Have you?"

Concho considered his response, answered only with, "I was in Afghanistan."

CHAPTER 26

Maria had reluctantly gone to work this morning after taking yesterday off and was spending the night with her ill mother in Eagle Pass. That would leave Concho alone this evening, and he decided to make a couple of stops on the Rez before returning to his empty trailer.

First, he drove over to the Kickapoo Traditional Tribe of Texas (KTTT) Sheriff's Office. He wanted to see Roberto Echabarri, the twenty-six-year-old head of the tribal police. Concho had been instrumental in getting Roberto appointed to the position, and the two of them had worked together on several cases now. They meshed well and had become friends.

After touching base with Roberto and the KTTT deputies and hearing that all was peaceful at the moment, Concho motored out of Kickapoo Village toward his oldest friend's place on the reservation. A couple of miles along a dirt road through a sparsely populated landscape took him to Meskwaa's.

Meskwaa was a tribal elder. He sometimes claimed to be over a hundred years old, though Concho figured it was closer to seventyish. His name meant red, possibly because his hair had once been tinted that color. Concho had known him as a child but only remembered him as gray. He'd been a friend of the lawman's grandmother and grandfather before their deaths. He'd served as a mentor to Ten-Wolves and presided over his naming ceremony.

Meskwaa lived in an old, cluttered trailer well off the beaten path, though he spent much of his time in a wickiup in his yard that he'd put up himself years before. Concho had helped build such huts when he was younger; someday, he'd do so again.

The Kickapoo traditionally constructed four types of wickiup: summer, winter, cook, and menstrual. The summer house was generally the largest. To build a wickiup, you began with desert willow or one-seed juniper posts sunk deep into the ground. You wrapped these in sotol stalks and trimmed saplings to make walls, binding it all together with pita twine woven from the fibers of the maguey plant. Mats of river cane and cattails were used to make the roof.

Wickiups had no windows and didn't require a smoke hole because the loose weave of the sotol stalks created plenty of ventilation. There was just one entrance, a doorway facing east, usually covered with a blanket. The inside area of the summer house was about two hundred and forty square feet, with the roof about six feet high along the center. Most also had an attached porch, called a ramada, which was open on three sides. Wooden benches on the ramada and inside provided space for sitting and sleeping.

As Concho pulled into Meskwaa's driveway and parked, he saw smoke drifting up from the wickiup. Leaving his coat in the truck, despite temperatures that hovered around forty-five degrees Fahrenheit, Concho strode across the wickiup's ramada and knocked on the outer wall of sotol stalks.

"Come ahead," a voice called.

The Ranger pulled back the heavy gray blanket covering the door and ducked into the room beyond. A fire burned in a circle of stones in the center of the space. Tatters of smoke drifted through the air. Meskwaa sat on a scarred old bench near the fire, his feet flat on the carefully swept dirt floor. He lifted both hands in greeting, then motioned toward a second bench across from himself.

At six feet four, Ten-Wolves couldn't stand up straight inside the hut. He made his way, bent over to the second bench, and seated himself. Despite the cold outside, it was hot and almost stifling within. Sweat beaded on his face. A tin bucket of water sat near the bench he'd chosen. A dipper protruded from it, and Concho used it to scoop up a swallow of lukewarm water.

"Thank you for hospitality," he said.

"Welcome," Meskwaa said.

Meskwaa proffered one of his filter-less cigarettes, as he typically did. Concho waved it off, as he always did.

"I am grateful you have found time to come see me," Meskwaa said. "I knew yesterday that you had returned from the city of Orleans."

"I spent the day with Maria," Concho explained. "And bought myself a new truck."

"Each more important than a visit to this old man, of course."

Concho grinned. "I knew you would still be here today. Meskwaa is eternal."

"True," the old Kickapoo agreed. After a moment, he added. "In the Crescent City, you lost much. But found much as well."

The Ranger sobered. "I found a half-brother and a half-sister I didn't know I had. You know the brother. The one called Bull Knife. He was on the reservation here for a while."

"I recall Bull Knife. But I thought he was Apache."

"Half. And half Kickapoo."

"What is your sister's name?"

"Eve. She did not seem to know how to take me."

"You are a rather large brother to suddenly find. In more ways than one."

"Yes."

"You also found another," Meskwaa added. "The woman who was once your mother."

Concho startled. "You knew?"

Meskwaa drew the cigarette from his lips, letting smoke trickle from his nostrils to mix in the wickiup with the smoke from the fire. He shook his head. "Only now. I can see it written on you. Cakiwiiskenoohihkwee. Sparrow Woman. She had ceased being your mother a long time before you 'found' her. I do not know if she were even Kickapoo still. For such reasons, I lost any sense of her."

Concho nodded. "She'd…had a stroke. She didn't recognize me anyway."

"I am sorry," Meskwaa said.

Ten-Wolves shrugged. "Nothing to do with you."

"I'm not sorry for the event. Such things are inevitable. I am sorry it has caused you pain."

Concho glanced away from Meskwaa for a moment, took a breath, then looked back. "Thank you."

Meskwaa lifted the smoking stub of his cigarette in acknowledgment but then changed the subject. "But now you are onto another of your cases, are you not?"

"Yes. A troubling one. It involves children. Kidnapped. Hurt."

The elder Kickapoo flinched. "An awful thing."

"Very much."

They sat in silence for a moment. Meskwaa's cigarette had burned down to his fingers. The heat didn't seem to bother him, but he reached over with his other hand and pinched the coal off at the end of the cigarette, and dropped it into his fire. He tucked the remaining butt into the pocket of his tattered red shirt.

"I don't suppose," Concho said, "that you've had any visions to help me find the man who set everything in motion?"

"I have had something, but it is not a vision, and I do not like it."

"Tell me."

"Two days ago. From afternoon into the night, I lost all awareness of you. It was as if a door had opened, and you had stepped through and closed it behind you. Later, you stepped back through and were here again."

"Here?"

"In this world."

"What could have caused such a thing?"

"Magic. Powerful magic."

Concho no longer waved off Meskwaa's occasional talk of magic. Too many things, unexplainable by all the rules of the physical world, had happened to him recently.

"The time frame you mention," he said. "It's when I was hunting the man named Jericho and was likely physically close to him."

"Jericho," Meskwaa mused.

"He also goes under the name Roy Simms."

The elder Kickapoo shook his head. "Jericho is closer to his real name. Though it is not his real one."

"I thought perhaps as much."

"This man is powerful and dangerous. By any name."

"Are you saying it was his magic that hid me from you?"

"I believe so."

"I thought the white man did not have any magic."

Meskwaa made a face. "I did not ever tell you such foolishness. All populations have magic. Some know it; some do not. It is different in all. If the whites did not have magic, it would not now be the Kickapoo, the Apache, the Cheyenne, and Sioux who lived on reservations."

"Aye," Concho said. Then: "Perhaps I am learning. As you said, I would. I rode with Jericho for hours on a bus. I knew he was dangerous. In a way, most people are not. You might say, I sensed his power. When I dozed, I even dreamed of him as Maneto."

"Ah," Meskwaa said. "Maneto. The horned serpent. But," he raised a gnarled finger in warning, "he is *not* Maneto. You identified him as such because it is what you know. But if he is any devil, it is a white man's devil. Something you have not seen before. Or at least did not recognize."

"Something you do not recognize either?"

Meskwaa drew another cigarette out of the small red leather sack he carried them in. He stuck it between his lips and lifted a small flaming stick from the fire to light the white cylinder of tobacco. For a moment, the flame limned the old man's face, flickering along the folds of the wrinkles and leaving darkness in their depths.

"I do not know what he is," Meskwaa answered. "But I will warn you of one thing. Beware the black dog."

The blanket flapped over the door to the wickiup. A cold gust of wind sniffed inside and brushed Concho's neck. His hair stood up.

CHAPTER 27

Jericho's cell phone rang. He picked it up from the pas-senger seat of his car, saw the caller ID, and swiped to answer.

"I was wondering when you'd call," he said.

"Haven't had much to relay, but I've got something now."

"Do tell."

"Concho Ten-Wolves visited Mandy today. Is the girl going to be a problem for us?"

"Not at all. Let the good lawman visit as much as he wants. He'll get no more information from her than what I want him to have."

"It seems she's developed a certain bond with our Ranger friend."

"Doesn't matter. Mandy can only tell him what she knows. And I control everything she knows."

"If you're sure?"

"I am. I'm more concerned with Max Keller."

"Who?"

Jericho drew in a deep breath. "He's Ten-Wolves' boss in the Texas Rangers. Not a very pleasant fellow to speak with."

"You talked to him?" The voice on the phone sounded alarmed.

"I did. But don't worry. I used a burner phone."

"What did you talk about?"

"Ten-Wolves, of course."

"And?"

"Mainly, I got a clear impression of Keller's character."

"So, how can he cause us harm?"

"Keller is a liar and manipulator. Even if he does what I told him to do, he'll be working on a way to turn things to his advantage. Which could upset my plans for our Ranger friend."

"What plans are those?"

"All in good time," Jericho replied before swiping the call dead.

***

Ten-Wolves pulled up to his trailer in the early evening. He called it a trailer though the standard name was "modular home." It had no wheels and had never moved on its own. This was the third trailer he'd lived in on this spot—the first with his grandmother, a second which had burned, and this one, which even had a small back deck the others had lacked. He'd yet to have time to use it for much, but he looked forward to reading in the sunshine and maybe getting an outside barbecue and doing some grilling.

Climbing out of his truck, he went inside. A sixteen-ounce ribeye sat thawing on his counter. He'd set it out this morning before leaving the house and now stuck it in the oven on broil. He stepped over to his dining room table, where he'd laid out the pieces of wood and the tools he'd picked up over at John Gray-Dove's shop.

It was time to start on his new bow.

His first bow had been carved from the wood of an Osage orange tree growing right on the reservation. Since the tree had been dying anyway, he'd taken it all down and roughed out several blank staves to store and season for potential future bows. That future had come.

He'd already trimmed the blanks to the proper length. A bow had to fit its user, and the best way to measure such was to hold one end of the stave against your right hip, then stretch your free arm out at a forty-five-degree angle and position the other end of the stave in your palm.

After he'd cut the blanks to the right length, he'd used the machine lathe at Gray-Dove's to shape the proto-bows, creating relatively flat staves that were thicker in the middle and tapered toward the ends. Now, he stepped out onto his back deck with a belt sander to create the final shape and to notch the ends where the bowstring would attach.

The makers of bows in the ancient way had used flint or obsidian scrapers to work the weapon into shape. They'd polish the results with sandstone. He'd made his first bow that way, and it had required many days and superhuman patience. This time he decided to let modern technology help him speed the process.

Abruptly, he remembered the steak in the oven and rushed back inside. It was overcooked rather badly, but he ate it anyway, washing it down with sweetened iced tea before returning to his work.

The next step in the bow-making process involved the application of deer sinew to the back of the bow. Deer were a sacred animal to the Kickapoo, hunted ritually whenever a child was to be named or some other special occasion marked. Concho had gathered or been gifted the sinews from many such hunts and stored them against a time of need—such as now.

He'd set the sinews to soaking before he'd left this morning. He pulled these out and laid them across his table on a big wooden cutting board. Bowmakers of the past would have chewed these sinews with their teeth to soften and pulp them, but he'd found working them over with a pestle did much the same job.

After the sinews were prepared, the big Kickapoo slathered the back of the bow with glue. To provide a good clinging surface for the adhesive, he'd left that section of the stave a little rougher. He also used modern glue, which was much stronger than what his ancestors had made from rendering the hooves of horses or buffalo. As soon as the glue was on, he began layering on the sinew, stringing it along the wood in parallel lines, with the ends overlapping near the tips. As the sinews dried and shortened, the bow would begin to bend into its characteristic shape.

The glue and sinews would have to dry before he could do anything more with the bow, so he sat it carefully down on the table on top of some spread newspapers. He had several other items to work on. He'd use deer hide and buffalo horn to strengthen the bow. The hide had come with the sinews from local hunts, but he'd gotten the horn from a park ranger friend who worked at Caprock Canyons State Park, which housed the official bison herd of Texas.

He first cut the already cured hide into appropriately sized strips for binding to the wood. Next, he put a final polish on the bison horn, which had already been jigsawed into four curved pieces to be fitted over sections of the bow stave. He laid out his bowstring, which—in another nod to modernity—had been purchased from a place that made custom strings using today's tough synthetic materials.

As he worked, his memories began to take him back to earlier experiences with bows. He remembered being seven and learning to shoot with a short bow Meskwaa had made for him, shooting at paper targets on which the outline of a deer had been drawn.

That reminded him of his first actual deer hunt, at age nine, when he missed a shot due to over eagerness after a two-hour stalk to get in position. It was a lesson in patience he wouldn't forget.

And he remembered, suddenly, with vivid intensity and full surround sound, the first time he'd used a bow in combat.

CHAPTER 28

AFGHANISTAN, 2010

Concho's twelve-man ODA (Operational Detachment Alpha) followed some Taliban fighters into the hills. Such was always dangerous, but with risk came the possibility of a payoff. They located a cave in a narrow valley, its wide black mouth both a threat and a promise.

Half a dozen enemy fighters opened fire on the ODA as they worked down the valley, pinning them down temporarily. Russ Adelaide, the squad commander, called in an airstrike. A chopper came, like something out of Apocalypse Now. *Rockets flared; the stones erupted around the mouth of the cave. Amid the flame and smoke that followed, all gunfire from the enemy ceased.*

Concho and his friend, David Lanoue, were on point. They worked forward, leading the ODA. No firing discouraged them. They reached the cave, found it partly collapsed. The bodies of two Afghanis lay dead in the rubble. But there'd been more than two doing the shooting a few moments before.

Concho pulled away some of the fallen rock from the cave mouth and slipped cautiously inside. A tang of gunpowder and rocket exhaust lingered in the air. The first thing he saw was a wide dark tunnel continuing on into the depths of the mountain. No doubt, how the other Afghans had slipped away. The second thing he saw was a pile of boxes and bales of supplies stacked against one wall of the chamber.

Jackpot!

He called for Adelaide. The commander joined him. Lanoue crawled in, too. They examined the supplies. Some foodstuffs. Canned and boxed goods mostly. But a lot of it consisted of weapons and ammo—just what the US military command would most appreciate. It would make for good visuals on the TV news.

On top of a wooden crate of LAWS rockets rested an unusual weapon for modern warfare. It was a longbow, forged of black metal, with a synthetic quiver lying beside it containing fifteen black carbon arrows with wicked red and silver broadheads. Concho picked it up, wondering who among the Taliban was a fan of such historic weapons. Or at least, modern interpretations of ancient weapons.

"Looks like it was waiting just for you," Lanoue said with a grin.

Concho grinned back, then slung both the bow and quiver over his back. "Silent but deadly," he said.

Adelaide interrupted. He called in the rest of the ODA and pointed at two soldiers. "Turk, you and Nguyen. Call it in and get a chopper out here to take some videos and load these supplies. The rest of us. We're following the tunnel. Probably more supplies ahead. But we move carefully. Likely to be bullets ahead, too."

"You sure this cave is gonna keep standing?" Lanoue asked Adelaide.

The commander shrugged. "Let's hope so. But let's keep any shooting to a minimum. We don't want the ceiling coming down."

Everyone nodded. A pair of soldiers named Petry and Ricks took the lead now. The rest of the men followed. Taking the comment about "shooting" to heart, Concho slung his M4A1 carbine

over his back and pulled the black bow into his hands instead. He
was already wearing his warpaint.

As the tunnel darkened, men began to attach flashlights to
the barrels of their rifles using Velcro. A hundred yards into the
mountain, the cave branched to the left and right of the main
chamber. Adelaide wasted no time. He sent Concho, Lanoue, and
a trooper named Simmons up the tunnel on the right, three others
up the left, and kept the rest with him as they penetrated farther
into the mountain.

Concho took the lead for his group, relying on the lights of the
men behind him to show the way. The tunnel they were in widened at first and generally trended upward. Soon, enough daylight
filtered in for the Ranger's good eyesight to pick out the lay of
the land. He motioned for Lanoue and Simmons to turn off their
flashlights.

Good thing. Just yards farther up the tunnel, Ten-Wolves heard
the sound of voices speaking Dari. He signaled the men behind
him to silence and crept forward, the bow held ready, with one
arrow nocked and a second hanging between the last two fingers
of his left hand.

The tunnel curved to the left; more light came from around the
bend. It was natural light rather than artificial. Concho eased to
the corner and glanced around it. A wide beam of sun shone down
from above through a chimney opening to the surface. In that pool
of dusty light, two Afghanis worked at the jammed mechanism of
an AK-47.

As bad luck would have it, one of the men happened to be
looking toward the exact spot where the Ranger's face appeared.
He cried a warning to his friend and grabbed for a second AK-47
slung at his side.

Concho drew back the arrow in his bow and loosed it in a frac-
tion of a second. The razor-sharp broadhead on the arrow tore a
gaping hole through the man's throat and sparked into the stone
wall behind him.

The second man stood dazed in surprise for a second, then dropped the useless rifle and clawed for a pistol stuck in his belt. Concho twisted the last two fingers of his left hand upward, positioning the feathered end of the arrow he held there against the nocking point of the string. His index finger slid over the nocked arrow; his second and third fingers slid beneath.

He drew the string back and released. The arrow zipped into the Afghani's chest and punched out the back, taking along a piece of lung and the top of the aortic valve with it.

The Taliban fighter's dark eyes grew wide. He had his pistol half drawn but now dropped it and grabbed for his chest. His hand hit the feathered tip of the arrow still embedded in his body. He shuddered, then slid slowly to earth.

Concho loaded a fresh arrow and stepped into the lighted section of the tunnel. Simmons and Lanoue followed. The three men stared at the bodies. Lanoue glanced up through the rock chimney overhead.

"Still twelve to fifteen feet underground," he said. "My turn to take point."

Concho stepped to one side. Lanoue moved past him, his M4 at the ready position. The tunnel narrowed beyond, and the men had to turn sideways to squeeze through. It was a particularly tight fit for Concho, who felt stone scraping unpleasantly at both sides of his body.

The tunnel widened abruptly, dipped down and back up a sharp little slope to a wider opening that let in the sun. Lanoue started up the slope, motioning his companions to wait.

Lanoue took a step, and another, lifting up on his toes to see over the rise of the slope to the outside. A sudden barrage of bullets whipped into the cave, spanging off the walls and sending stone chips flying.

Lanoue grunted, stumbled backward, and started to fall. Concho dropped his bow and caught his friend. He spun to turn his back to the gunfire, his big body hunched over his smaller col-

league.

"I'm hit!" Lanoue said.

Concho squatted, laid the other Ranger on the dirt floor. "Simmons," he hissed.

Derick Simmons had medical training. He plunged forward to drop to his knees beside Lanoue, pulling the pack off his back to fumble for his medical kit. Lanoue had been hit on the inside of his left leg. It must have been a ricochet because the wound looked almost like a knife slash. Judging from the spray of blood, it must also have hit an artery.

Concho looked away, back toward the slope leading up to the outside world. The firing from up there had stopped. A voice called out in heavily accented English:

"American. American. You trapped. You give up now. We are many. We let you live. Else we kill you all."

Concho didn't believe the voice. He called back, also in English. "Come get us."

"We've got a problem," Simmons said.

Concho looked back at the medic. The man's pupils were widely dilated. The pulse throbbed in his neck. His hands were bloody where they'd been probing Lanoue's wound. Next to him, the injured trooper lay on the ground panting, groaning through gritted teeth. His face was ashen.

"What?"

"The femoral artery's been cut," Simmons said.

"Clamp it!"

"Can't! The severed end must have withdrawn back up into the abdomen. I can't reach it! Can't get my hand in."

"Cut a bigger hole."

Simmons nodded. He fumbled in his medkit and pulled out a scalpel. "Can't give him morphine, though. His BP will bottom out."

"Do it!" Lanoue said, his voice hoarse with fear.

Simmons leaned forward, then hesitated. Sweat beaded his

face. The scalpel rattled in his hand.

Concho snarled. "Hold on, brother," he said to Lanoue. "This is gonna hurt."

Without further hesitation, the Army Ranger stabbed two fingers of each hand into Lanoue's wound. He tore it wider. Blood spurted a foot high, spraying a scarlet stream into his face and across his chest. Lanoue screamed, arched his back, and passed out.

"Clamp it!" Concho snapped at Simmons.

Simmons stuck his hand into the gore of Lanoue's leg, pushing his fingers up into the bloody wound.

"Got it!" he said triumphantly. His other hand held a forceps. He fed this into the wound and locked it around the severed end of the artery, which he'd managed to get hold of. Lanoue's hemorrhaging stopped.

Concho spun back toward the mouth of the tunnel, a snarl distorting his face. He reached down and picked up the black bow where it lay in a pool of his buddy's blood. Pulling an arrow out of the quiver on his back, the Ranger seated it firmly, then rose to a crouch.

"American!" the voice called from outside.

"On my way," Concho muttered low.

Blood dripped down his face. He was coated in it as if it were warpaint made from the gore of a friend. Moving silently but with speed, he charged up the slope toward the glint of sunlight. As he leaped into the open mouth of the cave, he saw three turbaned fighters standing against some rocks only a dozen feet away. They weren't expecting an attack, though all had rifles in their hands.

As they glimpsed the giant, blood-soaked apparition that appeared before them, two of the men froze. The third turned and ran. Of the two remaining, both jerked on their rifles, starting to raise them into firing position.

Concho shot the one farthest away with an arrow that tore into his gut. The man gagged on his scream. The Ranger shifted his grip on the bow, lifting it as he lunged toward the last man standing. The man swung up his AK-47, pulling the trigger before the weapon was level.

Bullets puffed into the dust around his legs as the Ranger charged forward. He twisted the bow up over his right shoulder and swung hard as if swinging for a home run. The metal bow smashed across the left side of the Afghani's face, hammering it to one side and sending spittle and teeth flying.

The man folded like a fitted sheet and struck the ground in a heap of dust. His jaw was broken, but he clung to consciousness. His eyes blinked up at the blood-stained American soldier standing over him.

Concho drew an arrow over his shoulder, nocked it. With a snarl on his face at the thought of his wounded and possibly dying buddy, he took aim at the downed man at his feet. The Afghani's eyes pleaded; the G.I.'s arms shook with tension.

Concho let out a shuddering breath. Abruptly, he relaxed his pull on the arrow and let the bow go slack. He glanced across the rocky field in front of him. The man who'd fled was still running with the dust rising behind him. Concho dropped to his knees and zip tied the wounded man's hands and legs.

Slinging the dark bow over his shoulder, he stepped back into the cave. Lanoue wasn't out of danger yet; he'd lost a lot of blood. They needed to get him to the surface stat and call for a chopper evac.

Strangely, Robert Frost's most famous quatrain popped into his head, modified by the fever rage of combat. He muttered out loud to himself:

"War is terror, stark and steep, but I have duties to keep and miles to go before I sleep."

As the war in Afghanistan faded back into his mind, Concho glanced at the clock on his trailer wall. Hours had passed. He felt exhausted. When he looked at the work he'd done, he found

Kickapoo symbols incised on the bow and on the bison horn in
his hands. He didn't remember making those symbols, though the
tools used to engrave them lay on the table at his fingertips. It
wasn't the first time such an experience had happened to him.

He pushed back in his chair. It would be a couple of days anyway before he could do more with the drying bow. He texted Maria good night and went to take a shower. Bed followed.

A phone call at 5:00 AM ripped him up from a sound sleep.

PART THREE
BLACK DOG

CHAPTER 29

In the hours before Concho was awakened by an early morning phone call, Jericho went to work. His plan was for an impromptu performance, a spur of the moment nocturne. Yet, he would still bring the same care to this short vivace as he brought to a symphony.

In early afternoon, he left his new refuge for a drive to Weslaco, Texas, a growing town of some forty thousand souls in Hidalgo County, which lay almost at the very southern tip of the United States before the land became Mexico.

As with most towns, Weslaco had a mixture of affluent and blighted neighborhoods. Google had provided Jericho with the location of the neighborhood he wanted, a street of upper-middle-class affluence, although not the richest avenue in the city. It was called Holly Street.

Jericho slipped unnoticed into that neighborhood and parked his Miata at the curb among other vehicles of middling to higher expensiveness. Darkness had arrived by now, and the temperature had cooled into the high forties. Jericho's velour tracksuit did not look out of place as he locked his car and did a few stretches to loosen his muscles.

After a moment, he began to jog down the sidewalk, past well-maintained houses, and watered lawns. Holly Street could almost have been "anywhere" street USA. Except for the fact that many houses had Spanish roofs and other small "south of the border" touches, little here proclaimed: TEXAS. No mesquite and no cactus. Oak and walnut trees predominated, and even some palms. A few flower beds still had blooms, mostly roses and other exotics to this climate.

After he'd worked up a little sweat, Jericho slowed to a walk but continued to stride purposefully. As he well knew, when you look like you're going somewhere, people generally leave you alone. This kind of neighborhood would get a few cruise-byes from the police every night, but they'd be looking for someone out of place. A black man perhaps. Or a Hispanic laborer. Maybe a man with long hair. Jericho wouldn't get a second look. He fit in.

He passed a mailbox with 1410 written on it and glanced casually across the road to see 1411 Holly Street. The house at 1411 stood two stories of wood and painted white. With several tall oaks standing close. It had a garage. Closed. In the driveway out front sat a brown Dodge Ram 3500 pickup with dual back wheels.

Overkill, Jericho thought. He doubted the owner spent much time hauling heavy loads. He probably drove the vehicle back and forth to work on paved highways, but the truck would make him feel like a *working* man.

A wooden fence, treated but unpainted, ran down the left and right sides of the home. It probably extended around the back. But the front had only a hedge of winter-barren rose bushes separating it from the sidewalk.

Jericho walked another block, then crossed Holly Street and started to jog slowly back up it toward his car. He passed 1411 again and took a closer look. The rose bush hedge was about three feet high. Manageable. As long as he prepared himself.

The most important question was whether the owner had installed a security system. Jericho doubted this particular owner had given in to the urge to *secure* himself. He'd be too proud and confident in his own abilities. And, companies that installed security often put up a little sign out front to advertise. No such sign existed here, but Jericho wouldn't know for sure about any alarm system until he got close. That would have to wait until later in the night.

Jericho jogged back to his car. He unzipped his velour jacket and placed it on the passenger seat beside him before pulling out of his parking space. For the next couple of hours, he drove the streets of Weslaco, familiarizing himself with any and all ways out of the town. By 11:00 PM, he was parked again on Holly Street, several blocks down from 1411.

He'd never been one for team sports but had been on the track and gymnastics team of his high school, competing in various individual events. Most people who saw him misjudged his athletic prowess. He liked it that way. At 11:15, after loosening up and checking to see no one was around to report him, he took a standing high jump over the rose bush hedge in front of 1411.

He landed softly on a grass lawn shedding its green color for the winter. Standing frozen for a moment against the backdrop of the rose bushes, he studied the house. No lights came on in or outside the house. No motion detectors, it seemed. At least not in the front.

The curtains over the front bay window weren't even pulled. Jericho could look in at a formal dining room where a single chandelier style light burned over the table. He wondered if it were left on all night. Quite possibly.

The only other light was a dim glow behind some closed curtains in an upstairs room. He had a feeling his target sat in that room. Jericho chuckled quietly to himself. Up late working on something nefarious, no doubt.

Jericho smelled diesel fuel from the big Ram 3500 to his left. He smelled the rose brambles against which he stood. Many people had told him you couldn't smell things like brambles and thorns. They were wrong. Such things smelled like desolation, like despair. He loved the scent, but now was not the time to enjoy it.

He darted forward to the side of the house, then worked his way toward the backyard. By 11:30, using tools taken from the old-fashioned leather doctor's bag he carried, he'd jimmied the lock on the rear door and stood in 1411's kitchen. No alarms went off. Even if there had been a silent one, he would have felt it. He smiled and started up the stairs.

At 11:42, he injected the sleeping wife of the house's owner with a little something to *keep* her a drowse through any noise that might soon follow. At 11:49, he stepped through the open doorway of the only lit room in the upstairs. He'd moved silently, and his target sat with his back turned to him at an old writing desk scribbling by hand on a lined yellow office tablet.

Jericho drew the black and gold MR73 from the Kangaroo pocket of his tracksuit and cleared his throat. The man spun around in his chair, a look of surprise on his face. The surprise faded quickly into the purity of outrage. The man started to stand up, and Jericho cocked the hammer on the MR73.

"If you do anything other than what I tell you, I will shoot you," Jericho said. "And after, I'll sodomize, rape, and strangle your wife. Sort of in that order. But if you cooperate, everything will be just fine."

"What do you want?" the man snapped. "Money?"

Jericho smiled again, broadly. "I can see you aren't quite ready for tonight's performance. But you will be."

Behind him in the doorway, he heard the low, snuffling growl of the black dog, who'd just arrived to play its part.

A little later, as Jericho put the tools he'd brought in his doctor's bag to good use, the man finally embraced his role. He begged, "Please! You said everything would be fine."

Of course, by that time, the man's tongue had been removed, so the words were distorted as he gargled in blood. Jericho understood the meaning of the mutterings, however. He responded soothingly but honestly:

"Art is always a lie revealing the truth."

***

The call that dragged Ten-Wolves out of sleep came from Raul Molina, his friend in the Texas Rangers.

"Raul!" Concho said, with alarm bells shrieking into his awareness. "What's going on?"

"It's Keller!"

"Keller? What's he up to now?"

"Nothing. He's dead!"

"Dead," Concho said, aware of repeating everything Raul said to him but too discombobulated to stop.

"Murdered!" Raul added.

Concho beat the urge to repeat that word, too. Instead, he asked:

"Where? How?"

"At his house. Sometime around midnight, I'm hearing. As for how I haven't seen the scene, but I'm told it's pretty gross."

"What about Keller's wife?"

"Alive but shook up. She found the body. After."

"You saying she slept through it?"

"Apparently, she was drugged. While she was already asleep, she woke up around 2:30 or so. Went to find out why her husband wasn't in bed. Found him in his study. She called Dalton Shaw."

Shaw was Max Keller's second in command. He'd be the one to call.

"How did *you* find out?" Concho asked.

"I was on dispatch duty. Got the order to send units. When I asked what it was all about, one of the men who responded explained it to me."

"I see." Ten-Wolves took a deep breath and released it slowly. "Anyone have any idea who might have done it?"

"Plenty of people didn't like Keller, but…."

"But what?"

The sound of Raul scratching at his bearded face carried even through the phone. The moment dragged on.

"What?" Concho repeated, a little sharper.

"There was…a message. Written on the wall behind Keller. Written in his blood."

"Morbid," Concho said, though his thoughts were racing along more personal pathways as he anticipated what was to come.

"The message said, 'You're welcome,' Ten-Wolves."

"Damn!"

CHAPTER 30

Concho got the phone number for Dalton Shaw—who would be the new acting head of the Texas Rangers Company D—from Raul Molina before the two friends disconnected. He tried the number immediately but got redirected to a voice mailbox. He left his name and number and a single statement.

"I believe I know who killed Max Keller."

Afterward, he paced back and forth through his house until realizing he was only playing into Jericho's hands. Surely, it was Jericho who'd killed Keller. He would want the Ranger upset.

Concho fixed himself breakfast but only ate a little. He tried to work on his bow but found it a struggle to focus. He was on his back deck, letting the cold seep through his t-shirt while morning sunlight slowly filled up the bowl of the world when his phone rang. He snatched it from his pocket, saw Dalton Shaw's name, and answered.

"Yes, Chief Shaw?"

"Ten-Wolves," Shaw said. "I'll expect you in my office as soon as you can get to Weslaco. Understood?"

"Yes, Sir."

"Good," Shaw said before hanging up.

Concho shaved and showered. He put on new tan khakis instead of the jeans he usually patrolled in and a white, long-sleeved cotton shirt. For the first time in a long time, he wore a tie, a yellow one from the meager collection hanging in his closet.

His Texas Ranger hat had burned up with his old truck in New Orleans. He considered whether to stop and buy another one on the way to meet Chief Shaw but decided not to take the time. It would feel odd to him anyway since he hardly ever wore it.

Leaving the reservation around 8:00 AM, he hopped on TX-44 East out of Eagle Pass and arrived in Weslaco after about a five-hour drive, parking in front of the Texas Department of Public Safety building at 2525 North International Boulevard in Weslaco. He'd only been here a few times, but he remembered where to go.

The Texas Ranger offices teemed with activity. Much more than usual, and certainly because of Max Keller's death. No police unit ever took the death of one of their own nonchalantly. That went double for the Rangers.

Everyone in the office stopped what they were doing when Concho entered. If they hadn't known him before, they knew him now. Faces and postures were neutral, neither hostile nor friendly. Someone pointed him toward Dalton Shaw's office. He knocked on the wall beside Shaw's open door, but the acting Chief was already motioning him inside.

"Close the door," Shaw said.

Concho did so, then stood at attention in front of his new commander's desk. He studied Shaw while Shaw studied him. Keller's second in command stood about six feet and probably weighed around two hundred pounds. His hair was dark, with a few strands of white. His eyes were dark gray and calculating.

Shaw wasn't a huge man but still exuded a certain physical presence. He'd been a golden gloves boxing champ when younger. Even at rest, his biceps bulged his shirt sleeves.

Although Concho had met Shaw before, the two had never exchanged more than a few words. Shaw was still a cipher. He'd be competent, certainly. And something of a political animal if he'd survived this long under Max Keller's command. Other than that, any guess was as good as another.

"Sit," Shaw said, pointing to the chair across from him.

Ten-Wolves glanced at the chair. It was big and sturdy. He sat. "Thank you, Chief."

"Still 'Assistant Chief' at the moment."

Concho nodded.

Shaw's hands rested on the laptop keyboard on his desk. He pulled them back and shut the computer's lid down. "You didn't like Chief Keller much, did you, Ten-Wolves?"

"No, Sir."

"And the feeling was mutual, wasn't it?"

"I believe so, Sir."

"Why do you think that was? On his part?"

"I don't know, Sir."

Shaw snorted lightly. "Perhaps you don't *know*, but you have an opinion. I'd like to hear it."

"Chief Keller took over after I'd already been confirmed as a Ranger. I don't think he liked the idea of having a Kickapoo in the ranks. I suspect he also didn't care for my skin color."

Shaw's gaze never wavered. "Tell me why you didn't like *him*."

"Is that an order, Sir? I don't like to speak ill of the dead."

"Consider it an order."

"Other than that, he was prejudiced against me for something I had no control over; I thought he was more concerned with his own ambitions than with the welfare of the Texas Rangers."

Shaw nodded. He leaned forward and placed his elbows on his desk; steepling his fingers, he stared over them. "Chief Keller spoke to me quite often about you. And you're right; he didn't like you. He never mentioned to me anything about you being Kickapoo. Or black. He said you were slovenly. That you never wore a tie, that you flouted the traditions of the Rangers, and you never wore a hat. That you were a wild card, a maverick. That you didn't follow the rules."

"Some of those things are true, Sir, but I've never disrespected the traditions of the Rangers. I don't often wear the hat because I'm not riding the range under the blistering sun. In a fight, it falls off. In a moment of focused intensity, it sometimes distracts. But I'm a Ranger, and I will never forget it."

Shaw took a deep breath and leaned back in his chair. "Tell me who you think killed Max Keller."

***

Meskwaa felt restless and uncomfortable, which was rare. Normally, the Kickapoo elder was completely at ease inside his own skin. The smallest part of his discomfort was the cold. His Kickapoo ancestors may have originated in the northern great lakes region, in areas of forest and marshes and winter snows, but Meskwaa had lived his entire life in southern Texas and northern Mexico.

In his youth, he had not minded the area's few truly cold days, but youth was long behind him now, and every winter chill seemed to bite harder. This morning he'd left his wickiup, where he spent most of his time, and went into his trailer instead, where he turned on the white man's heater. He was disappointed in himself, but the warmth surely felt good.

The bigger part of his discomfort came from another source than the weather. Something was wrong on the reservation, and he couldn't *see* the cause. Meskwaa had visions. Many times throughout his life, those visions had helped save members of his tribe from disaster or even death. But now, his mind was blank.

No, not blank. Blocked. It was as if someone had sewn him into a black shroud and blinded his eyes with layers of gauze. And whoever had done it was no Indian. No Kickapoo. That should not have been possible.

Only a few times in his experiences had he met anyone whose magic was powerful enough to blind him this way. Never had such a one been anything else but an Indian. This was... Well, he did not know who or what it was. Even that was opaque to him.

And so he fretted, and fidgeted, and strove to see, while he feared that someone or something walked freely as a beast across the land of his people. And there was nothing he could do about it.

CHAPTER 31

"Tell me who you think killed Max Keller," acting Chief Dalton Shaw had said to Concho.

Concho considered his answer. "Before I do, Sir, I wonder if you might tell me about the scene of Chief Keller's death. The details might help me be sure of my thoughts about the killer."

"I suspect you already know your name showed up at the scene. Written in Keller's blood?"

"Yes, Sir."

"Raul Molina told you about the crime scene?"

Concho didn't want to get his friend in trouble. "I'd prefer not to say, Sir. And all I heard about was the name."

Shaw lifted his hands in the equivalent of a shrug. "It doesn't matter. I would have told you anyway."

Ten-Wolves nodded.

Shaw hesitated. He rubbed his mouth with his hand. "It's not pretty. I've been a Texas Ranger for a long time, and it's the worst murder scene I've encountered."

Concho winced. "Sorry to hear, Sir."

Shaw puffed out a quick breath and put both hands on his desk. "Keller was crucified. Strapped down across his desk. On his back with his arms spread to either side and tied to the legs of the desk.

Both shoulders were dislocated in the act of being tied. His legs were bound to the other legs of the desk. His clothes had been cut off with scissors and tossed aside."

"Any idea how the perp managed to overpower Keller? Not likely he would have submitted to being tied down that way."

"The coroner thinks he was injected with something like propofol before being tied up. Likely the same thing given to the wife. It's also possible the perp threatened Keller's wife if he didn't cooperate."

"What else, Sir?"

Shaw shook his head and swallowed as if bile were spurting into his mouth as his memories of the scene came back. "He was skinned in places. Long strips of skin were removed on his chest, arms, and legs.

"He was...he had his lips and tongue removed. And his genitalia. The genitalia were placed on his chest, but we didn't find any of the other removed tissue at the scene, so the perp likely took it with him. There was something else. I don't know why, but it seemed even worse."

"What was that?"

Shaw scratched at his nose. "The skin of his belly had been slit open and sewn back up to leave a pouch of skin. There was something inside the pouch. You could see its outline through the skin. It was his badge."

Concho winced again. "Which direction was his head facing. If you remember?"

"Why?" Shaw asked. "Is it important?"

"Maybe."

"It was south. He was oriented north to south on the desk."

"I see."

"So," Shaw said, his face still screwed up as if he'd bitten into something distasteful. "This help with your thoughts on the killer?"

"It does. The sewn-up skin pouch particularly so."

"Well?"

"Have you seen the recent report I recorded on a child kidnapping case?" Concho asked in response to Shaw's query.

"I just finished listening to the whole report this morning. Are you saying it has something to do with Chief Keller's death?"

"I believe so. I think the killer was the kidnapper mentioned in that report."

"Roy Simms?"

"He's used that name. But he seems to go more often by Jericho."

"So why do you suspect this Jericho?"

"Partly because of the use of my name at the crime scene. Partly a feeling. The badge sewn under the skin cements it for me."

Shaw made the connection. "During your investigation of Jericho's house, you found a boy whose lips were sewn shut. The one killed by the FBI."

"Yep."

"So, whoever killed Keller. Maybe this Jericho. Wrote your name at the scene. I admit to being very curious about that. But surely you have more than one enemy who'd like to implicate you in some way. The Aryan Brotherhood, for example. From the reports I've read, they've tried before."

"Yes, Sir. But Jericho wasn't trying to implicate me. I believe he thought he was helping me."

Shaw flashed an eyebrow. "That's going to require some explanation."

Concho considered how to explain. He started with:

"I don't believe Jericho is completely sane. I think the coincidence of me being on the bus where he intended to kidnap a child was not a coincidence to him. I'm convinced he knew who I was when he first saw me on the bus. Probably from local news reports. I believe he thinks there was some kind of...*meaning* behind my being there."

"Meaning?"

"A connection between the two of us. In his mind. I believe that's why, as I said in my report, he called to tell me where to find the girl, Toni. And about the human trafficking ring."

"So he's trying to…help you? Make you more famous than you already are?"

"Strange as it seems, yes."

"He's looking at you as some kind of ally?"

"I'm clawing at thin air here, Sir, but I don't think as an ally. More as a…well maybe an 'honored foe.' If that makes any sense."

"Logically, it doesn't," Shaw said. "But if he's insane, then I can see where it might make some sense to him. But what made him think killing Max Keller would help you?"

"He seems to have looked into my background. Although it's not common knowledge, there's no real secret about the animosity between myself and Chief Keller. Maybe he picked up on that. Maybe somehow, he knew Keller had suspended me. His note. It read, 'You're welcome, Ten-Wolves.' He's saying he did it for me, and I should be grateful."

Shaw seemed to consider his next words carefully. "Eventually, the news outlets are going to get hold of that message. They're going to run with it, and it's not going to look good for you. It's worse that you've previously had good press for the Eagle Pass Mall affair. The only thing people enjoy more than a hero is a fallen hero."

"I know, Sir. I remember the quote, 'you either die a hero or live long enough to see yourself become the villain.'" He grinned wryly. "I didn't think the villain part would happen so soon."

"It hasn't happened yet, but there'll be questions. The most important question *I* have is how it helps us that the killer believes in this connection of yours?"

"Because he's going to contact me again, which will be my chance to zero him. It may be the only chance we have since I doubt he left any other clues at the murder scene."

Shaw laced his fingers together across his stomach. "Right. If that happens, you know what to do."

"I'll let you know immediately, Sir."

Shaw puffed out a short breath. He leaned forward in his chair to rest his palms on his desk by his laptop. "I want you on this case full-time. If Jericho contacts you, be ready to respond in whatever way helps us. But be careful. He's shown himself to be a violent man, and it won't take much to turn him from 'helping' you to trying to kill you."

"Yes, Sir."

Shaw folded his laptop case open as a signal to end their conversation. Concho rose. As he started to turn toward the door, Shaw spoke again, softly.

"You were right in your thinking about Keller, by the way. He never said it in so many words, but it was clear to me he didn't like your color or your heritage. That won't be a problem with me. Honoring the best ideals of the Rangers is a very different issue and one I won't see flouted."

"I understand, Sir. And I agree with you."

"Good. You're dismissed. Bring this Jericho to justice."

"I think Jericho has forgotten one important thing about the Texas Rangers," Concho said.

"Oh?"

"That we have another name. *Los Diablos Tejanos.*"

"The Texan Devils," Shaw said.

"Yes, Sir. But I'll remind him."

Both men smiled.

CHAPTER 32

It was almost 3:00 PM by the time Ten-Wolves returned to his truck outside the Department of Public Safety. Despite sunny skies, the cold had deepened. He flicked on the heater in his Ford.

Though food had no aesthetic appeal to him after hearing what had been done to Max Keller, his stomach growled and grumbled with emptiness, and he needed food for fuel. He stopped at a Golden Corral for a late lunch. He filled his plate from the buffet with meat loaf, pot roast, and fried chicken. He added a loaded baked potato and several refills of sweet iced tea. Normally, he would have enjoyed every bit, but now he ate almost mechanically, shoving food into his mouth while his thoughts were elsewhere.

Finally, with his stomach quiescent rather than snarling like a hungry grizzly, he headed for Eagle Pass. It was dark when he drove onto the reservation. He'd spoken with Maria Morales on the phone, telling her he'd likely be home around 9:00. She'd promised to be waiting at his trailer with a good supper prepared. He drove quickly, looking forward to some peace with Maria after a troubling day.

Pulling into his driveway, he noticed the small tin flag was upon his mailbox. He hadn't mailed anything, so it must have been put up by the mailman, maybe to indicate something left for him. He stopped to see. Inside was a square red envelope, greeting card size. His name was written neatly on the front but with no return address and no stamp.

Christmas card, he thought. *'Tis the season.'* For some people, at least. He was not a big holiday kind of guy.

One of his friends must have dropped it off rather than spend money on a stamp. He plucked it out of the box before pulling the rest of the way into his yard and parking beside Maria's blue Ford Focus.

Lights in the trailer spilled a warm glow through the windows into the cold. Concho smiled. He stepped through the door, carrying the Christmas card, and Maria ran to greet him, smiling and lifting up on her toes for a long, heated kiss.

She wore a loose gray sweater and jeans that hugged her legs and bottom. He scooped her off her feet and carried her laughing back into the kitchen. When he put her down, he tossed the card onto the bar. The two kissed again.

"You taste like fried chicken and tea," Maria murmured.

"You taste like sun-flavored bacon," Ten-Wolves replied.

Maria laughed a second time and punched him lightly on the shoulder as she pulled away. "I hope you're hungry. The pork loin is almost ready. I made cornbread, too."

The oven sizzled; the smell of bread and Maria's lilac-scented shampoo tanged the air. The day's ugliness slipped away.

The lawman smiled happily. "You're an angel."

"And you're a devil," Maria countered. "And as a devil, you need to light a fire while I finish cooking. It's a little chilly in here."

"As you command," he said, grinning.

She grinned back, and he turned toward the fireplace in his combination den and dining room. He didn't use the fireplace often; it didn't get that cold here most of the time, and the heater worked just fine. But he built a fire on occasion for romantic reasons and kept the fireplace ready just in case, with wood and kindling on the grate.

He crouched down and opened the flue, then started tearing a sheet of newspaper into strips to use as tinder. He was about to light it when Maria said:

"What's this card?"

"Christmas greetings, I guess," Concho said over his shoulder.

"From whom?"

"Don't know. Why don't you open it and see."

He touched a match to the edge of a strip of paper, saw the flames leap up and the strip curl and blacken. A piece of wood started to smoke. He smelled the pepper scent of the flames.

Behind him came a tearing sound as Maria peeled open the card. A choked gasp followed. Something dropped on the floor. Maria's voice followed, "No, no, no!"

He dropped the match into the fireplace and spun around, still in a crouch. Maria was backing away from the bar. Her heels clicked on the linoleum. Her eyes were bright and wild. The Christmas card lay red on the floor.

Concho lunged to his feet, crossed the distance to Maria in a few strides. He grasped her shoulder. "Maria! What is it?"

She looked at him, fear and shock twisting her face. She pointed at the card, which lay face up. Concho looked closer. Santa Claus adorned the front of the card. A small plastic baggy had slid out of the card. It was still sealed, but something pinkish nestled inside it, something surrounded by a reddish fluid. It took him a moment to realize he was looking at a human tongue.

***

Concho sat on the couch in his living room, with Maria's hand in his. Men and women moved back and forth purposefully through his trailer. Some wore the letters FBI on their jackets. Some had Coroner or KTTP Sheriff's Department on theirs. Photographs were snapped. Samples were taken.

A man walked out carrying an evidence bag with the tongue and the Christmas card in it. The card had also contained a handwritten note, which Concho had discovered by using the tip of a pen to open it. He'd taken a picture with his phone.

Roberto Echabarri, Chief of the Kickapoo Traditional Tribe of Texas police force, approached the couch. With him came Della Rice, FBI field agent.

"You say the tongue belongs to Max Keller?" Rice asked.

"Pretty sure. He was killed last night, and his tongue was missing."

Maria abruptly let go of her lover's hand and stood up. Her face had been slowly regaining color but now turned gray again. "Bathroom," she said.

Concho watched her go and bit his lip. When he looked back around, both Roberto and Della were gazing at him with sympathy.

Concho gave a quick sketch of what he knew. Rice took notes. Echabarri didn't but wouldn't forget the details.

"No stamp on the letter, so this Jericho got someone to hand deliver it," Echabarri said.

"He dropped it off himself," Concho replied.

"Maybe, but we've had patrols out all day and evening, and no one has reported anything or anyone unusual. It's not easy to get onto the Rez without being noticed. Unless you're just going to the casino."

Concho pulled out his phone, swiped over to his photo gallery. He showed Roberto and Della the picture he'd snapped of the note inside the card. It was written neatly, in cursive. He read it out loud to them.

Dear Concho,

In case you weren't sure who took out Max Keller for you, I thought I'd offer a keepsake. Knowing you, you'll probably turn it into your fellow law officers. But, really, you should keep it. Make it the start of a rare collection.

I know you've killed before. And have convinced

yourself those killings were justified. My own killings have also been justified. It's only that my sense of morality is broader than yours. Therein lies the freedom I enjoy while you bear heavy chains.

Only in such freedom will you discover the transmundane. Only then will you find the power you don't even know you seek. I've given you a chance here to unlock that power. Don't waste it.

By the way, the woman who waits for you is a true beauty. Do not worry. Out of respect for you, I will not touch her. Would that you had granted me the same respect with my family. Perhaps in the future, you will do so.

For much the same reason, I did not take Keller's wife. You are not ready for such a dramatic disruption of your current morality. But that time is coming. Soon.
– Jericho.

CHAPTER 33

As Concho finished reading Jericho's note, his fingers closed tightly in anger around the body of his phone. A creaking sound from the device warned of an impending collapse. The Ranger forced his grip to relax and took a deep breath. He looked up at his friends and colleagues.

"So, you see, he was here. Outside my house. While Maria walked unaware within, I'll kill him for that."

Roberto remained silent. Della Rice added, "I'll pretend I didn't hear what you just said."

Concho looked down as if lost in thought.

"What does transmundane mean?" Roberto asked after a moment.

The question brought the lawman back to the now. "It's something that lies beyond the world as we know it. I think he's talking about magic. He's at least a little bit crazy. If not a lot. I believe he thinks there's some supernatural connection between the two of us. Just not sure what."

"Scary," Roberto said.

"Schizophrenia, you think?" Rice asked.

Concho shrugged.

"That note was awfully well organized for a psychotic," Rice added.

"What he is, is dangerous," Concho said.

"His imagined connection to you also offers us hope of catching him," Rice said.

"I know. But so far, he's stayed a step or two ahead of us."

Rice nodded. "We'll get him. One way or another."

"Yes," Concho said grimly. He placed his phone on the table in front of him so he wouldn't crush it in his fist.

***

After everyone else left, Concho drove Maria home—in her car, watching carefully for anyone who might be tailing them. He spent the night at Maria's apartment, despite the fact that her double bed would barely accommodate them. He had to sleep with his legs drawn up to keep his feet from hanging over the bottom.

In the morning, while Maria showered, Concho made her breakfast, then drove her to work. He left her car in a well-watched section of the parking lot and called a cab. His first stop was Piero Almanza's bar—*Evil Ways* in English. Piero was his old friend from the Army Rangers.

Concho called ahead. The bar wasn't open yet, but Piero told him to come by anyway. The ex-Ranger opened the door himself and led Ten-Wolves through the empty barroom and through a blue interior door in a blue wall.

The big space beyond the wall was a combination bedroom and gun room. An unmade double bed stood in one corner, with a TV mounted at the foot of it. The rest of the room was full of gun racks, and tables with various weapons in various stages of disassembly spread over them.

Piero motioned his friend to a chair and sat across from him. "Your voice on the phone sounded troubled," Piero said. "What can I do for you?"

Concho studied Almanza for a bare moment. He was a tough-looking hombre, in his mid-forties and about an inch under six feet and built compactly with dark hair and eyes. A set of three facial scars lent him a sinister cast that wasn't entirely undeserved.

The two men had served together in Afghanistan, though not in the same ODA. As was the case with Ten-Wolves, Almanza had a mixed heritage. He was a quarter Cherokee, and perhaps it was the shared native blood that had helped jumpstart their friendship. Shared values and dangers had cemented it.

"I'm worried about Maria," Concho said. He told Piero about Jericho and about the tongue and note left in his mailbox—while Maria had been in the house nearby.

Piero nodded his head at the revelations, though he said nothing just yet.

"Jericho has done his research on me," Concho continued. "I'm sure he knows Maria works at *The Mall de las Aguilas*. He can follow her home from there anytime. I can't spend every moment with her. And that would be as likely to attract danger as not. The man wants *me*. I need to keep his attention *on* me and away from her."

"You have, of course, warned her of the potential danger," Piero said.

"I have. But she's a civilian. She doesn't really understand the nature of danger. Or how to recognize it."

"And you would like for someone to keep an eye on her? To make sure she is safe?"

"Yes."

"You know no one's safety can be guaranteed. No shield exists without a weakness."

"I know. But I have to do everything I can to minimize that weakness."

"Then it is agreed," Piero said. "I will arrange for Maria to be watched." He smiled crookedly. "Sometimes even by me. I will make sure she is as protected as she can be."

Concho reached across the table where they sat and grasped Piero's wrist. He squeezed hard. "Thank you, old friend," he said fiercely.

"I will not say it is nada," Piero replied. "It is a thing between friends. Do you wish her to know or not know?"

"She'll be more careful herself if she doesn't know she's being protected, and that's an added level of security."

Piero nodded. "Thus it will be."

Concho rose from his chair. "Thank you again."

Piero shrugged. "I know you would do the same for me."

"I would."

***

After leaving Almanza, Concho took the waiting cab home to the reservation. With daylight as his ally, he walked his yard and studied the ground around his mailbox. A few scuffs marred the dirt near the box, but the land was too dry to take good impressions. Nor were there any signs of unexpected tire tracks along the road leading to his trailer. Jericho seemed mysterious in every aspect of his life.

Returning to his trailer, he found the glue on his bow dry enough to allow further work, and he put the finishing touches on the weapon and on a dozen arrows, six of them headed with flint and the other six with the black shine of obsidian. He felt better when the weapon was done and was carrying it to his truck when his cell phone rang.

"Hello?" he said.

"Ten-Wolves," Earl Blake said.

"You got something for me?" he asked the coroner.

"Why don't you drop by. And bring that good-looking FBI agent with you."

"You mean Will Bolin?" Concho jibed.

Blake snorted. "You know who I mean."

Concho grinned and was glad for the momentary lightness of feeling. "I think I do." He glanced at the time on his phone. It was already after 2:00 in the afternoon. "We'll be there within the hour. Maybe less."

"Good." Blake hung up.

The Ranger called Della Rice. "Can you meet me at the coroner's office in Eagle Pass?" he asked.

"What's up?"

"Blake has something to tell us. He specifically asked for you."

"Oh?"

"I think he likes the cut of your jib."

"I don't even know what that means, and I'm not gonna ask. I'll meet you there in half an hour." She swiped off.

CHAPTER 34

The Eagle Pass coroner's office was a one-story, L-shaped building at 1995 Williams Street. Concho arrived about 2:45 and waited in his truck because of the cold. Della Rice tooled into the lot a few minutes later, alone in her Dodge Durango.

Concho met her as she climbed out of her SUV. She wore black dress slacks with short heels and a long-sleeved white silk blouse over which she'd thrown an open and stylish black linen jacket.

Except for Concho's Ford and Rice's Dodge, the parking lot was empty of cars. A plastic grocery bag blew across the lot like a modern-day tumbleweed. Ten-Wolves wondered where Blake parked. He led the way inside. A chime announced their presence. That was new since the last time he'd been here.

The front office featured an empty desk with a phone and computer on it. A table behind the desk held various blue binders full of who knew what, as well as a nearly empty coffee pot. To the left of the desk, a hallway ran back into the building. A gruff voice, recognizable as Earl Blake's, called from that direction.

"Come on down!"

Concho led the way again, turning right at the first door along the corridor. Blake sat behind a typical metal office desk loaded with manila folders and reference books. Shelves behind him held more books, with filing cabinets against the right-side wall.

Blake looked to be in his fifties, though he might be older. He was on the heavy-set side and mostly bald, with a still thick white beard. His right hand held a laboratory beaker about a third full of some thick black sludge vaguely resembling coffee. He studied his visitors from behind a pair of bushy eyebrows. His gaze lingered longest on Della Rice, who certainly had a bit of a statuesque thing going. Then he motioned them to sit.

The same two chairs from the first time Concho had visited were still here. Neither looked particularly suited to a man of his size, but he selected the one he'd used before and settled gently into it. It crackled a little but held up. Rice took the other chair.

"There's coffee out front if you want it," Blake said. "Cups, too."

"Thanks," Della said, smiling. "But I'm good."

"And I'm already topped off on crude oil today," Concho said.

Blake shook his head. "If only you were as funny as you think you are."

"Guess I'll have to keep practicing."

"You do that," Blake replied. He sat down his makeshift coffee mug and picked up a sheet of paper lying in front of him. He didn't bother to look at it, though. "First, the stuff you already know. The tongue belonged to Max Keller. Or the two thirds of it I have here do. The DNA match is conclusive. It was sliced off neatly with a very sharp instrument. Almost certainly a scalpel."

"How easy is it to get a scalpel?" Concho asked.

"You can order 'em off Amazon. But, the way it was used, I think we might possibly be dealing with someone with medical training."

"Very useful," Della Rice said. "Maybe a med school dropout. We can check for potential matches. Ten-Wolves said this Jericho was in his early to mid-thirties. That should narrow our search."

"*Possibly* has medical training," Concho said. "No guarantee he doesn't work as a butcher."

"No," Blake said, "but there's something else to support the medical training theory."

"Oh?" Rice asked.

"I found a tiny fragment of black material in the wound."

"What kind of material?" Concho asked.

Blake laid the sheet of paper he was holding down and leaned over beside his desk. He lifted into view a black leather satchel that reminded Ten-Wolves of the medical bag Doc Adams had carried on *Gunsmoke*.

"This kind of material," Blake said. "The kind of medical bag doctors used to haul around with them. Back when they made house calls. Your killer apparently has such a bag. And, in my experience, it's not unusual for doctors or wannabe doctors to collect this sort of thing."

"Really, really helpful," Della said, sounding excited.

Concho glanced over at her with a skeptical eye but said only, "So, can the FBI run some checks on locals who've either completed or dropped out of medical school around here in the last eight to ten years?"

Rice frowned. "Why local? You never mentioned that before."

"I was just realizing; Jericho must be from South Texas. It's the accent. I was thinking about the college-educated people I know from around here. Folks like Earl. They lack a strong accent, but a touch always remains. Jericho had that touch. In the times I spoke to him."

Della slapped her palms on the arms of her chair. "Then we have a lead. Maybe a thin one but better than we had when we walked in here." She smiled at Earl Blake. "Thank you, Doctor Blake."

"My pleasure, Ma'am," Blake said.

Concho felt his eyes rolling just a little. "If you two are finished buttering each other up, I wonder if the good coroner has anything to tell us about the bodies found at Jericho's farm."

Della gave him a glare. Blake made a face but sat the medical bag back on the floor and picked up a thick manila folder off his desk. He didn't bother to look inside it as he said:

"Yeah, I do. I've been consulting with Frank Port up in Kinney County. I've had a look at all the forensic evidence he's gathered. We're agreed there were six bodies in the pond. Some mostly bones. Some with preserved tissue from being buried in the mud."

"Buried?" Rice asked.

"Gators will do that with prey they don't want to eat all at once," Concho said. "Stick 'em down in the mud under a tree limb or wedged under a rock."

"Yes," Blake said. "But the alligator had definitely been eating on the bodies. They're so torn up it's impossible to know if they were mutilated after death the way Max Keller was."

"I'd heard there were two men and four women," Concho said.

"Yes, that's pretty clear."

"Ranging in ages from twenty-five to sixty."

Blake shrugged. "That's what Frank Port thinks. I generally agree, but it's hard to tell. Frank believes the men were stabbed and the women strangled. I did find enough neck tissue on two of the women to see ligature marks suggestive of strangling. No way to be absolutely sure, though. The men were probably stabbed with a blade, but the tearing of the tissue after death makes it hard to know."

Concho let out a heavy breath. "And that's it?"

"All of it," Blake said.

Ten-Wolves pushed himself to his feet. Della Rice rose as well but leaned across the desk to offer her long-fingered hand to Blake. Blake stood up to take it with a beaming smile on his face. A few minutes later, the Texas Ranger and the FBI agent stood together in the parking lot outside.

"I'm surprised you didn't flip your hair at him," Concho said to Rice teasingly.

The woman laughed. "Just because I don't flirt with you doesn't mean I don't know how to do it," she replied. "Besides, maybe I like the cut of *his* jib."

"And now I'm the one who doesn't want to know what that means."

Rice laughed again, then took a breath and sobered. "All right," she said. "I'll get started looking into the possible medical school connection. That'll keep me busy a while."

"Let me see any list of possible suspects you come up with."

"You going to be able to tell anything from a list of names?"

"Maybe. Sometimes there's a pattern in a perp's use of aliases."

"Gotcha," Rice said. "Will do." She flipped her hair at him and climbed into her Durango with a grin.

Concho chuckled as she drove off. He climbed in his truck and headed for the reservation. There was someone he needed to talk to.

CHAPTER 35

Concho pulled into Meskwaa's driveway. He was sur-
prised to see no signs of smoke rising over the old man's wickiup,
but lights burned in the trailer, and when he stepped out of his Ford,
he heard the heater running.

Well, it *was* cold. The lawman shivered in his light jacket. He
started toward the trailer. After 5:00 PM in December, after the
end of Daylight Savings Time, it was already nearly dark. Only
along the western horizon did any sun linger, and its rays were
long and red.

The Ranger knew people who became melancholy at this time
of year, as winter darkness closed the days down early. He normally did not feel such himself, but today was an exception. A sadness
seemed to perch on his shoulder and whisper of futility in his ear.

He shook the feeling away as he knocked on Meskwaa's door. It
opened almost immediately. Meskwaa beckoned him within. Ten-
Wolves stepped into what Meskwaa sometimes called his "White
Man's Home." It had been a while since he'd visited the elder
here. It made him wonder.

"Are you well, Uncle?" Concho asked as Meskwaa closed the
door behind them.

The old man slightly shivered as he pulled an old red blanket more tightly around his shoulders. "Only a bit tired," he said. "Come on into the kitchen." He turned and threaded his way through his combination living room/workroom.

Concho followed, frowning. The room was more cluttered than the last time he'd been here. A few feathers had fallen from a basket and not been picked up. Unfolded clothes lay spread on the couch. A tower of books leaned against a wall.

Along with the smells of leather and grease, of juniper and sawdust, and a medley of dried plant odors, the acrid smell of cigarettes lingered. Concho's heart sped a touch. He'd never known Meskwaa to smoke inside his trailer.

They entered the kitchen, which was warmed not only by the trailer's heater but by a working oven. It was almost stifling, and Concho took off his coat and hung it over one of the wooden chairs around the old, nicked, and yellowed Formica table.

Meskwaa sat. He fumbled his red cigarette pouch out of his pocket but placed it on the table without choosing a smoke. He looked almost embarrassed as he glanced up at his visitor.

The Ranger felt his jaw muscles clench as his teeth tightened together in worry. He forced them to relax. He pulled out a chair for himself and gently sat. Meskwaa was truly getting older. Throughout Concho's years on the reservation, the old man had been eternally the same. But no one resisted aging forever.

For a long while, Meskwaa had been the only Kickapoo to offer any public support or affection for Concho. He'd certainly been a mentor, perhaps even a surrogate father. Ten-Wolves did not like to think of him aging, suffering, hurting.

"Perhaps you should get a nap," he said. "I can come back another time."

Meskwaa waived the words away. "I am merely winter cold, not grave cold." He chuckled, sounding like his old self again now. "Not yet, at least."

Concho took a breath. "Where's Dog?"

Recently, a half-wild wolf-dog hybrid had adopted Meskwaa.

The two had been frequent companions since. The old man had clearly developed a strong affection for the animal, and the dog seemed to return the feeling.

"He is hunting. Somewhere around. He likes the cold better than I do. He'll return soon enough."

"Good." Concho wasn't sure what to say next, but Meskwaa knew.

"I had thought to visit you today," the Elder spoke. "But I knew you would come to see me."

"You wanted to talk about something?"

"I believe we both need to speak of things."

"You go first."

Meskwaa nodded. "Our topics are related anyway."

"Jericho!"

Again, Meskwaa nodded. "Yesterday. In afternoon and evening. Into the night. I felt... No, that is not right. I could *not* feel. For a time, my sight was blinded. Not my eyes. I speak of the extension of vision that has been with me all my life."

He reached out and clutched the younger man's wrist; his thin fingers were gnarled but strong. "Such has not happened to me in ages. Except...."

"Except recently. When you said, I disappeared from your awareness. When I was close to the man named Jericho."

Meskwaa released Concho's wrist and drew back. Again, he fiddled with this smoking sack but still did not take out a cigarette. "Yes," he said. "Only after I remembered that incident did I begin to understand. It was Jericho who was here. On the reservation. It was his magic blinding me."

Despite the heater and the oven, a chill coursed up Concho's back. He took a breath. "He *was* here. He left...something in my mailbox. The tongue of a man he killed." Concho's fists clenched. "I *wasn't* here. But Maria was. She was at my home. Only feet away from this...devil."

Meskwaa blinked. "I can tell that you, too, sense the danger surrounding this man. I wish there were a way to help you."

"Perhaps there is," Concho said suddenly.

"Tell me how and I will do it."

"The blindness. When Jericho was close, you were blinded. When he was close to me, you lost your sense of *my* presence. If this holds true, you'll know if he comes on the Rez again. Or if I get anywhere near him."

Abruptly, Meskwaa sat up straighter in his chair. "Yes. This might work."

"Tomorrow morning," Concho said. "I'm going to buy you a cell phone with my number programmed in it. I know you hate them, but with any luck, you'll be able to warn me immediately next time Jericho is around."

"For you, I will do it," Meskwaa said.

Concho smiled and rose from his chair. "Now, I think it's time for you to eat something. What have you got baking in the oven?"

"It is only on for heat."

"Then I'll cook something. You have eggs? Bacon? I know you have a skillet."

"Eggs and ham and peppers. There may be cheese. But I do not know if I have enough to feed an army."

"You inviting the neighbors? There aren't many around."

"By army, I mean you," Meskwaa said.

Concho laughed. "I'll bring you groceries with the cell phone tomorrow."

Meskwaa shrugged. He finally pulled a cigarette out of his small bag and stuck it between his lips. He lit it with a match scraped to life on a thumbnail and smoked while the Ranger made him supper. For a while, they were both content.

CHAPTER 36

Around 8:00 PM, Concho left Meskwaa's place and drove back toward home. Meskwaa's fridge had contained a dozen eggs, and they'd eaten six of them in an omelet with diced ham, cheese, sliced bell peppers, onions, and wild mushrooms. At least, Concho had tried to make an omelet. He'd ended up with scrambled eggs, as was usually the case. It ate just the same.

As he drove through Kickapoo Village on the way to his trailer, his eyes caught the glow of the Kickapoo Casino, and on the spur of the moment, he turned up Lucky Eagle Drive and pulled into the casino/hotel parking lot. He wasn't quite ready to go home yet and spend the next few hours alone worrying about Maria and Meskwaa and too many others.

Entering the gambling floor, he was recognized. A spontaneous wave of applause erupted from among the patrons. The news must be out about how he'd help break up a human trafficking operation. It had probably been on TV, which was part of the reason he hadn't been watching the tube. He didn't like seeing himself as the reporters wanted to portray him. He hadn't done anything heroic; he'd just done his job.

The clapping embarrassed him enough, so he almost turned and left. But he liked the idea of running away even less than the attention. He exchanged ten dollars for quarters and headed for the slot machines. On Friday evening, the place was busy. Bells and whistles and clinking coins. The swish of shoes on carpet and clothing on bodies. The creak of chairs and slurping of drinks. Voices laughing and cursing.

Normally, Concho found the constant noise an irritant, but somehow, tonight, it became a comfort. He didn't even mind the congratulations and slaps on the back from people who stopped to thank him for his service. It all provided him with a sign that the normal human world wasn't all gone away, and he wasn't left alone in the ruins with the monsters.

He'd just won a small jackpot at a slot machine when he noticed someone watching him. They weren't being coy about it. They stared. Admittedly, Concho's size made him stand out among the casino crowd, but the watcher stood out even more.

He appeared to be a religious man, a monk or friar, dressed in a gold robe that evoked the image of Buddhists meditating in the temple. He knelt in a chair across the room, but his eyes never left the Ranger.

Concho scratched his chin, then scraped the last coins of his jackpot into a plastic cup and rose. He walked straight over to the monk, or whatever he was. "Can I help you?" he asked.

The Monk's face was serene. He was probably not yet thirty. His bloodline was Asian. Perhaps Chinese. His shaved head glistened in the light. His brown eyes focused on Concho's. He was under six feet tall but strongly built.

"I was told you might come here tonight," the Monk said.

"By whom?"

"He did not give me his name. Merely retained my services."

"And what services would those be?"

The Monk offered a very faint bow without dropping his gaze. "I am supposed to...kick your ass."

"And that's it?"

"Yes."

Ten-Wolves chuckled. "How much does a good ass-kicking go for?"

"Five hundred dollars."

"Hmmn. Quite a lot of money. But I thought monks didn't care much for filthy lucre."

"Even monks must eat. And find a place to sleep out of the cold."

"This man who hired you. Describe him."

"Taller than I. Brown hair. Very straight white teeth."

"And his eyes," Concho said. "They had a ruby tinge. Like a scorpion's stinger."

The Monk inclined his head in a slightly deeper bow.

"His name is Jericho," Concho said. "Not the kind of man you want to work for."

"I have already taken the money."

"Give it to me and tell me where he is. I'll make sure it's returned."

The Monk unfolded slowly from the chair and placed sandaled feet on the floor as he rose. "It is too late. He is long gone now, and I would have no idea how to find him. You surely know this place better than I. Where might we conduct our business uninterrupted?"

Concho tapped his badge. "I could arrest you for threatening an officer of the law."

"Are you such a man? If so, both Jericho and I have been mistaken about your character."

"Did he tell you why he wanted my ass kicked?"

"He said you needed to learn humility. That your arrogance would cost you when you could least afford it."

"And you're supposed to take me down a peg? Ever hear the saying that a good big man beats a good small man every time?"

"Of course. I grew up in the most American city of them all."

"Cleveland?"

"Hollywood. Land of the silver screen."

Concho grinned. "In that case, I'm your huckleberry."

"*Tombstone* is an overrated movie," the Monk said.

"Now it's on! Follow."

The stairs up to the second-floor conference area was closed off by a velvet rope, but the security guard standing near it knew Concho and waved him past. They went up and turned left into a conference room. Ten-Wolves flicked on the lights. The room was about to be refurbished and was empty. The carpet had already been pulled up, leaving a hard linoleum floor like a makeshift dōjō.

Concho took off his jacket and tossed it in a corner. He unbuckled his gun belt and placed it down carefully on top of the jacket. The Monk kicked off his sandals, and the Ranger reciprocated by removing his boots, leaving on his white socks. He turned toward the other man and rolled his head and shoulders to loosen up.

"How about you give me a name."

"Philip Lue."

"Well, Philip." Concho shifted into a Georgia accent, "Say when!"

Lue sighed. "You going to quote Doc Holliday from *Tombstone* for the rest of our time?"

"Maybe. Why?"

"Because I'm beginning to think it's not worth five hundred dollars."

Ten-Wolves chuckled. "*In pace requiescat.*"

Philip Lue took a stance—legs spread, one arm straight, pointed at Concho with a closed fist, the other hand curled over his shoulder.

"*Kungfu?*" Concho asked.

"*Wushu.*"

Concho stood loosely, legs slightly apart, hands hanging open at his sides. "Army Rangers," he said.

Lue offered a slight smile. "I have defeated many military-style fighters."

"Remember." Concho gestured at himself and then at Lue.

"Big man, little man."

Lue was not as patient as he should have been. Or perhaps the goading had gotten to him. He darted forward, moving fluidly, confidently, swiftly. His hands blurred as he launched an attack. Concho blocked.

Lue spun, leaped, lashed out with a foot. Concho blocked. Lue dropped to a crouch, tried to sweep the Ranger's legs. Concho backpedaled on his toes. Lue straightened into his original stance. His face was no longer completely serene but showed a hint of surprise.

"You are very quick for such a big man," Lue said.

"Maybe you should quit while you're not ahead."

Lue said nothing but came gliding to the attack. Concho did not retreat. They met near the center of the room. Hands and feet became blades. Strikes and punches flew. Impacts thudded with the slap of bone on flesh.

Lue scored one solid hit, the side of an open hand against Concho's cheekbone. As they broke apart, the Ranger reached up and touched the quickly swelling flesh. "Good one. But now it's my turn."

The Ranger snapped a hard kick toward Lue's chest. The Monk backed up. Concho charged. A blow snapped stingingly into his chest, but he powered through it. He swung a right. Lue ducked under it, tried to grab the wrist, and throw him. The Ranger avoided the grab. He brought up a knee hard into Lue's right leg, driving it out from under him.

The Monk crashed to the floor. Concho stepped back.

Lue rolled away and twisted up on his feet. Again his face showed surprise. "You could have stomped me."

"Could have. But I don't wanna hurt you. You seem like a decent sort, and I know Jericho can be very persuasive. You should know, though, he's a killer. Literally!"

Lue lowered his hands. "I do not much like officers of the law. Particularly in Texas. They have a tendency to harass those who don't have a normal job and don't wear cowboy hats."

"So you were ready to believe I was an arrogant SOB who abused his authority."

"I suppose I was. But it seems I was misled."

"As well as being paid five hundred dollars," Concho added.

"That, too."

"How's the leg?"

Lue offered a shrug. "How's the cheek?"

"Smarts!"

Both men chuckled. Lue sobered. "A killer, you say?"

Concho nodded. "And a stealer of children."

Lue frowned. "I would not have believed it of him."

"Like I said, he's persuasive."

"Then perhaps I should tell you something to help catch him," Lue said. An instant later, he realized how he'd phrased his statement. He blurted hastily, "Don't say it. Don't say it!"

"You're a daisy if you do," Concho said, grinning.

Lue shook his head. "I set you up for that one."

"You did. But, I promise to stop if you tell me what you know about Jericho that might help us catch him."

"It was obvious from the way he hired me that he didn't care if I described him to you."

"He wanted me to know it was him."

"Yes," Lue agreed. "But there was something he conveyed that I doubt he intended."

Concho frowned. "Maybe. However, he's very deliberate in his actions. What was it?"

"Told you I was from Hollywood. It was more than just a place to live. My parents were associated with TV and movies. Mostly TV. Not as actors. Though they occasionally played extras when needed. Behind the scenes stuff. Costumes and props. My mother was quite a seamstress. My dad knew weapons. He sometimes served as an armorer."

"What?"

"A weapons specialist. The person who keeps track of all the prop weapons on a set. Maintains them, keeps them ready for action. Makes sure no one gets hurt with them."

"Ah. I understand."

"Anyway, I've been on a lot of sets as a kid. My parents wanted me to be an actor. I had some bit parts, but I never liked it." He shrugged. "Too much of an introvert, I guess. A big disappointment to my parents. Dad especially."

"Not that this isn't interesting and all," Concho said, "but I need to know what you know about Jericho. Besides, if you keep going, I'll start quoting *Tombstone* again. Kurt Russell's Wyatt Earp this time."

Lue offered a wry grin. "You're right; we don't want that. Jericho has been associated with acting and actors. I'm sure of it. He knows the lingo, the attitudes. I don't know if he's an actual actor, but he's been around the set."

Lue's words felt right. And they slid another piece of the Jericho puzzle into place. "Thanks," Ten-Wolves said. "That helps. I owe you." He grinned. "Not five hundred dollars' worth, but still...."

CHAPTER 37

Concho called Della Rice and Dalton Shaw to report Jer-
icho's potential involvement with film media. Slowly, a picture of
their target was forming. He headed home after to a dark and lonely
house. He missed Maria. As he pulled into his driveway, his cell
phone rang. He immediately understood who it had to be, even
though the caller ID showed him no identity.

He left the pickup and heater running as he swiped on the
phone and said, "Hello, Jericho."

"And the connection strengthens," Jericho said. "We are growing more attuned, Concho."

Concho bit back a bitter retort. If this "connection" Jericho
kept speaking of was the only way to keep contact with the killer,
he had to play along until they caught the man.

"So it would seem," the Ranger finally said.

"Have you stopped by the casino recently?" Jericho asked.

"Yes, I met Philip Lue."

A chuckle sounded through the line. "How did it go?"

"You didn't get your money's worth."

"Oh? No fight?"

"We fought. Until he realized you'd misled him. We parted as
friends. With both our asses unkicked."

Jericho's voice sounded almost gleeful in response. "I didn't really expect him to beat you. However, I hope my message got through?"

"That I'm too arrogant for my own good?"

"Indeed."

"Lue conveyed those thoughts."

"Then I'm pleased. Nothing personal, of course. We all need to relearn humility at times."

"Even the great Jericho?"

"Of course. I've learned the lesson over many times."

"Guess it doesn't take, huh?"

"We are an ancient and forgetful breed."

"On that, we agree."

"I suppose you turned the souvenir I sent you over to the authorities?"

"I did."

"Too bad. Could have been the nice start to a collection. Did you never take souvenirs during the war?"

"You mean like a necklace of rebel teeth?"

"Yes."

"Only an amateur or a savage does that kind of thing."

Concho's words must have stung. Jericho's voice lost its jovial edge and snapped with sudden irritation.

"I see my point about humility has already lost its sting for you. Of the two of us, which one is closer to the savagery of his ancestors?"

"I think the answer is pretty clearly you."

For a moment...silence. Then a deep, slow breath. Jericho's voice returned, calmer.

"You're trying to goad me. And you almost succeeded. You make a worthy opponent. It's too bad we have to *be* opponents."

"As long as you're killing people and kidnapping children, we will be."

"And if I should stop, we would become best of friends. Is that what you're saying?"

"The chances are pretty slim, I'll admit."

"Let me tell you a story, Ten-Wolves. One told to me as a child."

"I'm on the edge of my seat."

Jericho ignored the gibe. "Two dogs. One big, one small. The big dog just wanted to rest, but the little dog kept irritating him. Kept jumping on him, walking on him. Biting at his ears and tail. The little dog had sharp claws that scratched the big dog's face. One day the big dog snapped. He grabbed the small dog in his mouth and bit down hard. Broke its little neck and spine. Finally, the big dog got some rest."

"And the moral of the story is?"

"Leave Daddy alone."

"A horror story then."

"No, a cautionary tale."

"I must be the big dog."

"I don't think the story is actually about size."

"So, it's a metaphor," Concho said. "Which dog are you?"

Jericho's voice sounded pensive. "I'm not sure yet." He hung up.

***

Another early morning call brought Concho more bad news. This one didn't wake him. It came at 8:00, and he'd been up already for hours after a troubled night's sleep. He was working out when the chime came through on his cell, and he saw the name, Beth Pennebaker. Sudden fear iced his sweat.

"What's wrong?" he answered.

Pennebaker's voice thrummed with concern. "Have you heard from Mandy?"

Another chill swept the Ranger. "No? Why would I have?"

"It looks like she might have...run away?"

"*Run*away? Or been taken?"

"I think, *run*. Her parents called me just a few minutes ago.

They said Mandy wasn't in her room this morning. But all the windows and doors are locked from the inside. They'd also had a security system installed, and it was turned off. Had to be from inside."

"Did she leave a note?"

"No. Not that they've found anyway."

Concho's thoughts raced around in his head like crows mobbing an owl.

"What are we going to do?" Pennebaker asked. "She's...she's in no condition to be out alone."

"Did you call the police?"

"Her parents did. Before they called me, could she...have gone back to Jericho?"

"It's possible. Did she have a cell phone?"

"She did, but she left it behind on her bed. I guess she knew it could be tracked."

"She's smart."

"I'm on my way up to see them now. The parents. But I don't know what to tell them."

"Has she reconnected with any old friends since she's been home?"

"I...I don't know. She's still not being very forthcoming with me."

"We need to find out. If she didn't go to Jericho, she might have gone to a friend. Have her parents check her phone for any calls in or out, and let me know what you find. Also, have the police check out all the friends she had from before she was kidnapped. We'd better follow up every possible lead."

"But you don't think that's where they'll find her, do you?"

"No, I'm afraid not."

"What are you going to do?"

Some of the Ranger's thoughts came in to roost. "I've got an idea. I'll be in touch. Whether it proves out or not."

"OK," Pennebaker said.

Concho hung up without saying goodbye. If his idea had any merit, time was critical. He dried his workout sweat with a towel and ran to get dressed. In ten minutes, he was out of the house, in his truck, and on his way to Kinney County, Texas. On the way, he dialed the cell number for Deputy Perse Wiebke.

The woman answered on the third ring. "Concho?" she asked.

"It's me. I need a favor."

"If I can."

"You remember Mandy?"

"The young woman Jericho left behind at the truck stop?"

"Yeah. She's missing again. Her parents think she ran off."

Wiebke's voice sharpened. "You don't think so?"

"If she did, it's because of Jericho."

"She's going back to him?"

"Maybe. I have a hunch. A suspicion she might return to Jericho's farm."

"You want me to check it out?"

"I want to check it out, but I'd appreciate backup."

"I can do that. What's the plan?"

"I'm on my way now. Probably forty-five minutes out. I'm going to come in the back way, through Jericho's escape route. Can you get to the burned-out church? I noticed a place to park behind it out of sight. And if I call for help, you come running?"

"Gotcha," Wiebke said. "I'll be there. Before you."

"Thanks. And, by the way, don't know if anyone has told you, but we've got two vague clues as to Jericho's background."

"Oh?"

"A hint that he might have had medical training. And, that he seems familiar with the details and lingo of acting."

"You mean, like movies?"

"Could be. Or maybe just associated with a college drama troop."

"Interesting."

"Anyone come to mind?"

"Not yet," Wiebke said. "But I'll work the idea around in my head.

"Good."

"Anyone else joining us this morning? Say the FBI?"

"Not this time. It's just you and me."

"All right. I've got your back."

CHAPTER 38

Concho made one more call on the way to Jericho's farm.
He asked Roberto Echabarri to take some groceries and a cell
phone to Meskwaa and to program his number into the phone
and show the old man how to use it. Once that was done, he put
his cell away and began to compose himself for what he might find
at the farm.

Soon, he reached the *Old Rugged Cross* Church, which
marked the turnoff to Jericho's place. The walls of the church had
been built of stone and were still standing after the fire gutted the
building. The windows had been blown out by the flames, though,
and the door was gone. Concho saw no sign of Perse Wiebke's patrol car as he passed the place on the highway, but there was plenty
of room behind the building to hide a vehicle.

Concho slowed. About a hundred yards past the church, on the
left side of the road, a narrow turnoff revealed itself through the
weeds. He pulled his Ford into it and pushed ahead. A rutted dirt
trail just wide enough for a vehicle slanted down to the dry and
stony bed of a creek. The pickup rattled across it and pulled to a
stop at the base of the rise beyond.

Ten-Wolves climbed out. Wisps of white cloud stained the
blue sky. The day was bright with sunshine that didn't do much to

warm the air. It wasn't as cold as yesterday but cold enough. Concho kept his jacket on, though he left it unbuttoned. He checked his Colt Double Eagles in their holsters and turned his cell phone to vibrate.

A sparse grove of oak and cedar trees grew along the creek to either side of the trail. Most of the leaves had fallen from the oaks, and some of the cedars were browning from a lack of rain. The dryness had a smell. A single, out-of-season frog burred a forlorn call.

He started up the road, which Jericho had used as an escape route before. It angled up a short hill, and he went to his belly at the top. The farm came into view below, less than a hundred yards away. No vehicles and no sign of activity. But he hadn't really expected any, and the absence didn't dissuade him.

Slipping into the shallow ditch along the road, Concho worked forward in a crouch until the trail disappeared into the farm's backyard. He was less than thirty yards from the back door, where he'd entered the house the last time he'd been here. Seeing no movement at any of the windows, he lunged to his feet and sprinted to the three cement steps leading up to the back porch.

No sound of alarm came from within the house. Yellow crime scene tape blocked the rear screen door. He pulled it away and opened the unlocked screen, stepping through onto the cement porch.

Just as last time, the back door was unlocked as well, and he pushed through it into the same spotless kitchen he'd found before. The room was empty, and he moved into the hallway beyond, pausing to listen carefully. The house creaked. Old houses did.

The only thing that smelled different from before was the powder used to take fingerprints. The FBI must have doused everything in it, and the scent was still strong, though it hadn't helped much. They'd identified the prints of Mandy and the young man, Jeff, and had found two other sets of prints, believed to be Jericho and his partner Wilbur. Neither of those had shown up on any database search.

He worked his way down the hallway and turned into the dining room. The five mannequins were gone, taken as evidence by the police. The heavy curtains had also been pulled back, allowing the room to fill with sunlight.

The stairs to the second floor arose here. He could neither hear nor smell anything unusual up those stairs. And he got no sense of any presence above. He started carefully up. A step creaked under his boots, and he stiffened. A faint click sounded that he couldn't place. Maybe just another random noise from an old house. He waited a full minute. When nothing further came from above, he worked his way to the top.

Everything on the second floor was much as it had been before, except there was no dying boy here now. The body had been removed, though the chalk outline lingered. The large room at the top of the stairs remained nearly devoid of furniture. The bullet-shattered window at the front had been boarded up by someone.

The doors to the two other rooms remained open, as before. Concho stepped lightly across to the first room. It was clear. He moved to the second room, the bedroom, where he'd grabbed a quick nap. This one wasn't clear.

Mandy lay bound to the bed, flat on her back. She wore tennis shoes, jeans, and an overly large black cotton t-shirt. She appeared to be unconscious, perhaps drugged, though the rise and fall of her chest showed she was breathing.

There was nothing else in the room except for the broken grandfather clock he'd seen before. He rushed to the bed. Mandy looked pale but two fingers pressed to the pulse in her neck found it strong and sure.

He used his thumb to roll one of her eyelids up. The pupil was constricted. He was no doctor, but he'd read that propofol, a common anesthetic, caused some pupillary constriction. She must have been drugged.

He grasped her shoulders and shook her. "Mandy. Mandy! Wake up!"

A click sounded behind him. He spun, right hand streaking for a Colt.

"Nuh-uh," a voice said.

Concho froze at seeing the double bores of a shotgun pointed at his midsection. At a distance of ten feet, the shot would cut him in half and probably kill Mandy behind him, too.

The man holding the shotgun was dirty and unkempt. He wore a shabby pair of overalls over a brown and yellow flannel shirt. Behind him, the grandfather clock had been shifted aside, and the black mouth of a secret compartment showed. Concho cursed himself. He'd never even considered that the farmhouse might have a hidden room. Knowing Jericho, he should have.

"Be still as a cigar store Injun," the man said, gesturing slightly with the shotgun.

"Wilbur, I reckon," Concho said. The man was just as Mandy had described him, heavy, filthy, and nearly bald.

"Guilty," Wilbur said. "And I here I got the drop on you. The great Jericho couldn't do it, but I did."

"Maybe *you* should be in charge."

Wilbur snorted. "Yeah, mebbe so."

"Is Jericho here?"

"Nope, did this my own self."

"All on your lonesome?"

"Got a couple friends to help with the heavy liftin.'" He called out loudly. "Tim, Strick, get out here."

Two men pushed free of the secret compartment. Each carried a lever-action .30-30 rifle. Probably Marlins. If the order in which Wilbur had called them forth was correct, Tim was a smallish red-head with meth-mouth, and Strick was a skinny Hispanic with heroin eyes.

"A couple of heroes there," Concho said.

Tim snarled at the insult; Strick didn't even blink. Wilbur chuckled. "Enough to bring down the great Ten-Wolves," he said.

"Guess I can't argue with you there," the Ranger said. "What did you give Mandy? Is it something she's going to come out of?"

Wilbur shook his head impatiently. "She'll be fine. Just some-thin' to calm her down until we get her to Jericho. *If* we decide to take her to him, that is." He gestured at the man called Tim. "Take those zip ties I gave ya and put one around this Injun's wrists. Behind his back."

"Injun?" Tim asked. "Don't look like no Injun to me. Looks like a spook."

"Whatever," Wilbur snapped. "Jus' do like I tell ya."

Tim mumbled but handed his rifle to Strick and pulled a jum-bo-sized zip tie out of his pocket. The Ranger eased one step to-ward the three men and turned slightly. He dropped his hands to his sides as if abandoning any thought of resistance. But his move-ments took him out of line with Mandy, so if the shotgun fired, she wouldn't get hit. He shifted his weight onto his left leg and glanced out the window next to him. The roof of the back porch lay just beneath, with the ground a short drop farther.

"Too bad they took away the gator," Wilbur said. "Would a enjoyed hearin' ya scream while he ate ya. But don't matter, we gotcha now."

"Don't count your crocodilians before they're hatched," the lawman replied.

"Huh?"

Concho didn't answer as Tim stepped up behind him. The red-head grabbed his left wrist and pulled it backward. Concho twist-ed his hand free. Tim cursed and reached for it again, but he had to lean forward to make that grab, putting him directly in front of the shotgun's bore.

Concho latched onto Tim's left forearm. At the same time, he whipped his body around and curled his free arm around Tim's neck.

"Hey!" Wilbur shouted.

His finger tightened on the trigger of the shotgun, but he hes-itated with Tim in the way. Still clutching the redhead, Concho threw himself violently backward through the window.

CHAPTER 39

Glass and wood shattered under their combined weight as Concho hurled himself and the red-headed thug out the window. The tail of a lace curtain whipped across his face for an instant, and then they were through, bursting into the open, falling.

Concho twisted his body in mid-air, pulling a struggling Tim beneath him. They whammed hard into the roof below. Tim cried out as his back struck the roof and his skull bounced off the shingles.

Ten-Wolves rolled, taking the two of them off the roof just as Wilbur fired both barrels of the shotgun through the busted window. The heavy bolt of lead tore a hole where Concho had been a moment before, shattering wood and shingles.

Concho hit the ground beneath the roof on his side. The impact wrung a groan from him, and he gasped for air as his body spasmed in pain. Tim gave a low moan. He lifted his arms, let them flop back to the ground.

"Cain't...cain't feel my legs," the redhead murmured.

Concho struggled to his feet. His back burned; his face stung. Everything hurt. But he was alive. His left-hand Colt was still strapped into its holster. The right-side one had fallen out during his tumble but lay on the ground a few feet away. He scooped it up.

Wilbur was screaming commands from the second floor at the man named Strick, no doubt. "Get down there! Get down there! He's gotta be hurt. Finish him!"

Concho bent over Tim. Tears stained the red head's cheeks. "Help me," he pleaded. "I cain't feel my legs."

"If I live, I'll call an ambulance," Ten-Wolves snapped. "But that's a big if at the moment."

Tim flailed at Concho, trying to grab his arm. "Please!"

The lawman shook off the man's grip and turned toward the house. He ripped open the screen door and rushed onto the porch. Behind him, Tim muttered desperate prayers to Jesus. Then, from above, Wilbur called to him through the broken window.

"Better give up now, Ten-Wolves. Else I'm gonna hurt the little lady. I'll wake her up first, so she knows what's happening."

He didn't answer. Wilbur couldn't see over the edge of the roof to where he'd fallen. Let the man think he was hurt badly. Or dead. Concho stepped through the back door of the house into the kitchen. Two doors led into the room. Strick might come by either one if he came at all.

Concho pulled off his encumbering jacket and tossed it aside. He fumbled in his jeans pocket with his left hand and pulled out his smartphone. The glass was cracked but briefly showed his reflection. The scratches across his cheeks from the window and his fall were sticky with blood, turning his features into a war face. He ignored it, swiped the phone. It came on. He'd already set the number for Perse Wiebke's phone and pressed it now.

Ringing.

Wiebke answered. "Yes." Her voice sounded odd, but he didn't have time to ask why.

"I need that backup. Be careful. Two men with guns."

Before the deputy could respond, running footsteps sounded in the hallway, coming toward the kitchen. Not bothering to hang up, Concho stuffed the phone back in his pocket and swung up the Double Eagle in his right hand.

A human figure came flying into the kitchen. Concho's finger tightened on the Colt's trigger, but he held fire. It was the torso of a mannequin, painted silver. Had to have come from the hidden compartment upstairs.

Strick must have thrown the dummy. Heroin eyes or not, the man didn't seem crazy enough to come through into the kitchen himself. The Ranger backed toward the other doorway into the room, then turned and stepped through.

He found himself in the dining room now, with the stairway to his left. No one could see him from above unless they came down the steps. But if he moved to the stairs himself, he'd become visible and vulnerable. He hesitated, unsure of his best option. Where was Deputy Wiebke? He should have heard her sirens by now as she rode to his support. Nothing.

A voice whispering from above distracted him. Wilbur's voice. "Strick! Strick! You see him? What's going on?"

Wilbur must be leaning over the upstairs railing. Concho made a decision, an uncalculated risk. He grasped his Colt with both hands and stepped suddenly into the open, twisting to gaze toward the stairway landing above him.

A gasp sounded from a dark figure at the head of the stairs. *Wilbur!* The big shotgun hung in his hands, but instead of swinging it to bear, he dodged backward away from the railing.

Concho already had his pistol up. He fired twice, the bullets cracking loudly in the quiet of the house. The first bullet splintered the railing where Wilbur had leaned and wrung a cry from the desperate gunman. It didn't stop him, though. The second bullet plowed harmlessly into the ceiling.

Concho stepped into the corner of the room beneath the stairs. Gunsmoke stung his nostrils. He dropped to a crouch. From the hallway at the other end of the dining area came movement. He shoved his Colt out in front of him, but nothing happened.

A cell phone rang and was instantly silenced. Ten-Wolves heard indistinct mumbling. Wilbur must have called Strick. They were planning something. And he wasn't in a good position to respond.

Time ticked over, counted in heartbeats.

"Strick!" came a shout from above.

A shape came falling over the upstairs railing. For a sickening instant, Concho thought it was Mandy. His gaze tracked the form. It thudded to the floor, and an arm went spinning away.

Another mannequin!

Strick burst into the room from the hallway. His .30-30 was leveled, and he pulled the trigger. The shell smashed stairway splinters into Concho's face. He ducked, returned fire. It wasn't a clean hit. The .45 slug tore through the meat of Strick's biceps, spraying the wall behind him with scarlet. The rifle spun from the man's grasp.

Strick yelled. Concho hesitated. The man was disarmed.

A second shot came from elsewhere and caught Strick in the side of the head. The man stumbled sideways and dropped. Concho swung his pistol toward the source of the shot that had killed Strick. He saw a flash of green nylon from a jacket, then a face above it framed with blonde hair. A deputy's badge glinted.

Wiebke!

He hadn't heard the front door open or the deputy come in. But she was here now, the cavalry arriving. He signaled her to stay back, then pointed at the stairs to indicate another perp above them.

As if he'd cued Wilbur, the man's cursing voice sounded: "Ya got 'em both. Damn you, Ten-Wolves! But I still got the girl. You come up here…. Or anyone even comes close, and I'll open her from hips to head with this shotgun."

Concho straightened. "You hurt the girl, and I'll hurt you worse," he shouted up the stairs. "Throw down the shotgun and come out. I'll make sure you get a fair trial. We all know you were just doing Jericho's bidding."

"You're a liar, Ranger. But it looks like a standoff. My car's in the barn. Keys in it. Pull it up and park it in front of the house and back off. I'll take Mandy with me and let her go as soon as I'm away."

"Not a possibility, Wilbur!"

"You're pushin' me in a corner, Ranger. You ain't gonna like what happens."

Ignoring Wilbur, Concho signaled Wiebke that he was coming around. He slipped into the kitchen and circled down the hallway to where the deputy hovered in the doorway of the dining area. It kept him out of Wilbur's line of fire. Wiebke awaited him, her face pale. She looked upset. But she *had* just killed a man.

"You all right?" Concho asked.

The woman shook her head. "Not really." She wiped her mouth on the back of her hand. "Sorry I was late. But...."

"What?"

"Jericho! He was here." She shook her head. "I mean, at the church. I was in my car. Heater going but with the window down to hear better if there were any shots. He just...just walked up and put a pistol in my ear. I didn't hear him coming." She shuddered slightly.

"What happened?"

"He was with me. When you called, he *told* me to answer the phone. Cocked the hammer on his pistol first, though. I didn't... I couldn't...say anything. Warn you."

"I understand. What did he want?"

She shook her head. "I don't know. He held the gun on me for a few minutes. Told me not to look at him. I was talking, trying to convince him to let me go. He didn't say anything. So I turned my head just a little, and he was gone. He moved like you. Silently. I didn't know he'd left. Or where he went to. For all I know, he's somewhere around this house now."

"OK," Concho soothed. "It's all right. We'll keep our eyes open. We'll deal with Jericho. But first, we have Wilbur upstairs. He's got Mandy tied up. He'll hurt her unless we can stop him."

"How? We can't go up the stairs against that shotgun."

"There's another possibility. Out back. There's a way up to the kitchen roof. And a broken window into the room where he's holding Mandy. Give me four minutes. Then talk to Wilbur. Distract him. I'll get up on the roof and surprise him from the window."

Wiebke nodded. "Might work. But be careful and keep an eye open for Jericho." She shuddered again. "I can't believe he didn't kill me. Why didn't he?"

Concho dropped a comforting hand on the woman's shoulder. "We'll get him, and you can ask him yourself."

The deputy took a breath, got hold of herself. "OK. Four minutes. I can do it."

"I know you can." He squeezed her shoulder, then moved away down the hallway toward the back door. A tall AC unit sat just outside the kitchen. He could use it to climb onto the roof and make his way to the room where Mandy was held.

He stepped out the back door, easing it shut so Wilbur wouldn't hear the noise. His glance was drawn to where the man, Tim, lay with his broken back.

Tim wasn't there.

CHAPTER 40

Concho stiffened in surprise as he realized Tim's body had disappeared. The man couldn't have walked away with a broken back. But where was he, and who had taken him? The Ranger's keen gaze studied his surroundings, searching for some clue.

The farmyard itself was mostly barren dirt, with a field of dried grasses dotted with clusters of sagebrush fading away into the distance. Ten-Wolves wondered. Was he being watched from somewhere in that immensity? He felt no sensation of eyes upon him.

Taking a moment, he studied the ground where Tim had lain. It might have been barely possible for the man to *crawl* away, but the ground showed no signs of such. Scuff marks around the site were plentiful, and some of them were his own prints.

He couldn't derive any clear story of what had happened from the marks, though. And he had little time to study the scene. The four minutes he'd arranged for with Perse Wiebke were ticking away. Right now, Mandy was more important than what had happened to Tim.

The Ranger stepped from under the cover of the porch to where the AC unit crouched against the house. It was turned off and silent. Concho climbed up on it and from there slithered carefully onto the roof, moving slowly and carefully to avoid any noise that might attract Wilbur's attention in the room just above.

Rising to a crouch, he clung close to the wall and waited. He had a good time sense. At least three and a half of his four minutes had fled. Thirty seconds to go. Right on cue, a muffled voice called out from within the house. He couldn't understand the words, but it had to be Perse Wiebke doing what he'd asked her to do—corner Wilbur's attention so Concho could slip unnoticed up to the same window he'd hurled himself out of earlier.

No answering voice came from the room above, but footsteps edged across the floor. Concho inched forward toward the window, drawing his right-hand Colt. The tail of a lace curtain still hung out over the broken frame and occasionally flapped in the breeze.

"Who is that? Whatta ya want?" Wilbur yelled. He wasn't talking to Concho.

More words came from Wiebke inside. Concho could tell it was a woman's voice but couldn't make out what was said. Wilbur seemed curious, though. His footsteps echoed as he moved even farther away from the window.

When the man called again, he must have been right at the door of the room or had actually stepped through it. "What the hell!" he said clearly.

Concho lifted his head, peered in over the sill of the window. He scanned left and right. Mandy lay bound and unconscious on the bed to the left. Only drugs could have kept her knocked out through all the shooting. To the right was the dark opening into the hidden room. Wilbur was nowhere to be seen.

Concho hadn't expected the man to actually leave the room but now was his chance. He straightened, threw one leg over the sill, and lunged inside. From beyond the door came Wilbur's sudden yell:

"Hey!"

Then came a shot from a pistol rather than a shotgun. A clatter followed, metal striking wood. Next came a loud crashing, as of something large tumbling down the stairs.

Forgetting Mandy for the moment, Concho threw himself across the room and out the door, his pistol ready. He reached the head of the stairwell. Deputy Perse Wiebke stood at the bottom, staring down at the dead body of Wilbur.

The man's shotgun lay at her feet. A wisp of smoke curled from the barrel of her service pistol. She glanced up at him, her green eyes shining in the light. Her face fell as she saw him; she shook her head and slowly holstered her .38.

"He pulled down on me," she said. "I didn't want to shoot him. I know we needed to ask him questions. But…."

"You did what you had to do. I'm surprised he came out of the room, though."

"Maybe because I'm a woman, he thought he could buffalo me."

"Maybe," Concho agreed. "Can you call it in?"

"I will. What are you gonna do?"

"Release Mandy. And there's a secret chamber up here we didn't know existed. I'm gonna check it out."

"Be careful," Wiebke said. "Jericho may still be around."

'You too," Concho said. "And I'm pretty sure he is." He told her about Tim's missing body out back.

She winced in surprise and turned to go. Concho stepped back into the bedroom to check Mandy. She was still sound asleep but breathing well. He considered whether to unbind her but wanted to check out the secret room. If she woke up and he was gone, she'd surely run. Reluctantly, he left her tied a little longer.

Still holding a Colt in his right hand, the lawman strode over to the chamber. It didn't take long to figure out how the setup worked. The grandfather clock was hollow when he knocked on its side. It didn't actually touch the floor but sat on a small platform suspended a quarter inch off the floor. It served as a door for the hidey hole.

The clock/door was already partially open. Concho pulled it wider and saw the latch on the wall inside that would hook it closed when engaged. The area beyond lay dimly lit by sunlight trickling through cracks in the wall, but an electric bulb dangled from the ceiling, and a light switch stood on the left side. Concho flicked it on, and the space jumped into bright clarity.

The bedroom next to Mandy's room must have had a false back wall. A narrow corridor about two feet across ran behind it, between that room and the house's true outside wall. The area had been left bare and unfinished. It was empty but ran all the way to the far side of the house.

Concho's shoulders were as wide as those of a padded NFL linebacker, but he squeezed into the space and began to ease toward the far end. He had to holster his gun.

Dust motes danced around him. He fought a sneeze. The place smelled musty, though he detected some kind of oily scent that must have originated from Wilbur's presence here.

With his back against the outside wall and his chest brushing the inside, he worked all the way to the end of the little corridor. No secrets revealed themselves, but he wasn't convinced he'd found everything. He studied the wall.

A nail caught his attention. He tugged on it, and it came free. A click sounded, and a line of shadow appeared in the wall. He put his fingernails into the line and tugged. A two-foot-wide rectangle of wood came free to show him another secret area behind it. This one wasn't empty.

***

Roberto Echabarri left the Sheriff's office on the Kickapoo reservation about mid-morning and drove out to see the tribal elder, Meskwaa. In the backseat of his SUV, he hauled two bags of groceries: eggs, milk, bacon, bread, hamburger, steaks, and chops.

As a favor to Ten-Wolves, he also took along a Nokia 3310, about the simplest cell phone he could find, and one considered virtually indestructible. Meskwaa could be pretty tough on electronics.

Although a cold front was supposedly headed this way, today was a little warmer than yesterday so far, and as he pulled into Meskwaa's yard, he saw smoke rising from the Elder's wickiup. Leaving the groceries for now but with the Nokia tucked into the pocket of his jeans, he climbed out of his vehicle and knocked on the side of the hut.

"Come!" a vibrant voice hollered from within.

According to Concho's morning call, Meskwaa had looked a little old yesterday. He sounded strong this morning. Roberto pulled back the blanket covering the wickiup's entrance and slipped inside. The smell of fire engulfed him.

In the hut's center, a flame burned bright. Dry wood gave off only a little smoke, which drifted toward the ceiling to be drawn out through the loose construction of the cane and cattail roof.

Meskwaa sat cross-legged on a bench on the far side of the flames. His eyes brimmed with refracted gold. On the ground near his feet lay the old man's wolf-dog. It rose when Roberto entered and huffed a warning. Meskwaa calmed the animal with a hand to its ruff. It lay back down and put its head on its paws.

"Come and sit," Meskwaa said to Roberto, gesturing toward a second bench. "Drink!" he pointed to the pail of water sitting nearby.

Roberto nodded and obeyed. He took a polite sip of the cold water, then drew the cell phone out of his pocket and held it. "Concho was called away this morning," he said. "He asked me to bring you some groceries and a cell phone."

Meskwaa held out his hand, and Roberto placed the Nokia into it. The policeman pointed out a couple of features, how to get to a pre-programmed number and how to dial out or answer a call.

Meskwaa nodded throughout. "Thank you."

The Elder had barely looked away from the fire during their conversation. The flames seemed to consume his attention. He was dressed oddly as well, in ceremonial clothes rather than his usual attire. A red breechclout hung over buckskin leggings. His bony chest showed through a fringed vest, but he'd draped a bright red blanket over his shoulders. A beaded leather band held back his gray hair.

"Is everything all right?" Roberto asked.

"I do not know." Meskwaa gestured toward the fire. "What do you see there?"

Roberto looked to where the Elder pointed. Flames crackled and hissed. Embers whirled. Orange and red threads danced across the wood while gossamer swirls of smoke lifted.

"Only the fire," Roberto said.

Meskwaa shook his head. "I do not think so. And now, watch and see."

Roberto frowned but did as he was bid.

Meskwaa selected Ten-Wolves' number and left it on the screen without dialing it. He lifted the phone in both hands and made a casting gesture as if to throw it into the flames. Roberto almost shouted a protest, but the Elder drew the phone back at the last second before releasing it. Roberto saw nothing enter the flames, but suddenly they roared higher as if whipped by an invisible wind.

The dog surged to its feet in a fit of growling. The fire swayed back and forth, and now the orange and red streamers capered about like miniature devils. A puff of grayish-black smoke spouted upward.

For an instant, Roberto felt sure he saw a face in the smoke. No, a shifting sea of faces. One might have been Ten-Wolves. The others he did not know. The dog's growls ratcheted higher.

The smoke cloud drifted toward the ceiling, steadily darkening. The faces melted together. And then Roberto saw something else. A black dog snarling down with bleeding maroon eyes.

Meskwaa's wolf-dog went nearly berserk, snarling, snapping. Its lips dripped foam. Roberto felt sure the animal would have hurled itself after the smoke image if the elder Kickapoo had not grabbed it firmly by the ruff. The smoke cloud burst against the wickiup's roof, dissipating through the cracks. The wolf-dog calmed a little, though it remained on its feet, growling low and trembling.

"What... What was that?" Roberto asked Meskwaa. "Surely, I didn't see what I thought I saw."

The old man turned his head to meet the young police chief's gaze. "Faces. And a black dog," he said.

"Yeah. What was it? What did you do to make that happen?"

"I did nothing," Meskwaa said. "But you must do something."

"What?"

"Concho is in danger."

Roberto startled. He made a quick decision and reached for the phone Meskwaa was holding. When the old man handed it to him, he pressed call for the number on the screen. It rang and rang... and nothing. Handing the cell back to Meskwaa, he drew out his own and swiped the same number. Again, multiple rings and nothing. He glanced at the Kickapoo Elder with worry on his face.

"You need to find him," Meskwaa said. "Do you know where to look?"

Roberto chewed at his lip for a second. "Not for sure. But I think I know how to find out."

"Do it. And please hurry."

CHAPTER 41

The newest secret chamber Concho stared into was only about ten feet deep and barely two feet wide. In it were piled the separated limbs and torsos of a dozen mannequins. Three *complete* mannequins leaned against the wall behind the pieces. Their faces shone with dim light. Two were adult sized and gendered, at least for their top halves. One was male, the other female. The third was somewhat smaller and also gendered as a male.

The two biggest models were clothed, the man in a suit and tie and the woman in a low-cut black satin evening gown dulled by a film of dust. Only the smaller mannequin was nude. The five mannequins Concho had seen when he'd first entered this house days ago had been unclothed. And —it suddenly occurred to him—they'd also been genderless. Neither male nor female. He couldn't come up with a single reason at the moment for those differences.

Taking out his cell phone, Concho pressed the button on the side to bring up the cover screen. He wanted to photograph the hidden room. The phone didn't come on. He frowned, tried it again. The screen remained black. He must have damaged it, possibly from rolling off the roof. The screen had been cracked after, but he'd used it at least once to call Perse Wiebke. Huffing in frustration, he stuffed the phone back in his pocket and grasped the arm of the closest mannequin, the smallest of the three. He pulled it toward him. It rattled as if something were inside. And now he noticed another difference between this one and the ones he'd seen downstairs before. These three had been modified, with holes for eyes and slits for mouths.

At first, Concho thought the holes and slits had merely been stabbed into the shapes, but a closer look revealed contours. They'd been carved to look like true eye sockets and real mouths.

As Concho tried to turn around with the mannequin in the narrow chamber, he glimpsed a latch on the wall next to a trash can full of candy and food wrappers. Apparently, Wilbur—and maybe the others—had been hiding in this chamber for a while, though they'd likely left the area when no one was around. He wondered if Wilbur had been here when the initial raid occurred. No way to know now.

Pressing the latch emitted a faint click, and the wall opened with a creak. He pushed against it, and another hidden door rotated back. Concho stepped out into the second bedroom, still pulling the mannequin behind him. In this room, the secret doorway was hidden by a full-length mirror rather than a grandfather clock.

Leaving the chamber open, he tucked the mannequin under his left arm and strode out of the bedroom. He stepped back into the first bedroom, where Mandy lay, and paused. Perse Wiebke had returned. He frowned.

Wiebke must not have heard him approaching. She seemed oblivious to him as she leaned over Mandy and studied the girl carefully. She grasped the unconscious Mandy's face and turned the girl's head, stroking a purpling bruise over the cheek with one finger.

Concho cleared his throat.

Wiebke jumped and spun around, then burst into nervous laughter. "You scared me," she said. Her voice sobered as she asked, "How did you get out here? I thought you were back in the secret chamber?"

"I was. But there's another door opening into the next bed-room over. I came out that way."

Wiebke nodded. She added, "Local cops are on the way. I called Della Rice, too. She'll be here. Says it'll take a while."

"Good. We'll need the FBI. And suddenly, my phone isn't working." He patted the pocket where he'd stuffed the non-functioning cell phone.

Wiebke cleared her throat. She glanced back at Mandy before returning her gaze to the Ranger. "I was just checking over our hostage here." She pointed at the bruise on the girl's pale cheek. "Looks like this Wilbur character worked her over a little. At least her clothes aren't torn, and there are no scratches on her I can see. I don't think she was sexually assaulted."

"Yeah, I don't think so either. From what I understand from Mandy, Wilbur may have had leanings that way but held them at bay out of fear of Jericho."

Wiebke swallowed harshly. Then, "What have you got there? Another mannequin?"

"A different kind." He turned the shape around to show her the face.

She gasped as she saw the eyes and mouth. "What?" she asked.

"I don't know. There are two more back in the chamber. Both larger. And dressed. One as a man, one as a woman."

Wiebke shook her head. "I don't know what that means."

"I don't either. But I suspect it's a critical piece of information we need to know to catch this killer."

From the bed, Mandy cried out as she awakened from her drugged sleep.

***

As Roberto Echabarri left Meskwaa's house, he called another number in his phone. Della Rice, Special Agent for the FBI, answered.

"Hello, Sheriff," Rice said. "What can I do for you?"

"Agent Rice. I'll get right to it. I'm worried about Concho Ten-Wolves. I just tried his phone and got no answer. You have any idea where he might be?"

"Actually, I do. I'm on my way to see him right now. I think he's OK, though. I just got a call saying he was at Jericho's farmhouse and had found something for us to look at."

"You got a call from *him*?"

"No, from a woman named Perse Wiebke. She's a deputy over in Kinney County, where the house is located. She went in as backup for Ten-Wolves. Maybe she was calling because of his phone issues."

"Maybe so. Makes me feel a little better. Would you mind if I drove up to join you?"

"No. That's fine. You know where it is?"

"Afraid not."

"All right. Well, I'm driving, but I'll have my colleague text the address to your number.

"Sounds good. Thanks!"

***

"No, no, no!" Mandy cried out. She thrashed against the ropes binding her. Her brown eyes sprang open. She seemed hardly to recognize the Ranger standing beside her.

"It's all right!" Concho said. He thrust the mannequin against the wall and quickly sat on the edge of the bed to grab her shoulders. "You're safe. Let me get you free."

Mandy's gaze focused. She calmed. Concho drew a razor-edged hunting knife from the sheath on his belt and sliced through the nylon ropes securing Mandy's hands to the sides of the bed.

As soon as they were free, the girl sat up and threw her arms around Concho. Tears began to drip. Ten-Wolves slid his arms around the girl in return and awkwardly patted her shoulder. It kept him from being able to reach the ropes constraining her ankles, though.

"I'll get her feet," Perse Wiebke said as she stepped toward the bottom of the bed.

Mandy jerked her legs and shouted, "No!"

Wiebke froze. Concho tugged loose from Mandy's grip and slid to his feet. He glanced at Wiebke, who looked shocked, then back at Mandy as he leaned over the foot of her bed and sliced through the ropes holding her ankles.

The girl quickly swung her legs off the bed and sat up. She hugged herself as she looked up at Concho. "I knew you'd come," she said.

Concho gave her a nod. "I'm glad I could be here. Deputy Wiebke helped me out."

Mandy glanced at Wiebke and frowned before looking away. She muttered a reluctant, "Thanks." Then: "Where's Wilbur?"

"Dead," Concho replied. "And the two men with him are out of commission, as well."

Mandy blinked several times. "Good!"

Ten-Wolves chose his next words with care. "You know, Mandy, I don't mind helping people out, but I'm not a big fan of doing things twice."

Mandy's shoulders shook. She looked down, and it seemed as if she'd burst into tears again. She managed to hold it back. "I know," she said in her small voice. "I'm sorry."

"What were you expecting to happen?"

"I...I thought...Jericho would be here. It was Wilbur instead. I mean, I thought Wilbur would be here. But only with Jericho. Jericho would never let him mistreat me."

"What made you decide to run? And why now?"

Mandy wouldn't look at him. She kept speaking in her small voice. "Wilbur called me. I don't know how he got my number. He said Jericho needed me, that the family was broken up. Or gone. Jeff was dead. Jericho was nearly alone. And he...needed me."

"But you know what he is," Concho said, exasperated.

Mandy glanced up with a glare in her eyes. She quickly turned that glare on Perse Wiebke and held it. The deputy flushed in what looked like irritation, but she got the message.

"I'll wait outside for the others," she muttered.

She turned and stomped loudly from the room. Mandy watched her go before looking at the Ranger.

"I know Jericho has...killed people. But he never hurt me. Or hurt Jeff. He wouldn't have hurt that girl, Toni."

"Never hurt you?" Concho exclaimed. "He stole you from your parents when you were ten years old. He sewed Jeff's mouth shut. For goodness' sake. What would he have to do to you to *hurt* you?"

"He sewed Jeff's mouth shut as a lesson," the girl said heatedly. "He would have removed it soon enough."

"And you'd rather be with him than with your own parents?"

"You don't understand. I don't know who to *trust*!" Her shoulders slumped, and she began to sob.

Concho's emotions shifted back and forth between exasperation and sympathy. He finally sat down beside the girl and put his arm around her. "It's all right. Tell me."

Her sobs gradually faded. She took a deep breath and let it out. "I don't know who to trust," she said again. She looked up. "Except you. I trust you."

"I appreciate it. But why don't you trust your parents?"

"I...I overheard them talking. Mom...my Mom. She said they'd never intended to have me. That I was an accident."

Concho winced inwardly without showing it to the girl. "It's not uncommon for people to have children when they weren't expecting it. I know my mother wasn't expecting me. But that doesn't mean they don't love their kids and try to do the best they can for them. Your parents seem pretty nice to me, and I'm generally a good judge of character."

Mandy sighed.

"And there's Beth Pennebaker," Concho continued. "Don't you feel like you can trust her?"

Mandy shuddered. The lawman's chest grew tight.

"I... There's something I haven't told you," Mandy said, using her small voice again.

"What?" Concho asked. He tried to keep his question calm. It wasn't easy.

"I lied to you about one thing," Mandy continued. "When I told you one of the mannequins was Wilbur."

"I know it wasn't."

Mandy glanced up. She looked surprised. "How?"

"I could just tell you weren't giving me the whole truth."

"Why didn't you say something?"

"Because I knew eventually you'd tell me."

Mandy looked down again and twiddled her fingers back and forth in her lap. "There was another person who visited us. Not often, but sometimes. A woman."

"Not Beth Pennebaker?"

Mandy shook her head. "I don't think so. But...." She looked up again. Her eyes glistened with tears. "But I can't be sure. I *can't* be sure of any woman. It could be your FBI friend. It could be my mom, for God's sake. She never spoke. She always wore a black veil and long dresses that covered her completely. I don't know who she is, but she seemed close with Jericho. But...meaner. She scared me. Jeff and me both. And she could be anybody."

CHAPTER 42

The sound of sirens closing on the house ripped Concho's thoughts as he considered what Mandy had just told him. Shaking his head but with nothing to say, he turned and started toward the stairs, signaling Mandy to follow. They were standing in front of the house with Deputy Wiebke when the first state troopers rolled in.

Explanations followed. Concho informed the officers about the two bodies inside, about the secret chamber that shouldn't be disturbed until the FBI arrived, and about the missing perp—Tim, the redhead with the broken back. The police began to do their jobs, and Concho went to fetch his pickup and bring it up to the house. Mandy stayed right with him, as she'd done since she awakened.

"We should call your parents," Concho said as they walked toward the truck. "They'll be worried."

Mandy sighed. "Can we wait just a little while? I need to think of what to say." She shivered. "It's getting colder."

Concho had no jacket to loan the girl. He glanced up at the sky where banks of gray clouds had gathered. "Supposed to be a cold front moving in," he said. "We'll likely get sleet. Maybe even snow."

"I wish it would snow. Cover everything. Make it all pure and clean."

Ten-Wolves could feel where the girl was coming from but made no response. She needed to figure out for herself how she was hurting others and hurting herself. They reached the truck. Concho lifted Mandy up on the driver's side so she could climb into the vehicle and slide over. He climbed in after her and pulled a thick green blanket out of the extended cab to give her. She tugged it around herself, and he pinned the front so she wouldn't have to hold it closed with her hands.

After pulling a coat out of the cab area for himself, he started the engine and plugged in his non-working cell phone in hopes it was just a lack-of-charge issue. The phone beeped, but nothing appeared on the screen to indicate the device was charging. He grunted but left it plugged in.

As he slipped the Ford F-150 into drive, Mandy suddenly exclaimed from the passenger seat. "Why is there blood in the back of your truck?"

Concho twisted his head around. Mandy had gotten up on her knees in the seat and was looking out the rear window. As the Ranger followed her gaze, he saw a thin smear of crimson across the top of his toolbox. He couldn't see into the bed below the box.

"Stay here," he snapped, throwing the truck back into park and bailing out.

He stepped past the big toolbox to glance into the pickup's bed. A frown creased his face, and his heart sped its beat. A hacksaw with a yellow handle lay in the bed. He recognized it. It had been taken from his toolbox, which was seldom locked.

As his gaze focused, he picked up a red discoloration on the saw blade. Pieces of tissue clung to it. He stepped instantly away from the truck, and his right-hand Colt flashed into his fist. He turned in a circle, studying his surroundings.

"What is it?" Mandy called from inside the truck.

"Stay there!" he snapped as she started to climb out.

He stepped over and turned off the engine, then pulled out the keys and locked Mandy inside. Again, he scanned his surroundings. Nothing seemed out of place. His ears heard nothing but the soughing wind. His nostrils flared, and he recognized the hint of blood in the cold air.

Keeping his pistol handy, he stalked around the truck. In the ditch, near the back of the Ford on the passenger side, he found what he expected to find. Bile rose in his throat. He spat into the dirt.

"What is it? What's wrong?" Mandy called again from inside the truck. Her voice sounded distant.

Concho glanced toward her, motioning for her to stay put. He didn't want her to have nightmares about the scene in the ditch. Despite the violence he'd seen in his life, he thought he might have nightmares of his own from this moment.

Tim had been laid out flat on his back with his arms spread. He must have been unconscious, perhaps from the pain of being carried here with a broken spine. His hands had been severed at the wrist. The cuts were jagged, done in a rush with the hacksaw taken from his truck, and then tossed back into the bed when the killer was done.

Tim would have bled out from his wrists but had been given no time to die that way. His throat had also been sawed open. Pinkish blood still bubbled slowly from the wound. Whoever had committed this murder must have taken the hands with them. There was no sign of them. Nor any sign of the killer.

"Is it...is it the red-headed guy?" Mandy called.

Concho nodded, then called out. "Yeah. He's dead."

"Are you sure?" Mandy asked.

Concho returned to the truck and opened the door. "I'm sure."

Mandy stared at the Ranger as he climbed in and drove the Ford slowly up the dirt road into the backyard of the farmhouse.

"Did Jericho do it?" the girl asked when he parked.

"I don't know, but probably."

He climbed out, offered his hand to Mandy. She took it, and he pulled her out of the vehicle and led her toward the back of the house. The door into the kitchen opened before he could reach for it, and Della Rice stepped out. The FBI had reached the scene. And they'd brought along some unexpected assistance.

***

"Glad to see the Kickapoo Nation has arrived," Concho said to Roberto Echabarri as the two shook hands.

"Meskwaa was worried about you," Echabarri replied. "He tried to call you with his brand-new cell phone and couldn't get through. I couldn't either."

"Phone's out. "I think I broke it jumping out a window."

Echabarri arched an eyebrow, a trick Concho envied.

Della Rice frowned as she studied the scratches on his face. "You look a little worse for wear."

"We've got three dead bodies and more questions than we had before," Concho said. "So yeah, I'm a little worse for wear."

"Three bodies?" Rice asked. "I only saw two."

Perse Wiebke came out of the house to join them. Ten-Wolves gestured down the road he'd just driven up. "There's another in the ditch. About seventy-five yards down. Very ugly. You should all have a look at it, though."

Rice, Echabarri, and Wiebke stepped around the truck and started down the road. Concho trailed, with Mandy beside him. As they approached the site of the body, Wiebke began to slow and look queasy.

"I...don't think I can handle it," she said, stopping. "I've already seen two corpses today. Don't wanna see another."

Concho nodded. Wiebke had actually killed the other two, and she had to be feeling the effects. "Understandable," he said. He glanced at Mandy. "You stay here beside the Deputy."

"No! I—"

"I'm not arguing," Concho snapped. "I'm ordering."

The girl opened her mouth to protest but shut it again as she

saw the expression on his face. She stood awkwardly, looking anywhere but at the Deputy, while the rest of the crew continued on
another twenty yards.

"Oh my God!" Della Rice exclaimed suddenly. She stopped in
her tracks.

The only sound Roberto Echabarri made was a gagging noise
as he quickly turned away and leaned over to spit bile from his
mouth.

Rice covered her own mouth but studied the corpse. She finally backed away and walked over to Concho, patting Roberto on
the back as she passed. A gray pallor underlay the normal bright
brown of her skin.

"That's harsh," the FBI agent said. "Looks like with a saw, no
less."

"*Mine*," Concho said. "A hacksaw taken from the toolbox in
the back of my truck. It's still there."

Rice winced. Roberto joined them. He still looked nauseated
but seemed to have controlled his urge to vomit.

"Who killed him?" the Kickapoo Sheriff asked.

"Almost certain it was Jericho. Deputy Wiebke said she saw him
down near the burned-out church before everything started up
here. He must have been staking the place out. It was particularly
brutal because the man already had a broken back. It had to be
agony for him to be carried down here to die."

"Carried or dragged?" Rice asked.

"No drag marks," Concho said. "He was picked up and carried."

"This Jericho pretty strong?" Echabarri asked.

"Don't think he had to be that strong if you know how to carry
someone. And Tim was a pretty skinny guy. Probably weighed no
more than one-fifty."

"You think he's still around?" Rice asked. "Jericho, I mean?"

"Could be," Concho said. "He seems to be pretty good at remaining unseen."

Both Rice and Echabarri studied the surrounding landscape with suspicious eyes.

"Should have brought a dog," Rice said.

"Yeah," Concho replied, nodding.

"Wiebke said *she* killed the other two," Rice added.

"I hit the Hispanic perp with a shot, but it was Wiebke's bullet finished it. The other one's named Wilbur. A long-time ally of Jericho's, apparently. Wiebke shot him when he tried to pull down on her."

Rice frowned. "Where were you?"

The Ranger turned and pointed at the broken second-story window of the house. "Sneaking in the back way to get the drop on him. Never had the chance."

The three law officers walked back up the road to where Wiebke and Mandy stood, neither of them looking at the other. Rice turned an irritated gaze on the young girl, who shrank back under that attention.

"All this because of you," Rice said, directing the words at the girl.

Mandy shook where she stood. She didn't say anything but glanced at Concho as if hoping he'd defend her.

"Wilbur called her," Concho explained. "Tricked her. I think she's learned her lesson."

Rice never looked away from the girl. "I hope so!"

"Did you see the secret room?" Concho asked.

"Not yet," Rice said. "Heard your truck and came out back."

"I'll show you the insanity of it." He led the way back to the house with Mandy and the others trailing him.

CHAPTER 43

Concho showed the other law officers both entrances to the secret chamber upstairs. He pointed out the two clothed mannequins in their little nook and the half-filled trashcan showing that Wilbur, at least, must have been living in the bolt hole for a while.

He then introduced them to the mannequin he'd pulled out of the hole, pointing out the eye and mouth modifications that gave them a more life-like appearance. As he moved the dummy back and forth, the rattling sounded again from inside the left leg.

"Something stuck in there?" Rice asked.

"Seems so," Concho said. "Let's find out."

He drew his hunting knife and leaned down.

"You sure that's a good idea?" Rice asked. "Damaging evidence?"

"Not sure. But I'm gonna do it anyway."

He hacked the toes off the mannequin with the knife blade. When he tilted the shape forward, a small object fell out of the hole and clinked like a coin on the floor. Concho remained bent over to study it. The others joined him.

"A tooth!" Echabarri said. "Encased in Lucite. Is it human?"

"I think it is," Concho said.

"It's awfully small."

"A baby tooth," Rice said.

No one looked comfortable at the thought of a baby tooth hidden inside the mannequin.

"I think you're right," Concho said to Rice.

"He killed a...." Roberto started.

"Maybe not," Concho said in answer to the Kickapoo Sheriff's unfinished statement. "Kids lose these on their own. We'll need to get the coroner to look at it. Maybe he can give us some idea how old it is."

"This case keeps getting weirder," Rice said.

"I've got a feeling we haven't seen the weirdest yet," Concho replied.

***

The coroner arrived to examine the bodies, then released them to be taken away. He also examined the tooth found inside the one mannequin and identified it as a baby tooth, though he could make no judgment on how old it was.

Both the other altered mannequins rattled with something inside, but the coroner denied any request to open them on the premises, insisting they be taken back to his office for examination. He promised to contact both Rice and Ten-Wolves the moment he got any results.

Deputy Wiebke headed off after the bodies to make her statements about the shootings. Concho, Rice, and Echabarri, with the assistance of several other officers, searched every room in the house, looking for more secret chambers. They found none, though that hardly meant there weren't any.

After finishing up inside, Concho headed for his truck, where Mandy waited for him with the doors locked and other police officers around. The promised cold front had finally bullied its way into south Texas. Heavy gray clouds thickened the sky. The wind whistled in his face as he left the already cold house. He pulled his coat collar up and looked down to avoid the spicules of sleet carried by the wind.

Mandy was fiddling with the radio when Concho climbed into the truck. The engine was running, the heater on. The warmth felt good. "You doing OK?" he asked. "Want something to eat?"

"Yes and no," the girl answered, giggling a little. "I fixed your phone, by the way."

"What?" Concho picked up his cell, which was still hooked to the charger. The screen came on when he swiped it. "How did you do that?"

Mandy shrugged. "I didn't really do much. Just forced a restart on it."

"Ah. You turned it off and back on again?"

She giggled again. "Essentially."

Concho hefted the phone in his hand. "Thanks."

"Your screen is cracked, though. You'll have to get it replaced before long, or it'll freeze up again."

"Will do. Let's call your parents."

Mandy sobered. "I'd...rather not."

"I'm going to call them. Don't want them to keep worrying. Then I'll take you home."

"I'd rather stay with you."

"That's just not possible. Why are you concerned about going home? Is it the trust issue you talked about before?"

The girl dropped her hands into her lap. Her ebullient mood of moments before had dissipated. "I guess," she said.

"Talk to me."

Mandy looked out the window as she spoke. "Mom and Dad. They used to...fight a lot. When I was a kid."

"I can see how that would bother you."

She looked at him, then dropped her gaze. "Mostly, they fought about me."

Concho felt the girl's agony. He wanted to offer comfort but decided the best choice was to treat her as an adult.

"*What* about you?"

"That they'd planned on school and trips. Things like that. And I messed it all up by coming along. I was already thinking of running away when Jericho showed up."

"Definitely harsh. But as I said before, it's not unusual for parents to feel that way. Doesn't mean they don't love their child."

Mandy shrugged.

Concho sighed. "My mother left me with my grandmother when I was about a year old. I never saw her again until just a little while ago. She'd had a stroke. She couldn't talk or communicate. I'll never be able to tell her how I felt or how I survived. I'll never know whether she…cared."

Mandy was staring at him now. Her eyelids glittered with unshed tears. "I'm so sorry," she said.

"You have a chance I won't have. To talk to your Mom, to both your parents. To tell them what you just told me and see how they respond. Only then will you know for sure why she said those things. And what all her feelings were. People are complicated. They're not just an extension of *our* wants and needs. They have their own baggage to carry."

Mandy nodded. "All right," she said.

"All right what?"

The girl offered a small smile. "All right, let's go home."

***

After calling Mandy's parents to let them know he was bringing their daughter home, Concho called both Della Rice and Roberto Echabarri to show them his phone was working again.

Rice had something to tell him. "I forgot in all the excitement at the house, but we've been running down your idea that Jericho might be someone with medical training. Given an age between twenty-five and thirty-five, we've got three hundred and four men who attended at least one year of medical school in Texas before dropping out or who graduated but never practiced. Of course, Jericho could have attended medical school elsewhere. It would take weeks to get all that data. If we even could."

"Jericho is a Texan. South Texan. I'm sure of it from talking to him. He's got the accent. Educated but not gone. I bet if he went to medical school, it was here."

"Well then, of the three hundred and four, eleven have died of various causes. A lot of the others have moved away from the state. We've got thirty-one still living in Texas, and we're in the process of trying to track those down now. I'll send you the list."

"Send me the dead ones, too."

"Why?"

Jericho has passed himself off once under a dead man's name. Roy Simms. Maybe he's done it before."

"Good point," Rice said. "I'll send you that list too, and we'll run a check to see if we turn up any inconsistencies."

"Thanks. Stay in touch!"

The last person Concho called was Dalton Shaw, his new boss in the Texas Rangers organization. He reported on what had happened.

"You feel like you're making progress?" Shaw asked after.

"Slow. But yes."

"Then keep hammering it."

"Yes, Sir."

"Congratulations, by the way. I guess."

Concho frowned. "For what, Sir?"

"You haven't seen it?"

"I guess not. I don't know what you're talking about."

"The *Texas Monthly* article?"

"I don't typically read *Texas Monthly*, Sir. What article?"

"The one about you," Shaw said.

CHAPTER 44

Jericho stopped at a Walgreens Pharmacy to get Tylenol for a headache. As he walked back toward the checkout counter, he passed the magazine rack, and a cover headline grabbed him:

Hero Ranger!

He pulled the issue of *Texas Monthly Magazine* off the shelf for a closer look, and a big smile cracked his face as he saw a cover photo of no other than Concho Ten-Wolves. He tucked the issue under his arm.

As he paid for his purchases, the thirty-something woman at the counter remarked on the cover.

"Good lookin' man. He black or what?"

"He's half African American and half Kickapoo. From down around Eagle Pass. I actually know him. A good friend. And definitely a hero."

"He the one saved that little girl from human traffickers over by Brackettville?"

"Yep."

The woman swiped the barcode for the magazine and put it in a plastic bag for Jericho. "Cool," she said. "You a Ranger, too?" She took the money Jericho handed her and gave him the bag with his change.

"Not a Ranger. But I am involved with law enforcement."

The woman smiled. "Wonderful! We need more folks like you. Keep doing God's work."

Jericho smiled back. "Be sure I will. Lots of good work to be done."

"Amen."

Jericho offered the woman a two-finger salute and took his prize out to his Miata. Without starting the vehicle, he pulled out the magazine and studied the cover. Ten-Wolves definitely looked larger than life in the image. He stared straight off the page with intense brown eyes, with muscular arms crossed over a broad chest. Other than the fact he wore a black, western-style hat in the image, the picture was an excellent likeness. He wondered where the magazine had gotten it.

The article itself began on page 114. Jericho turned there and began to read:

> *Texas Ranger Concho Ten-Wolves grew up on the Kickapoo Reservation outside Eagle Pass, Texas...*

Skipping what he already knew, Jericho flipped ahead:

> *The Ranger, along with FBI Agents and several local law enforcement officers, surrounded the compound where the human traffickers were holding nearly a dozen children. As they moved in, the desperate traffickers opened fire on the law officers, and a wild gunfight ensued. A witness at the scene described how Ten-Wolves, while under heavy fire, smashed down the back door and fought his way into the house to directly free several children threatened with imminent death.*

"Yes!" Jericho said, pumping his fist.

Two other pictures ran with the article. One showed Ten-

Wolves from his Army days, standing with three other men in
military garb with the mountains of Afghanistan filling the frame
behind them. The other picture must have been Concho's head-
shot from the Texas Rangers. It also showed him wearing his hat.

Jericho read the article's last few lines:

> *When contacted for an interview for this article, Ten-*
> *Wolves declined, saying only, "Thank you, but I was just*
> *doing my job. I don't need recognition for that." Well,*
> *we believe he does. Concho Ten-Wolves is indeed a*
> *hero. And there are too few of those around these days.*

Jericho closed the magazine and smiled to himself. "And you
owe it all to me!" he murmured. "About time to collect on that
debt."

***

As Concho pulled onto the main highway to take Mandy
home, he saw Roberto Echabarri's white SUV parked in front of
the burned church. He pulled up beside the Sheriff, rolling his
window down.

Echabarri rolled his window down as well. Their breaths
smoked in the cold.

"Thought you were headed home," Concho said.

"I was but then had second thoughts."

"What thoughts?"

"Meskwaa! He said you were in danger."

"The danger has passed."

"I called him while you were finishing up at the farm. He said
it hadn't."

Concho frowned. "He give you any details?"

"No, but for tonight at least I'm going wherever you're going."

"I'm just taking Mandy home." He gestured toward the girl in
his passenger seat.

"I'll follow. Afterward, we can convoy home."

Concho stuck his arm out the window, hand up. The storm spat sleet into his palm. He glanced up into the cloud-darkened sky. "It's getting colder," he said. "Windier. If it gets worse, the roads will start to freeze. You might not make it home tonight unless you go now."

"So I won't make it home," Roberto said. "Plenty of motels around."

"Suit yourself."

Concho rolled up his window and backed out onto the main road, then headed for Uvalde, Texas, and Mandy's parents. It was about a fifty-minute drive under normal conditions.

Echabarri followed.

***

The winter storm intensified, turning the conditions ab-normal. Traffic began to back up until everything slowed to a crawl. Concho kept his windshield wipers on high to combat a steadily increasing fall of mixed sleet and freezing rain. At least the truck's heater kept the vicious wind and cold at bay.

Despite the heater, Mandy huddled in her blanket and said almost nothing, even though Ten-Wolves tried several times to engage her in conversation. It was well over an hour before they pulled into the driveway of Lewis and Linda Callimore's duplex on the outskirts of Uvalde. Roberto Echabarri stopped at the curb behind them.

Concho helped Mandy out of the car, and they rushed up the slushy sidewalk to the front door. It was after 7:00 PM and deeply dark. The temperature continued to drop, and the wind to build. It whistled around the Ranger's ears and yanked at his hair.

Mandy's father threw open the front door as soon as the doorbell rang. He ushered his daughter and the lawman inside but seemed unsure on what to do then. Mandy's mother came running and threw her arms around her daughter. The father moved in to hug them both, and Mandy bore it without any overt enthusiasm.

"Let's go in the living room," the father said after a moment.

Mandy glanced at Concho with pleading eyes, and he followed as everyone moved into the living room and found spaces close to the fireplace. Half an hour passed with the Ranger telling the parents what they needed to know and supporting Mandy as she tried to explain her actions. Eventually, the crying and hugging receded, and Concho disengaged and headed for his truck.

The wind buffeted as he stepped outside. The bushes growing to either side of the doorway wore glistening hard shells of ice. Concho pulled his coat collar tight around his face as his boots crunched sleet beneath them. He stopped for a moment beside Echabarri's SUV.

Roberto cracked his window and shivered at the cold seeping in. "Saw a Motel 6 back up the road a couple miles. Had a vacancy sign."

"I'll follow you," Concho replied.

Twenty-five minutes found them in adjoining rooms at a Motel 6. They separated to make some calls, agreeing to meet again in half an hour to try and locate food. Concho called Maria and Meskwaa, assuring them both he was fine and would either be home tomorrow or would call again if the storm persisted.

Afterward, they found a nearby quick stop and were able to get a couple of hot dogs that had been baking under an artificial sun throughout the day. Roberto also picked up a copy of *Texas Monthly Magazine* with a certain Texas Ranger on the cover.

Concho shook his head when Roberto offered him the mag. "Mostly BS, I'm sure. Keep it."

Roberto grinned. "For the future Ten-Wolves Museum!"

Concho made a face. "Better to throw it in the garbage."

Roberto chuckled. "You really don't know how to take compliments, do you?"

"Find 'em mostly a distraction. And right now, I need to focus on catching Jericho."

"Maybe some sleep will put you in a better mood."

Concho didn't respond. They headed back to their motel, and the Ranger had a nice hot shower. A text message awaited on his phone when he got out from Della Rice. She'd sent him an email containing two lists of names: the thirty-one men still living in Texas who had attended at least one year of medical school here, and the eleven who had attended such a school but were now deceased.

Ten-Wolves signed into his email with his phone and called up the lists. He began to peruse them, spending some time with each name as he tried to conjure up any recognition or memories regarding people with that moniker.

The first list of thirty-one names raised no response from him. He didn't think he'd ever heard of any of them or crossed their paths. The second list was different. The third name on the list of the dead immediately triggered a response.

Eric Sands!

"Sands" was familiar. He'd heard that name recently in some context linked to this case. Then it came to him. He quickly swiped Perse Wiebke's number. She answered after a few rings.

"Concho? What is it? What's wrong?"

"Deputy Wiebke. Perse. Nothing's wrong. Something may be right. Before our raid on the Stone Creek ranch house, you mentioned that one of the previous owners was named *Sands*. Right?"

"Yes, Eli Sands."

"Did he and his wife have any children?"

"Mmm, I think they did. Seems maybe they had at least two. But I don't know for sure. Why? This have something to do with the Jericho case?"

"Maybe. Would you happen to know if *Eric* was the name of one of their kids?"

"I don't. I'm sorry."

"Can you find out? How many kids? And their names? It could really help."

"I can probably do that. There are folks around Brackettville who would remember. I'd like to know why."

"I'm going to ask you to indulge me for the moment. I promise I'll explain."

Wiebke sighed. "OK. For you. I'll start making calls right away. I'll let you know what I get?"

"Thanks. I owe you."

Wiebke chuckled. "I'll remember you said that. Let me get on it. I'll talk to you later."

They hung up together, and Concho paced quickly back and forth across his small room. For the first time in a while, he felt some excitement about this case. If Eric Sands was related to Eli Sands of Stone Creek, then quite a few puzzle pieces might fall in place together at the same time.

Concho texted Della Rice his thoughts on Eric Sands, and she texted back that she'd look into it as well. He tried to force himself to relax by practicing some deep breathing. Eventually, he began to calm and decided to try to sleep. He needed it.

Realizing he hadn't completely finished drying off after his shower, he did so now, then pulled on his boxers. He climbed into the motel's overly soft bed and tucked a .45 under the second pillow. For half an hour, he tossed and turned. Finally, sleep came with dreams.

CHAPTER 45

In the dream, Jericho's black dog stood at one edge of a battlefield littered with broken rifles, broken arrows, broken lances. The skulls of men and horses lay piled in mounds through which a bitter wind whistled. Concho stood across the field from the dog, his feet rooted to the ground as if he were a tree.

Between man and dog, a child of three or four wandered. He wore only a pair of torn shorts, and his light skin had turned almost blue with cold. Tears froze in his eyes before falling to the ground like miniature diamonds.

The black dog studied the child. At first, Concho thought the animal was planning to attack, and he struggled to free his feet from the earth so he could reach the child and protect him. He couldn't.

But the dog did not attack. It trotted to the child. The little boy turned and grabbed at the dog's smokey ruff. The animal curled itself around the boy as if to warm him. But the dog's eyes remained focused toward Concho. They were as green as the cold Atlantic but then flickered and turned a wine red. The beast's mouth was open and snarling.

Ten-Wolves awoke. He lay still for a long moment, seeking the meaning of the dream. It was close, so close. And yet eluded him.

***

Jericho made a phone call. A woman's voice answered.

"It's time," Jericho said.

"Time for what?"

"Time to give Ten-Wolves one last chance to join. Or die."

"He'll never join you. I've told you."

"You don't have the level of faith I have."

"But I'll be right. You'll see."

"So be it."

"OK. What do you need me to do?"

"It's simple," Jericho said.

***

Concho finally gave up on any quick deciphering of his dream. And on sleep. He rose and dressed. It was 3:57 AM. Putting on his heavy coat, he stepped outside. The wind had died down, but the cold had deepened, and the spicules of precipitation falling now were halfway between sleet and snow.

The last time he'd seen snow was December 7, 2017, the first time in his memory the white stuff had fallen on Eagle Pass, Texas. He was a little farther north here in Uvalde County, but snow was still a rarity.

Roberto Echabarri's room was next to Concho's. The light was off in the window, and he decided not to disturb the Sheriff. Nor did he want to call Meskwaa at this time of the morning. The old man needed his sleep. He took a walk instead to clear his head and maybe focus his thoughts. He headed along Highway 90 toward the outskirts of Uvalde.

Besides the Motel 6, several fast-food restaurants, and a couple of quick stop gas places clustered along this stretch of road, all were closed. Lights from the storefronts and from the streetlights set the night aglow. There was almost no traffic. The passing of his boots in the slush made the only sound other than the underlying hum of human existence almost always present in settled areas.

The Ranger took long strides to keep his body warm. He tucked his gloveless hands into his coat pockets and wished he'd brought a hat. He'd gone several hundred yards along the highway's wide shoulder when he realized he'd just passed the last streetlight. In front of him, the shadows deepened until they became an obsidian wall. He kept walking.

Blackness enveloped him. Only when he glanced back did he see the glow of the town, the glow of human presence. Ahead of him, the world might as well have turned to void. He could see nothing, smell nothing, and hear only the sound of his own breathing and the click of freezing rain hitting ground ice.

The wind dropped completely away. And now the click of sleet changed to the plop of snow falling and hitting. Huge flakes fell straight down from an immense sable dome overhead. An intense feeling of peace enveloped Concho, only to shatter an instant later as he heard a growl behind him.

He spun. A pair of coyotes stood in the road between him and the town. The glow of the last streetlight turned their fur golden, and the cold sharpness of the air created a halo of blue-white light around them. They stared at him, their shoulders hunched and their yellow eyes calculating. He relaxed. Coyotes had been known to attack children and pets, but they wouldn't risk taking on a full-grown man. Concho was a bit more than full grown.

"The night's big enough to share," he said loudly.

The smaller of the two coyotes yipped. Three other members of their pack slipped out of the shadows and joined them. Then four more. And another, and another, and another.

Concho's relaxation faded. Now there were a dozen of the animals. He still didn't expect them to attack him, but this wasn't as comfortable a moment as it had been before. He unbuttoned his lower coat buttons so he could reach his sidearm if necessary.

Now, another animal joined the pack. The others cleared a way for it. This was no coyote. It was twice as big as any of the others and with a shorter muzzle and ears. Its coloration was also different, with its golden-brown fur tipped with black. Some hybrid of coyote and dog. Such crosses weren't common but weren't unheard of.

The Ranger's heart picked up some speed. Dogs were much more likely to attack humans than coyotes or wolves. They'd lived with people long enough to lose much of their fear. Concho drew his Colt and let it hang down alongside his leg. Dogs also knew enough to be afraid of guns.

"You bring your crew after me, and I'll shoot you first," the lawman said to the new animal, which was clearly the pack leader.

The creature's tongue lolled out of its mouth as if it were laughing at him. Then its eyes abruptly dilated, and it shied backward. The other coyotes leaped back as well; they broke and ran.

The leader held its ground a moment, no longer staring at Concho but staring past him into the blackness beyond. Then it, too, turned and fled. Concho turned slowly to face whatever had scared the pack away. He thought it might have been a car coming. There was no car.

Twenty yards off, a thicker area of blackness, like an indigo knot of solidified air, caught his attention. It seemed to shift and sway, though such apparent movement was a common illusion created in the darkness under such conditions. What wasn't a common illusion was the feeling of something looming there, staring at him with no eyes he could detect.

"Who are you?" Concho asked.

No response.

"*What* are you?"

No clear answer came, but he heard something, a susurration, almost a whisper. Far away in the town of Uvalde, a siren shrieked. Concho glanced back instinctively, then faced forward again. The susurration had gone. The inky shadow had gone.

The snow stopped.

CHAPTER 46

Concho walked back toward town. The tithe of snow that had fallen had already melted. He could see no sign of coyote prints in the remaining slush, but he trusted his senses enough to know he hadn't imagined the animals.

The indigo knot of shadow was a different matter. Had anything truly been there? Meskwaa, the old medicine man, the tribal Naataineniiha, would have called him foolish for not believing. Meskwaa believed everything had meaning.

What Concho knew, or thought he knew, was that mysteries abounded in the world. And it was good to be open to them but not controlled by them. Meanings revealed themselves, eventually.

By the time he reached his motel, it was after 5:00 in the morning. Roberto's window remained dark. Concho entered his own room. He stripped and slid into bed. His walk had convinced him of the likely meaning of his dream. The child alone represented Jericho. The black dog protected him and would keep on protecting him. But who was the black dog? Could it be the veiled woman Mandy had spoken of? And who was that?

It suddenly occurred to him. If the veiled "woman" had concealed herself so thoroughly from Mandy, then the girl couldn't be absolutely clear if it *was* a woman or merely someone dressed as one. That doubled his potential suspects.

Concho closed his eyes. He couldn't think about all the implications now. He was too tired. This time he quickly fell asleep. It was after 7:30 when he awoke again. Because his cell phone was ringing, he immediately knew who it must be.

"Jericho," he answered.

The killer chuckled. "Of course, you would realize it was me. We are simpatico."

"Not in any way, shape, or form," Concho replied.

"You'll see."

"One of us will. Eventually. Why did you call me?"

"I saw the wonderful magazine piece on you. Quite an entertaining read."

"You expect me to thank you for your interest in my career?"

"I suppose I expected civility. But you don't seem to have that in your repertoire."

"Not for murderers and stealers of children."

Jericho tsk tsked. "Are you so unbending when it comes to Maria?"

"We're not talking about her."

"Of course not. That would make things personal, and I want to keep everything professional at the moment. But I did call to talk about a woman."

A roil of butterflies swept through the Ranger's belly; his heart sped. "What woman?"

"Deputy Persephone Wiebke. Your latest sidekick, shall we say."

"A good officer. Just doing her job. She doesn't have anything to do with this thing between you and me."

"I beg to differ. She has repeatedly inserted herself into our... thing. I've had a couple of chances to remove her from the equation. But I passed them by because I knew it would upset you. But now... Well, she's gone a bit too far."

"Say what you mean."

"Last night, our good Deputy began calling people. People I

know. Asking certain questions. Upsetting them."

"You mean asking people around Brackettville about Eric Sands?"

"Eric Sands is dead."

"You sure?"

Jericho's voice took on an irritated tone. "I didn't call you to talk about a dead man. I called about a living woman. At least she is for now."

"You don't need to hurt Perse Wiebke."

"You'll determine that."

"What do you want?"

"I think it's time we meet again in person and finish this."

"I agree. When and where?"

"North of Brackettville, there's a place called Alamo Village. Ever heard of it?"

"I think so. Some kind of tourist attraction, isn't it?"

"An old movie set. Built in the late fifties for the movie *The Alamo*. Starred John Wayne and Richard Widmark. You probably remember it."

"I saw it. A long time ago."

"It's a full set. Not just false-front buildings. Two sets, actually. There's the full-scale recreation of the Alamo fort and a Mexican-styled villa off to one side. The place *was* a tourist attraction for years, but it's closed now. I want to meet you in the villa. Not the fort. I figure you're in Uvalde after delivering Mandy to her parents. It should take you about an hour to get here, but it'll be a little longer before I get all my business taken care of. Let's say... noon!"

"Just like a western showdown," Concho said.

"Not a showdown. Unless you insist on it."

"And you'll have Perse Wiebke there?"

"She's already en route, as they say."

"And if I show up, you'll let her go?"

"We'll negotiate it. But if you don't show up, she *will* pay the price. And need I say, come alone. I hear helicopters or sirens. Or see police cars other than your Ford pickup, and I'll know you're playing fast and loose. I'll kill her."

"I believe you."

"I know you'll come armed. I'll have my own weaponry. But I'm trusting that you won't start shooting on sight. There is much we must discuss."

"I'm the curious sort. And I'll be trusting you, too. Not to shoot me down when I step out of my truck."

"Trust is a beginning," Jericho replied. He hung up.

***

Concho dressed. He was headed for his door when a knock sounded.

"It's Roberto," a voice said through the thin partition.

The Ranger let Roberto in out of the cold. The Sheriff held a cardboard fast-food tray with two sodas on it and carried a paper sack smelling of reconstituted eggs, American cheese, and sausage.

"Thought you might be hungry," Roberto said.

"You thought right."

Roberto tore open the bag and handed Concho two egg and sausage biscuits, keeping a third for himself. He passed over the drink as well, which already had a straw through the plastic lid. They ate in silence, except for the smacking of lips.

"Sun's up," Roberto said finally. "Forecast calls for more sleet tonight, but it's warmed up some now. Roads will be mostly clear. You ready to head home?"

"Not quite yet. I want to visit Mandy again. And check with Beth Pennebaker on something."

The social worker?"

"Yeah. Got a couple of questions to ask her."

Roberto finished the last bit of his biscuit and licked his fingers. "Need any help?"

"No. You get on back. You've got a department to run."

Roberto nodded. "All right. But you let me know if you need anything. And make sure you get home before the weather turns bad again."

Concho grinned. "I'll do my best, *Nekya*."

Roberto made a face at being called "mother" but didn't say anything else.

Within half an hour, Roberto was on his way, leaving Concho behind at the motel. The Ranger made a call, not to Beth Penne-baker as he'd hinted, but to Earl Blake, the coroner back in Eagle Pass.

"Ten-Wolves," Blake said. "You need bail money or some-thing?"

"Something," Concho agreed. "But not bail money. I wouldn't wanna owe you any filthy lucre. You might send someone to break my kneecaps."

"I don't know anyone tall enough to reach your kneecaps," Blake replied.

Concho laughed, then got to his reason for calling. "I was won-dering if you had anything to report on the mannequins from over in Kinney County? I know you were working with Frank Port there."

"Yep. Giving old Frank a hand. He doesn't like the weird ones."

"And you do?"

"I'm getting used to them. Anytime you're involved. And I've got some preliminary information. Planning on running more tests today."

"What kind of preliminaries, if I can ask?"

"Both mannequins had something inside them. We extracted them, and I'm working on DNA tests."

"So, it was living tissue?"

"Once living. Now encased in resin. Unfortunately, it's a com-mon resin you can buy at any art supply store. No way to trace where it was sold."

"What were the objects."

Blake hesitated for a moment. Then, "Not a pleasant thing. The male-gendered mannequin had a...well, an eyeball in it. It had been drained of the vitreous humor and pressed flat before being covered with resin."

Concho winced into the phone. "Right. Not pleasant at all."

"The female-gendered mannequin had a...." Blake took a long breath. "This is even worse. It had a nipple. Also enclosed in resin."

Ten-Wolves felt the sting of bile in the back of his throat and swallowed it down. "Anything else?"

"Enough testing to know the eye came from a man and the nipple from a woman. I don't have any further information yet. The tests I'm doing today may help."

"Thanks," Concho said. "I also wanted to give you some info."

"Do tell."

"I don't know for sure, but I suspect there could be some connection to a man named Eli Sands and his wife. They lived up near Brackettville. Died at least twenty years ago."

"I see. Not that I don't appreciate it, but why are you telling me this?"

"If you don't hear from me for more than twelve hours, call Della Rice and tell her what I just told you."

"Why don't *you* tell her? You going somewhere?"

"Maybe down a rabbit hole. And if I told Rice right now, she'd try to stop me. Or come with me. Can't have either of those."

"Gotcha," Blake said.

"Appreciate it. Talk to you later."

"Oh, Ten-Wolves!"

"Yeah?"

"Catch this guy."

"Giving it my best."

CHAPTER 47

Roberto Echabarri had no intention of returning to the Eagle Pass reservation just yet. He drove into downtown Uvalde to a rent-a-car place he'd noticed earlier. Leaving behind his easily identifiable white SUV with the Kickapoo Tribal Police symbol on the side, he picked up a dark gray Hyundai Sonata instead.

After, he drove back to the Motel 6. The exchange of vehicles took half an hour, and it was a relief to see Ten-Wolves' Ford F-150 still in the motel lot. He found a parking space in one of the fast-food joints across the street where he could keep an eye on the Ranger's room and truck.

He waited for whatever was to unfold.

***

Concho checked out of his motel around 10:00 AM and filled up with gas before leaving Uvalde and heading up Highway 90 toward Brackettville. He was giving himself plenty of time to reach Alamo Village for his rendezvous with Jericho.

The skies still glowered with gray, but the sleet had stopped, though the news claimed more was headed this way. The weak winter sun peaked through the scudding clouds every once in a while, sending a flash of jeweled purple light lancing down. The day had warmed enough to turn the ice on the roads to slush, and he made good time, only slowing for the bridges, many of which still had frozen spots.

Only once did he suspect someone might be following him. He ignored it. It wouldn't surprise him to find that Jericho had a car shadowing him. He kept on Highway 90 until his GPS told him to turn onto Highway 674. From there, he came to a dirt and gravel road winding through open grassland and stands of live oak and pinion pine. He reached a fence and a gate with signs reading NO TRESPASSING and KEEP OUT. The gate was open; someone had been trespassing.

Jericho.

Beyond the gate, the road made a V. To the right could be seen what looked like the walls of the fake Alamo. To the left, up a ways, were a number of buildings he took to be the villa Jericho had mentioned. He took that road and soon came to two stone pillars and a rickety wooden gate that looked like it would fall apart at a touch. The entrance to the set.

Concho parked about fifteen yards from the entrance. He climbed out. The sky had lightened a little but hung pregnant with imposing clouds. The temperature had risen to nearly forty degrees Fahrenheit. It was still cold, but he didn't want to be bound by a heavy coat. He pulled on his overly large bullet-proof vest and tugged a black windbreaker over it.

Opening the extended cab area of his Ford, he drew out a sack containing several items. One was a small metal tin holding red ochre. He screwed the lid off and dipped in his fingers, then streaked two lines of crimson beneath each eye before reclosing the tin and wiping his fingers on a handy towel.

He was already well armed, with a Colt Double Eagle .45 at each hip—extra magazines tucked into slots on his gun belt—and a bone-handled hunting knife in a sheath at his left side. He had a pocketknife stuffed in his jeans. Now, he pulled one more weapon from his truck. This was the bow he'd recently completed. He strung it, then hooked it over his shoulder along with a quiver of arrows.

Stepping through the gate onto the set brought him to stillness while he scanned the fake town. Although many of the buildings were deteriorating, the place was still impressive and gave one the feeling of slipping back in time to the 1800s.

One building was labeled a bank, another a hotel, and yet another a cantina. Near the center of the set was a church, complete with a bell tower, though no bell hung in it. A sign on another building brought him back to the present. It read "John Wayne and Old West Museum."

An eerie moan came from the direction of the church. He strode that way —and saw Deputy Perse Wiebke. A wooden table about three feet high stood just to the right of the entrance to the whitewashed adobe building. Wiebke stood on top of that table with her hands bound behind her.

A similar table rested to the left side of the entrance. A man stood on this one, again with his hands bound behind him. Both Wiebke and the man had ropes around their necks stretching up toward the red-tiled roof of the church. When Concho followed those ropes with his gaze, he found Jericho on the roof, standing easily with his legs spread and braced against the slope. He held a machete and a smile.

"Glad you could make it!" Jericho called. "I like what you've done to your face. All painted for war."

Concho ignored the killer momentarily and studied the scene. Wiebke was dressed in her uniform, her badge glinting dully under the gray sky. She looked defiant. The man wore tan pants and a white polo shirt. He was probably in his late thirties, not overweight but looking unhealthy with a face mottled in fear and sweat beaded in his hair despite the chilly temps. Neither captive wore a gag, and it was the man's moaning that had attracted Concho's attention.

The Ranger returned his focus to Jericho. The killer had tied the neck ropes of Wiebke and the unidentified man together and had hooked them to a pole inserted into the roof. If he yanked on those ropes, he'd drag both prisoners backward off their tables and likely snap their necks as they fell. Or they'd strangle.

"Yes, I made it," Concho finally called back to Jericho. "You can let the deputy go now."

"Not just yet. We have things to discuss."

"She's not part of this. It's you and me!"

"Not anymore."

Wiebke suddenly shouted: "I hope you brought an army with you, Concho! Enough to take this bastard down!"

The Ranger said nothing. Jericho laughed.

"Of course, he didn't," the killer said. "He came alone. Just like the good hero promised."

The bound man interrupted. "Help me! Please! He's going to kill me. And I didn't do anything."

Concho turned his attention to the man. Jericho laughed again and gave a little tug on the rope to tighten the stricture around the fellow's neck. He blanched in terror as he took a half step back on the table to compensate for the tug. The table wobbled. It was old and not sturdy.

"Didn't do anything?" Jericho called. "Now, Stu, you know that isn't true." Jericho looked back at Concho. "Meet Stu Tomasso," he said. "Stu was supposed to be at the little party you and that pretty FBI agent broke up over at Stone Creek. He was so angry at the car trouble, which kept him away. But the next day. After word got out, he was happy he'd missed. Why he even thanked God for his engine problems. Can you believe it? *He*...even thought someone up there," Jericho pointed at the sky, "was looking out for him. Hard to imagine?"

"So, he's a pedophile and a human trafficker," Concho said. He eased forward a step toward Perse Wiebke's table.

"Indeed."

"Then let him down, and I'll arrest him."

"No, no, no. Not that easy. *He* doesn't deserve easy. In fact, why don't you kill him, Ten-Wolves? I've got a throwaway gun we can plant on him afterward. And I know where you can find plenty of evidence to implicate him. Not a bit of it faked either. Certainly, no one will question a hero Texas Ranger taking down another scumbag. And if you do, I promise I'll let Detective Wiebke go right away. No argument or debate."

"Just like that?" Concho asked.

"Just like that."

CHAPTER 48

"Kill him and finish what you started at Stone Creek," Jericho said.

"I'm not going to kill anyone in cold blood," Concho replied. He took another short step toward the bound Deputy. Now he was barely six feet away.

"Cold blood! Hot blood! Who cares?" Jericho protested. "How many criminals have you already shot dead? What's one more?"

"It's not the same. I've killed to protect my life and other people's lives. And when I don't have to kill, I don't. He'll be arrested, sentenced, jailed."

"But no jail sentence will be punishment enough for what's he done. No *jail* will give his victims any satisfaction. Especially not the dead ones."

"Not for me to decide."

"Oh, so holy, aren't you?" Jericho said bitterly. "You ever think about the monsters that walk past you every day? The murderers of children. The rapists. And even if you could see them. Smell them. You wouldn't do a thing about it because you have to follow the *law*. You're too cowardly to act without some outside force backing you up. Well, I *can* smell them. And see them. I can *see* the rot festering inside Stu's skin. It's yellow as pus and full of squirming maggots. I see it everywhere in far too many. And I'm not afraid to act *before* these things commit their atrocities. That's the difference between you and me."

"The difference is that you're insane," Concho said. He took two more steps toward Wiebke. "And if you give up now, I won't kill you either. I'll see you get some help."

"I've already got help," Jericho said. He yanked hard on the rope, binding the necks of Perse Wiebke and Stu Tomasso.

Both captives stumbled backward as the rope tightened around their necks. Concho hurled himself forward. Tomasso's table was more rickety than Wiebke's. Its legs folded. The table collapsed, and Tomasso gave one quick, strangled scream before the rope snapped taut around his neck with brutal force.

Perse Wiebke's table stood up under the strain, but one of her feet slid off the back and dangled in the air. The rope tightened around her neck, but Concho was there; he grabbed her legs, lifted her up as the rope came fully taut.

The Ranger's hand flashed to his side and came out with his hunting knife. Still holding Wiebke's legs, he lifted up on his tiptoes and slashed at the rope above her head. The strands parted like butter under the keen blade, and he lowered the Deputy slowly to earth.

"Than...thanks!" Wiebke gasped out.

Concho pushed the shocked deputy toward the wall of the church. He glanced up. The overhang of the roof hid him from anyone looking down from above. He spun toward Stu Tomasso and realized there was no helping there. The man's neck had snapped in his fall. The rope had caught on the roof, and the man dangled, swaying back and forth with his feet just inches off the ground.

Ten-Wolves returned to Wiebke and slashed the ropes binding her hands. He offered her the Colt in his fist, then gave her an extra magazine to go with it. She took it reflexively. The Ranger stepped out from under the roof overhang and glanced upward for any sign of Jericho. The man had disappeared. Probably into the bell tower.

"Hate to take your gun," Wiebke said.

"You'll need it. Besides, I've got another one." He sheathed his knife and drew his second Double Eagle.

"Thanks," Wiebke said again. She shook her head. "I seem to be repeating myself."

"No problem. You OK?"

"A little shook up but all right." As Concho started to turn away, she clutched his arm. "I...I don't know what difference this makes now," she said. "But from listening to him, I think Jericho was probably an abused child."

Concho nodded. "I think you're right. But that doesn't give him a pass on murder and kidnapping. We've got to stop him. Hopefully alive. But...."

"I understand," Wiebke said.

"He have anyone else with him you've seen?"

"No, but I didn't know he'd already stashed that other guy here until he brought him out and stuck him up on the table. There could be more victims around. Or allies."

"I wouldn't be surprised. You know anything about this place?"

"Mostly what I've read. I came here once with my parents as a kid. It was hopping then. Museums, gift shops, shows. But the buildings? I only remember there was a bunch of them. They look pretty rickety now."

"And who knows where to start looking," Concho said.

"I think..."

"Think what?"

"He had us blindfolded before, but my blind slipped a little while we were inside the church. He had supplies there."

"What kind?"

Wiebke shrugged. "Boxes. I don't know what was in them. But he could still be inside. He seemed eager enough to hang us in front of it. Maybe it's significant to him."

Concho made a decision. "OK, we'll check the church first. There a back way in?"

"Yeah. I noticed. And all the doors are gone. You can walk right through."

"All right, I'll circle around. You stay here. Give me three minutes. Then come in the front. But watch yourself."

Wiebke rubbed her throat where the rope had clenched. "Bet on it!"

Concho turned away. He slipped through a gate of short wooden stakes between two adobe pillars. A square room off the side of the church had an open doorway that menaced with blackness. Concho darted past it and pressed himself against the wall.

The bell tower was right above his head, but he could neither see nor hear any movement there. Jericho had had plenty of time to climb down while Ten-Wolves saved Perse Wiebke from a hanging. The killer could be anywhere.

Concho continued around to the back of the church. Another open doorway watched him. He considered trading his Colt for his bow, but the quarters might be tight inside. Keeping the pistol leveled, he slipped sideways through the door into the interior of the church. A corridor led farther in, lit dimly by sunlight filtering down. An animal had been here; he smelled its musk.

He passed a door on the left, revealing a small room that might have been the priest's dressing area. It was empty now. He came to the main part of the church, the nave. This room was better lit by light falling through several high windows. His eyes had adjusted as well.

The nave was empty of any pews, but a man knelt in the center of the room. It wasn't Jericho. This man's skin was black; he was blindfolded. An instant later, Jericho himself stepped out of the shadows to one side. Concho swung his pistol to bear, but the killer's hands were up and spread. He had no gun but held something in his right hand.

"You're under arrest," Concho said.

"Not quite yet," Jericho replied.

Perse Wiebke materialized through the front door with her service pistol pointed at Jericho's chest and a grim look on her face.

"You don't have any choice in the matter," Wiebke said. "There's two of us."

Jericho ignored the deputy. He stepped gently into a beam of light falling through one window. Dust motes swirled around him and around the item in his hand.

"What's he got?" Wiebke asked.

"A detonator," Concho said.

"Indeed," Jericho said. "The church is wired. I press this button, and it comes down on top of all of us."

"Including you," Wiebke snapped.

"I'm prepared to die. Are you?"

Concho didn't lower his pistol but jerked his head toward the kneeling man. "Might as well get in all the introductions," he said to Jericho.

Jericho smiled and slowly lowered his arms to his sides. "Trey," he called. "You want to stand up and take off your blindfold."

The man called Trey pulled off the black cloth covering his eyes and threw it on the floor, then slowly rose to his feet. He was in his late twenties, probably six two and better than two hundred and twenty-five pounds. Lean as an athlete but muscled like a weightlifter. He glared at Jericho, then turned and frowned toward the others.

"Treymon Jones," Jericho said. "A name we all would have heard of by now if he wasn't a rapist of children."

"Ima kill you," Treymon said.

Jericho chuckled. "I told you, you'd get your chance. But right now, you're going to do what I tell you to do. Else I press the *little* button on this thing," he held up the detonator, "and the back of your head goes splat."

Treymon shuddered. He looked back at Concho. "This bastard drugged me and put a bomb in my head. Cain't do nothin' about it."

"Sorry to hear," Concho replied. He looked over to Jericho. "What game you playing now?"

"Treymon is even worse than Stu outside," Jericho replied. "He started with his own family. Then branched out to the kids of friends. Along the way, he picked up some impressive boxing skills, though." He made air quotes while adding, "'Coulda been a contenda,' as they say."

"Cut the bull!" Treymon said. He stared at Concho. "He want me to beat ya to death."

Concho frowned.

"To be precise," Jericho corrected. "I want to see our hero Ranger get his hands dirty. And maybe along the way, realize the power he has to bring a little justice to the world."

"Whatever," Treymon said. "Let's do this so I can get away from this freak." He started forward but paused as Ten-Wolves pointed his gun at him.

"If you win," Jericho explained to the Ranger, "and you still don't understand what I want from you, then you'll fight me. And if you win that one, you'll have your arrest, and our good Deputy Wiebke will become a hero right along with you. If you don't fight..." he shrugged. "I bring the house down."

"You think you can believe him?" Wiebke asked

Concho just walked around Jones and handed his Colt to the deputy. "If you have to, kill Jericho before you die."

Wiebke nodded; Jericho laughed.

Concho moved over to the wall. He shrugged the bow and quiver off his back and leaned them against the adobe. Next, He stripped off his jacket and bullet-proof vest and let them drop. As he turned back toward Treymon Jones, the man lunged toward him with his fists up.

CHAPTER 49

Roberto Echabarri moved in a crouch to the rear of Con-cho Ten-Wolves' truck. The big Kickapoo was a wary man. Roberto had trailed him from far back to keep from being spotted. As soon as he'd seen where the Ranger parked, he'd hidden his car behind a stand of Pinion Pines and made his way forward on foot.

Clearly, Ten-Wolves was up to something and planning on going it alone. But that meant Roberto's friend was putting his life in danger, and Meskwaa would never forgive him if he let the big Kickapoo face it alone.

Slipping along the side of the Ford pickup, Roberto duck-walked to a ramshackle wooden fence. Beyond lay an abandoned town. He'd first thought Concho was approaching a genuine small Texas village. On closer look, it was some kind of 1880s set piece. Maybe a movie set or frontier days tourist attraction.

He slipped past the fence into the shadows of some bushes and studied the layout ahead. Now, where might his friend be? He lifted the hunting rifle he carried and studied the layout through the scope.

As he panned past a building that looked like an old adobe church, he gasped. A dead man swayed on a rope hanging from the building's roof. Concho could always be found close to the action, but Roberto had open ground to cover on the way to his friend —and no idea who else might be waiting and watching.

***

Concho met Treymon's rush with a straight jab that slowed him down, but the man still got in a right hook to the ribs that made them want to walk off the job of protecting Ten-Wolves' vitals. The Ranger ducked a left and blocked a right with his shoulder. That blow knocked him backward two steps.

Treymon was immensely strong and almost as tall as Concho and clearly knew boxing. He danced a little, just enough to keep his balance under him. His fists were up and cocked, his head bobbing and weaving on a thickly muscled neck.

Ten-Wolves had his own training and a lot of experience. The two traded blows, none of them clean hits. Concho snapped a leg kick into Treymon's thigh. The impact jarred. The man stepped back and snarled:

"Box, damn you!"

"Whatever it takes to put you down," Concho replied.

Treymon rushed. Concho swayed aside and threw a right. The boxer ducked his head; the blow merely grazed the top of his skull. Treymon twisted his body and spiked a thumb toward the Ranger's eyes. The thick nail scraped a groove through the pad of flesh beneath Concho's right eye.

Concho ducked back, feeling the blood and the sting. He snarled himself. Treymon threw a roundhouse blow as he tried to end the fight. The Ranger was too fast. He ducked under the blow and slammed a right into Treymon's gut. The man gasped and threw himself backward. His eyes showed respect now. That punch had hurt.

The two sparred, trading blows. Treymon was fast himself and accurate with his punches. It was taking too long to wear him down. And, Concho knew, once he beat Treymon, he'd have Jericho to deal with.

Can't punch myself out. Have to hold something back.

Those thoughts were nearly his undoing.

Treymon landed a left to Concho's chin, driving him backward. A right haymaker meant to end the fight only grazed and stung the tip of the Ranger's nose. Concho backpedaled desperately, trying to keep his feet under him as Treymon slung blow after blow with all the muscles of his shoulders behind them

Such an attack couldn't last. Treymon slowed, and the lawman went on the offensive. He had reach on the boxer. He used it now, distracting his opponent with fast left jabs while powering up his right. He slung it.

Treymon saw it coming and dodged. He couldn't get completely out of the way. The blow cracked him in the jaw, thudding and stunning. Concho swept forward, grabbed Treymon's arm, and twisted it to throw him over a hip. The boxer struck hard, crying out as he hit the floor.

The man was tough. He bounced back up to meet Concho's rush. They stood toe to toe a moment, fists striking. A knuckle cut Concho's lip. His fist cauliflowered Treymon's ear. Treymon backed up. The Ranger's anger had been building; he waded in.

Treymon got in two short jabs. Concho shrugged them off and kept coming. He jabbed with a left, then a right. Both blows connected, pulping the man's lips. Treymon stepped back, his legs weakening a little. Concho threw a right that boomed into the boxer's jaw, twisting his head to the side. A follow-up left hammered the man's head back the other way.

Nearly out on his feet, Treymon slapped ineffectually at Concho. The Ranger threw a quick right. Treymon's trained reflexes thrust the blow aside, but Ten-Wolves was already spinning, leaping, lashing out in a roundhouse kick. His boot pounded into the side of Treymon's face with tremendous force, and the man stum-

A.W. Hart

bled sideways against the wall and slowly slid down into unconsciousness.

Concho panted for breath, his fists still clenched as sweat ran down his face and drenched his shirt.

"Well," Jericho said, clapping. "Didn't that feel good? Beating an evil man to within an inch of his life. Just one more inch, and you could get rid of Treymon forever. Make sure he never hurts another child."

Concho straightened slowly, struggling to catch his breath. "Seems like you enjoyed the fight more than I did."

Jericho grinned. "Gotta admit, I liked it. Why don't you finish him? It'll make you feel even better. I promise you."

"No!"

Jericho shrugged. He looked down on the unconscious Jones. Pulling two big zip ties out of his pocket, he fastened the man's feet and hands together before looking back at Concho.

"I guess it's you and me. By the way, if you think I'll be easy to defeat after Treymon, you've got another think coming. How do you imagine I captured him in the first place?"

"He said drugs."

"Not at first. A straight-up fight."

"So, let's do it," Concho snarled. "And if I win, you and Treymon are both going to jail."

"Sure," Jericho said. He tossed the detonator to Perse Wiebke, who caught it with a smile.

CHAPTER 50

Concho glanced from Jericho to Perse Wiebke and back. "Gonna have to stop saying I'm a good judge of character," he said dryly. "You were ghosting me all along."

Wiebke laughed. "All along. I'm Jericho's big sister." She pointed toward her eyes with two fingers. "If I were to take out these green contacts, you'd see the one family resemblance you'd recognize immediately."

"Those maroon, scorpion sting eyes."

"Scorpion sting. I like it."

Concho thought of his dream where the black dog's eyes had turned from green to wine red. The message had been clear; he just hadn't understood it. Perse was the black dog who'd long protected the child called Jericho.

"Your real last name is Sands, isn't it?" Concho asked.

"Wiebke now. I married. For a while."

"Persephone and Eric Sands," Concho said. "Children of Eli Sands. What was your mother's name?"

"Tara. She was quite the actress, and I seemed to have inherited the talent. And Eric was actually Eryx. From Greek Mythology. Everyone just called him Eric until he became Jericho. Our mother liked that sort of thing. We even had a Hestia for a while. She didn't make it through her first two years. Daddy got worse and worse over time in his...delights."

"So that's why there were five mannequins at the dining room table," Concho said.

"Bingo," Wiebke said.

Jericho was stretching for the fight. "Enough!" he snapped. "He doesn't need to know our whole backstory."

Wiebke glared at her brother. "You're the one started this thing. Against my advice. Don't be upset when it gets out of hand." She glanced back at the Ranger. "Mom wasn't quite as bad as Daddy, by the way. But bad enough. Good when they were gone."

"Which one of you killed them?"

"I did," Wiebke said. "It's what a big sister does. Protect her little brother. Took a while for me to get old enough to do it, though. By that time....." She shrugged.

Jericho chuckled, drawing everyone's attention. He stripped off his shirt and tossed it on the floor. Beneath, he was built like an Apollo. "She's a lot more deadly than I am," he said. "Most of the bodies in the pond are hers."

"But you take souvenirs," Concho said.

"I do. Touchstones of justice."

"You saying they were all pedophiles?"

"Or enablers."

"You could have gone to the law."

"I went to the law," Perse said. "At thirteen. "None of them believed a man would do such things to his son and daughter. Certainly not the rich philanthropist named Eli Sands."

"I'm sorry."

"Well," Jericho said. "No matter now. You ready?"

"One last question first. Who killed Tim, the red-headed thug from the house?"

Wiebke smiled. "I did. Really that's why I was late getting to you. Took the hands to make you think it was my brother."

"And you murdered Wilbur to keep him quiet?"

"Enough!" Jericho snapped. "That's two questions."

"Wilbur did suspect I was the woman in the veil," Wiebke answered anyway. "But mainly, I just wanted him dead."

Concho said nothing, only rolled his shoulders and neck, then stepped toward Jericho. "I'm wondering why I should fight, though. I'm not getting out of here one way or another."

Jericho shook his head. "Perse won't interfere." He stared at his sister until she nodded, then looked back at the Ranger. "You beat me; you can arrest me. I'll just have a bigger stage to convey my message. A public one. Perse will disappear. We've got it planned. But I don't think you'll win."

"I always do," Concho replied.

***

Concho had already absorbed a lot of punishment from Treymon Jones. Jericho was fresher. And took advantage of it. His knuckles sliced like blades. Concho was cut and cut again. Blood ran down his cheeks to mix with his warpaint.

"This doesn't have to be," Jericho said. "Your mother didn't abuse you, but she abandoned you before you were a year old. You should be on our side. We could do great things together."

Concho ignored the words; he stalked forward. For the first time in his life, he'd met someone faster. Jericho struck and was gone before the Ranger's blows could connect. It didn't matter.

"I don't see kidnapping children in my future," he snapped.

"Ha," Jericho responded. "You know Jeff? The young man from the house? I took him from his father when he was twelve. His 'father' had raped him nearly every day since he was eight. I saved him."

Concho snapped a kick at Jericho. The killer blocked, danced away.

"Jeff's father is in the pond, by the way," Jericho said.

"I'll be sure to remember that after I take you to jail."

"You're the one who's bleeding."

"What about Mandy? And Toni? They weren't abused."

"Not yet," Jericho said. He lunged in, swifter than a striking rattler. One open-handed blow pummeled into the lawman's left kidney, wringing a grunt from him. A second blow narrowly missed an eye.

"But you saw them both," Jericho continued as he backed away. "Beautiful, beautiful children. And innocent. How long would it have been before someone hurt them? No time at all, I think."

"Maybe. As horrible as that would have been. But maybe not. You had no right to take them from loving families."

"I claimed the right," Jericho said. He made his move.

Concho was waiting. He couldn't beat Jericho in a ranged fight. It had to be close, which meant he had to take damage to get close. As Jericho lunged, Concho didn't try to avoid, didn't even try to block. He met the lunge with one of his own.

A pair of savage strikes pounded into the Ranger's unprotected face. His lips split; his nose broke. The pain blasted along his nerves, but Concho's hands were held low and ready. He grabbed Jericho's belt with his left hand; his right snapped out and locked around the other man's throat.

With a roar of rage, Concho yanked Jericho off the ground, jerked him around, and slammed him brutally down on the floor. Jericho's left leg was twisted under him when he hit. The knee popped out of the socket. He cried out from the pain and from the shock of his skull rebounding off the ground like a cabbage thrown against concrete.

Concho dropped to his knees beside Jericho, his fists raised to pummel. He stopped himself. The man's eyes were open but hardly seemed to see. His body writhed as he struggled for the breath that had fled him. His hands flailed and dropped to his side. The fight was over.

Slowly, Ten-Wolves pushed to his feet. Blood dripped down his chin and drizzled onto his shirt. He snorted to clear his nostrils of it. He felt a hundred years old. Maybe a thousand. He turned toward Perse Sands. She lifted her hand with one of Concho's pistols in it.

"Now I'm going to kill you," she said.

"No!" Jericho croaked from the ground. "You promised."

Perse shook her head almost sadly. "Someone has to protect you from yourself, little brother. You're not going to jail, and I'm not going to leave the life I've become comfortable in. He's the only thing standing in our way."

She eared back the hammer on the Colt, though she didn't need to.

"No!" Jericho said again as he tried to push to his feet and fell back with a gasp of pain.

Concho's mind whirled but found no escape. Time to die. He straightened, focused his gaze on the woman.

"Freeze!" a voice screamed from the front doorway of the church.

Concho and Perse spun toward the sound at the same time. The Ranger glimpsed Roberto Echabarri's face.

Perse fired toward the door. Chips of adobe splintered as Roberto dropped to his knees and triggered the rifle he carried in his hands. The bullet plucked at Perse's uniform sleeve. She shifted her aim, fired again. Roberto cried out as he was struck and slammed sideways with his rifle falling away.

Concho was already moving. Not toward Perse but toward the wall where he'd leaned his bow and quiver. He plucked the bow up, nocked an arrow from the quiver. Perse twisted back toward him. The deadly hole in the Colt's barrel looked a mile wide.

Concho yanked back the bow's string and released.

Arrow beat bullet. The obsidian-headed shaft punched into Perse Sands' throat. Her eyes went wild. She pulled the trigger on the .45, but her aim had been thrown off, and the bullet whanged impotently into the wall over the Ranger's head.

"Noooooo!" Jericho screamed.

The woman collapsed slowly to her knees, gurgling. A thick

crimson liquid poured out of her mouth like red wax and dripped down to cover the sheen of her badge. She fell sideways, the gun dropping to the floor.

Concho staggered toward her. He scooped up both his own pistols. For an instant, his gaze met hers. She tried to say something, but he couldn't hear it through the rasping breaths.

He stepped away from her and moved toward Roberto. The Kickapoo Sheriff was alive. The bullet had struck his vest and ricocheted away, cutting an ugly wound across his arm. It bled but wasn't fatal.

"I'm OK," he said. "Watch Jericho!"

Concho squeezed his friend's shoulder, then turned back toward the beaten Jericho. Jericho was crawling on his belly toward his dying sister. Tears flooded down his face and dripped into the dust of the floor, leaving mud behind.

The man reached his sister. He scooted around until he could draw her head upon one knee. He held her there, crooning and smoothing her hair. She died with her eyes open.

Jericho turned his head toward Ten-Wolves. His scorpion-red eyes were bloodshot, his face stained. "Kill me!" he pleaded. "Please!"

Roberto spoke from behind the Ranger's shoulder. "I'll call it in. Outside."

"Yeah," Concho said. He listened to his friend leave and glanced down at the pistols in his hands. He looked at Jericho. At his scarlet hands. At his eyes.

"Kill me," the man begged again.

Concho wondered: would it be justice? Or mercy?

He holstered his Colts and pulled a pair of handcuffs off his belt.

CHAPTER 51

An ambulance arrived. A paramedic sewed up Roberto's wound and put four stitches in Concho's busted lip. He set the Ranger's nose and put Jericho's knee back in its socket.

The police had many questions. The FBI had more. But eventually, the last question was asked, and Roberto and Ten-Wolves headed out for Eagle Pass and the reservation. Concho called Maria. He didn't tell it all, only that he was coming home. She said she'd be waiting for him.

***

The man known as Jericho, and Eric Sands, and Roy Simms, and Mister Friendly, slumped in the back of an FBI vehicle taking him to jail. He still wore his sister's blood. His gaze stared out the window into the darkness. It wasn't dark to him; he could see by the light of the dead.

***

Maria Morales heard the pickup pull into the driveway. She ran through the house, throwing open the front door. Her eyes dampened as she saw Ten-Wolves step out of his truck and tread

slowly toward her, as if with immense exhaustion. She winced at
the bandages half-covering his face. Then she put away the tears
and put on a smile and welcomed her man home.

A LOOK AT KILLER'S CHANCE: THE GUNSLINGER BOOK ONE

FROM THE AUTHOR OF THE FAST-PACED AVENG-ING ANGELS SERIES COMES A NEW KIND OF WEST-ERN HERO...

Fourteen-year-old Connor Mack dreams of a life adventure while stuck plowing, doing all the chores, and being treated as a slave on the half barren family spread in East Texas. He plans to one day flee the beatings delivered by his hulking older brothers and lazy pa. But he knows if he does, he must take his twin sister Abby—who is not always right in the head—with him.

He gets his chance when River Hicks, a man wanted for the murder of a policeman in Fort Worth, rides in with a pack of bounty hunters on his trail. When the gun smoke clears, Connor has killed men for the first time, but he also knows this is his and Abby's time to escape their life of abuse.

Knowing the law will soon be on their heels, they follow Hicks—an outlaw driven by his own demons, and by deep secrets which somehow involve the Mack twins.

Conner has a lot of learning and growing up to do... and he has to stay alive to do it.

ABOUT THE AUTHOR

Charles Gramlich lives amid the piney woods of southern Louisiana and is the author of the Talera fantasy series, the SF novel Under the Ember Star, and the thriller Cold in the Light. His work has appeared in magazines such as Star*Line, Beat to a Pulp, Night to Dawn, Pedestal Magazine, and others. Many of his stories have been collected in the anthologies, Bitter Steel, (fantasy), Midnight in Rosary (Vampires/Werewolves), and In the Language of Scorpions (Horror). Charles also writes westerns under the name Tyler Boone. Although he writes in many different genres, all of his fiction work is known for its intense action and strong visuals.

CPSIA information can be obtained
at www.ICGtesting.com
Printed in the USA
LVHW042046230322
714164LV00011B/2646